Conversations with the King
D.M. Freedman

Copyright © 2020 D.M. Freedman

Skalater Press & Books—Cedarhurst, NY
ISBN: 978-0-578-75953-1
Library of Congress Control Number: 2020918534
Title: Conversations with the King
Author: D.M. Freedman
Digital distribution | 2020
Paperback | 2020

This is a work of alternative historical fiction. Some of the characters are based on real life personalities and some real life events. Names, incidents, places, and dialogue are products of the author's imagination, and are not to be construed as real.

Dedication

Elvis Presley's death was a milestone event in my young adulthood. I was a fan, but Elvis' music did not dominate my playlist. However, for many it was a life altering event. Like many icons, it was difficult to comprehend how a man with such talent could pass from this earth at such a young age. For those who could not easily comprehend it, there was a hope that maybe it was not true. Many of us have experienced the loss of a loved one or close friend. Sometimes, we "see" them on the street and our heart jumps for a second. We realize that we are seeing someone else, but a part of us cries out to the mirage in our mind and we yearn to have the opportunity to say one last thing to our close one.

Over the years, I've read of the many Elvis sightings and of course laughed them off. When I started this project, I took a preposterous idea and tried to create a possibility story. Getting into Elvis Presley's imaginary head was one of the most difficult things I have done as a writer. It was also one of the most painful, for I had to empathize with a person I had never met and to whom I had paid scant attention to growing up. Elvis was a sad and complicated person. I tried to give that sadness a place to be heard. It became my sadness and a sadness for me to work out.

I will never know what his ultimate life plans would have ever been. Who knows what would have happened had he lived. This story looks at one possibility and the reasons for how that fictional life would have come about. I tried to show Elvis' sweetness, his love and in the end his determination. It is a determination he may have never known he had in real life. I hope I did him justice.

I want to dedicate this book to my wife Chaya and my children Chaviva and Menachem. I also want to dedicate it to those who were murdered by the Nazis and Ukrainians in the town that my family originally came from. The story of Skalat portrayed in this book is based upon true events. The names of the victims were changed to protect their privacy. Other names with the exception of Mendel Tackett are the actual names. Their crimes should live in infamy.

The Skalat story reflects what was a systematic plan to kill the Jews throughout Galicia in Europe. I owe a great debt to Mr. Abraham Weissbrod, who lived through the slaughter and recorded a written history of the events which led to the decimation of the Jewish community there. His story formed the basis of the Skalat story in my book and although by now, he is long passed on, his account helped me to understand a little of my own legacy. Thank you Abraham and may you rest in peace.

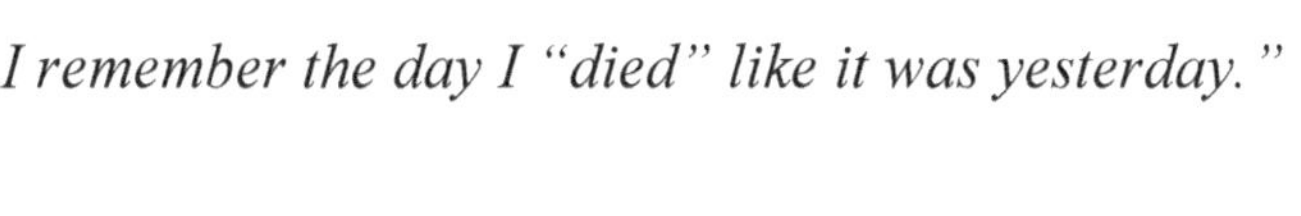

I remember the day I "died" like it was yesterday."

Prologue

It was an unusually chilly day in late October. The McDonald's in Dearborn, Michigan was very busy, as it was noon and people were coming in to grab a quick lunch. The restaurant was filled with teenagers from the local high school, so it was bustling and noisy.

The lines moved slowly but steadily up to the counter where people ordered, then picked up their tray or their bag with food and then moved on. On the line furthest to the right, a tall man with a long beard, wearing a black jacket and stocking cap waited patiently. Rubbing his hands together to get them warm, it was soon his turn to order. He looked down at the pretty teenager at the counter and ordered his meal.

"I'll have two Big Macs and an order of fries please, he said to her with his southern drawl. "Also, a large Coke and an Apple Pie."

She acknowledged his order, took his money, and returned his change. But she looked at him closely while returning his change and then stared at him as he stepped back. She turned to gather his order, returning back, looked at him and asked,

"To stay or to go?'

"To stay."

She went back to the service area and put his order on a tray. She came back to the counter and placed the tray in front of him. The man lifted it off the counter, looked at her briefly and went to find a seat. He settled into a booth in view of the counter. The teenaged girl kept looking up at him from the distance, but he being unaware, just opened his food and began eating. He was unsuspecting that he had become the subject of someone's repeated curiosity.

Finally, during a lull in the orders, his server called over to another girl working the line counter besides her. With a point of her pinky and a quick whisper, they looked over at the man. Whispering into her friend's ears, she pointed again at the man. Her friend looked up and then laughed.

"Silly girl, no way! It can't be him. He's been dead since last summer."

"I know that! Maybe it's some relative. The resemblance is eerie… I'm going to tell my Mom about this. She was a huge fan.

Chapter One

His head really hurt, and he knew it would be awhile before he would get some relief, so he put some water in the teapot and put it on the stove to boil. Soon, he heard the low whistle and shut off the fire. He prepared a coffee for himself and walked into the dining room to drink it.

"Good to see you again, Abraham", a voice boomed.

Abraham was so shaken he nearly dropped the coffee. He recovered quickly and looked in the direction of the voice. He saw a man sitting at the table half facing him. He had penetrating eyes, a long white beard and wore a long black coat.

"Do you remember me, Abraham?

"Of course, I do, Isaac"

"I scared you?"

"Well I wasn't quite expecting to see you at my table. Frankly, I was not expecting to see anyone". Tapping his chest lightly, "But I'm alright."

He put the cup on the table and stopped. The headache was gone.

Isaac smiled. "You have to admit it worked", he said with a wink.

"I guess it did"

"Why are you here?"

"I need your help"

"You . . need my help?"

"Yes"

Abraham nodded and sat down. "And how exactly can I help you?"

Isaac looked carefully at him. He looked deeply into his eyes. Then he sat back in the chair for a moment. Taking a deep breath, he leaned forward and reached across the table to take Abraham's hands in his.

"There is a man. A famous man. Very, very famous! He is in trouble. Terrible trouble! You should know that he is also a very sad man. Extremely so and very troubled. And soon, he will come to you to ask for your help."

Abraham looked perplexed, "Why me? And how will he know to contact me?"

"Don't worry about how! But you will know it when you are contacted. You are wondering why he will contact you, are you not?"

Abraham nodded yes.

"Because in your unique way will be able to help him.".

Isaac looked over at him and sighed deeply.

Abraham stood up and leaned over the table. "What exactly can I possibly do to help this man. A man I don't even know? You expect that I can do this?", he said angrily. "I am just an old man!"

"Oh, you are much more than that and you know it. You know how to live by your wits, even if you wouldn't want anyone to know that. You can help him. You know why? Because of what you learned escaping from Buchenwald."

"What are you talking about?" Abraham sighed deeply and sat back down again. He was silent for a few moments and then looked up at Isaac again. "Besides, that was a very long time ago." He looked down at his coffee cup and said nothing. Isaac just sat there in silence as well.

"I learned a lot of things in Buchenwald." He stopped again for a moment and sipped from his cup. Bringing it down slowly onto the table, he asked, "Exactly what could I use to help this man?

"What you learned to do to when you escaped."

"You can't ask that of me! No, not now! Are you telling me I am to help someone escape from somewhere?" Is that what you want me to do? Agh! Isaac, what I did to escape from Buchenwald… I don't talk about it to anyone, ever! I try not to even think about it. It haunts my dreams and that wakes me up." He paused to gather his thoughts which were running wild in his head. Finally he said to Isaac, "Why do you want me? I am an old man. I'm not meant for this!"

Isaac interrupted him angrily "Yes you are! You are exactly the right man for this! Why do you think I am here now? He looked across the table at Abraham and spoke softly, "Help this man to escape from a life of destruction and let him build a life of happiness and good."

Abraham shook his head, "And how am I supposed to do this? By myself?"

"You will not be alone. You will be the guide for others to get this man to the place G-d meant for him. There will be a time to get him out and there also will be a time when you will need to listen to the man himself. You will be the messenger and the guide for this man for the rest of your life and even after you are gone, he will remember, and you will be his guide. So, listen to what he needs and work out a plan to bring him close to you here in Brooklyn. Your old student Rabbi Fried will call you."

"And how is he involved in all this?",

Isaac didn't look at him. Getting no response, Abraham got up to rinse out his cup. When he turned back, Isaac was gone!

Chapter Two
Stan

"Let me tell you a story about my next-door neighbor. On the surface, he might seem to be a rather unremarkable fellow, but in reality, his story is the one every reporter wants to tell. And boy, oh boy, am I going to get to tell it to you. Not because I can. Because, believe me I can! Rather, I am going to tell you this story, to keep my word to this marvelous man. And most importantly because he agreed to let me tell it, when the time was right.

So, who am I that I get to tell this extraordinary story? I am Stan Eisenberg, a somewhat hotshot sportswriter, at least in my own mind and to some others, at the New York Daily News. To many in the know, it seems that I am always in the right place when a great sports story breaks in New York. If there is someone in the sports world with a story, I get it. I personally know all the owners, the managers, the coaches and the players. Before there were "Sports Doctors", there was yours truly. I am the expert when it comes to New York sports. For years, my column has run under the banner, "The Authority". Because in this town, I am the man, when it comes to talking about sports. Pretty big deal, don't you think? Ha! I also have written books about sports, as well as ghost written sports autobiographies with many famous players.

But I also have my share of demons. Unfortunately for me, the most problematic demon is my seeming incredible capacity to look someone right in the eye and tell them to go, you know... themselves. Given my profession, this ordinarily shouldn't cause too many problems. But for some inexplicable reason, I like to tell off the people most responsible for my success. I can't wrap my head around why I always seem to do that! Eventually, people get tired of dealing with "the man" despite the fact that I am that brilliant reporter and unusually dazzling teller of the story.

I do seem full of myself, Don't I? Well it belies the deep

disappointment I sometimes feel about myself.

Hey, and I had a wife as well. Trudy and I met on a blind date at a City College party and we were married for 24 years. We had a lovely apartment in Manhattan, raised two beautiful daughters, married them off and were left to live together. Not so suddenly, we both realized that we really didn't like each other. She quit first and asked me to move out four months after our youngest was married. I obliged her, because, well, the truth was, I didn't really care anymore and thought it would be more fun to be single. It wasn't! It was just the same old sad stuff. I moved into a tiny apartment on the Lower East Side and married my bar stool until my ulcer announced it could take no more.

I got sick. Really sick! The ulcer was the size of a pancake. Well that's an exaggeration but, when they were done cutting me up, I returned to that stinking apartment, where it would be months before I was able to go back to what I was doing before. My edge was gone, and I found that I had really started hating my life. I'd look out of my window onto Avenue A and get sick to my stomach. I had nothing! At least nothing that I had before. Just a sore belly, a tired apartment and none of the drive to get out there and be the man I once was.

Enough of the pity party!

So, let me tell you this story about my neighbor. How I got to be this man's neighbor is another story, probably best left to another time. But time being what it is, I'll tell you it anyway.

Soon after I went back to work, I went to cover a story about this young Orthodox Jewish man who was playing for the Brooklyn Cyclones. The Cyclones are a minor league team in Brooklyn. They play in a small ballpark in Coney Island. The Cyclone is the name of Coney Island's biggest attraction. It's an old wooden roller coaster built early in the 20th Century. People come from far and wide just to say they've ridden on the Cyclone. Hence the name of the team.

This kid played every day but Friday nights and Saturdays. He was tearing the cover off the ball and had become somewhat of a local celebrity. I went to interview him at his home in Flatbush, a quiet section of Brooklyn.

I finished interviewing him in his house and then walked down to Ocean Parkway. Now Ocean Parkway is one of the major roads in Brooklyn. It was a warm late spring night and before heading down to the subway, I decided to sit on one of these benches that are set up along the roadway. The benches are on these pedestrian islands that were built to separate the main traffic lanes from the residences that bordered the road. When I was a kid growing up in this neighborhood, there was a bridle path there for horses that you could rent from a stable in Prospect Park. I remembered that as a kid, I used to walk my dog on this bridle path. But now, it has been paved over for people to walk on and to ride their bicycles upon. Benches have been built for people to sit on. While sitting on one of those benches, if you weren't careful, you could easily fall asleep gazing at the passing traffic. It could be that hypnotic.

As a teenager, I would go out there every night with my gang of friends during the summer, to watch the pretty girls walking by and maybe if I got lucky, one of them would take the time to flirt with me. Now things are different. The neighborhood is mostly Orthodox Jews, but as I watched, it was obvious that behaviors don't change, just the outfits of the boys and girls. It was a beautiful evening and I enjoyed the warm breeze that was blowing down the parkway. All around me were young couples and their young children. Young girls dressed in long skirts sat on the benches. Young men in white shirts and black pants with their four fringes hanging out wearing black skullcaps. It was an idyllic scene. Everywhere I looked people seemed happy and connected. I longed for that. Deep, deep in my heart I longed for that. It had been a very long time since I had experienced it.

I had bought a sandwich in a local deli. Taking the food with me, I sat down to eat it on one of these benches. As I ate, I felt a little bit like when I was a kid again. It felt good.

I decided to walk around the neighborhood and take a look around. I had grown up nearby in an apartment building on East 3rd and Avenue P, so I knew the neighborhood pretty well. It had changed a lot since I was a kid, but outwardly it was still very much as I remembered it. I walked down Avenue P to East 7th Street and then turned and then on a whim turned up the street. As I moved on towards Avenue O, I saw a house for sale on my left. 1650 East 7th Street. It was the right side of this semi-attached house. I took down the realtor's number and decided I would call her when I got back to the office in the morning. The next morning, I made the call and set up an appointment to see the house the following Thursday.

So, the next Thursday arrived. I went back to Brooklyn and saw the house. Liked it right away and decided to put in an offer. My offer was accepted and three months later, on a blazing August morning, my moving van pulled up in front and the moving men started placing my things into my new home.

As I stood on the stoop directing the moving men, I could see some movement behind a curtain in the next-door neighbor's window. As I watched, I saw a woman looking out, and then she would disappear behind the curtain. A short time later, she looked out again. She kept doing this all morning, while the truck was being emptied. She never came out to say hello, she only looked out.

The moving men finished and now I'm in my new house in my old neighborhood. The thing is, I don't know anybody living there anymore, but I could care less. The block is quiet. Trees overhang the street. I have a little patch of grass in front of the house and a porch to sit on when this damn heat finally subsides. It's all right. The world is good for me again. I don't have to look out at the Manhattan filth. And I can walk to the subway to go to work. Not so bad!

The next morning, I get up, go to work, come home and start living a whole new life in this, my old stomping grounds. Except, I am no longer stomping. It's just home again.

Next comes the weekend and I see that the entire neighborhood shut down for the Sabbath. Families from all over are walking back and forth to synagogue or to visit each other. On Saturday afternoon, I step onto my porch and there is my next-door neighbor sitting quietly on his porch, staring at nothing in particular. I walk down the steps to walk over to the Avenue and as I pass him, I turn to wave. He doesn't wave back, rather he gets up and walks down the stoop and reaches out to shake my hand. So, I turned back to him and shook his hand. He looked me in the eye very closely. It kind of unnerved me. But I looked right back at him.

"Ah, my new neighbor! Hi, my name is Elijah Pressler, you can call me Elie." He spoke in a slow southern drawl and smiled broadly.

"Stan Eisenberg. I moved in a few days ago."

"I know! Stan or Stanley? Which do you prefer?"

"Either or. Most people just call me Stan. But whatever works for you, works for me."

He nodded.

"Elie, it's a pleasure to meet you. Is it Elie or Eli?"

"It's Elie, short for Elijah"

"Like the Elijah in the Bible?"

Elie smiled, "That's the one!"

"Elie, how long have you been living on this block?"

"My wife and I bought this house about 25 years ago. It is a really nice block. Mostly Jews like me, you know Orthodox. But some not! There are few Italian families living on the block but it's mostly just us Orthodox Jews."

Stan laughed, "Well I think you can see I'm not one of the gang." pointing to his head and the lack of a skullcap.

Ellie laughed as well, "it doesn't matter to me, I wasn't always Orthodox. In fact, I barely knew I was Jewish. I came to this life about 35 years ago and it's done well for me. So, I have a taste of both worlds. And I can appreciate both."

"Elie, what do you do for living?"

"I'm retired."

"Been retired long?"

"About 10 years."

"You don't sound like you grew up here. I hear a touch of the South in your voice."

"Memphis. I grew up in Memphis."

"I hear there is a big Jewish community down there"

"Not so big, but active!"

"And what did you do before you retired?"

"I was in the entertainment field", he laughed, "I was a Cantor"

"Really. For some reason I don't associate being a Cantor with being in entertainment, but I guess it is?"

Elie smiled sheepishly, "Yes, I consider it to be so. I've been doing it for a long time. I sing occasionally now, but that's what I did for a very long time."

"Did it pay well? I've heard that Rabbis and Cantors don't make so much."

"We got bye. I also did funerals and weddings and Bar-Mitzvahs, so, there was some money to be made. I taught Bar-Mitzvah lessons.... you know!" He shook his head and gave a quick laugh.

Elie turned to Stan, "And you?"

"I write for the New York Daily News. I'm a sports columnist. You may have heard of me. They call me the "Authority" when it comes to New York sports.”

“Oh, you’re that Stan Eisenberg! I read you all the time.” Visibly impressed, Elie said, “Wow, Stan Eisenberg. Nice to meet you.”

“The one and only! At least I think I am the only. At least, the only sports columnist with that name.”

Elie reached to shake his hand again, “Well it is a real pleasure. I love your articles; read them every time I see them in the paper. I am a huge fan.”

“Well, I’m glad you enjoy them.”

“You were sick, weren’t you? I didn’t see your column for a while.”

“Ulcers! Took me out for quite a while. But I’m back now and making trouble all over New York.”

“Glad to hear it. I missed your column.”

“Thanks, that nice of you to say.”

Stan turned to go. “Listen, I don’t want to disturb your Sabbath and I have to cover a game. But it was a pleasure to meet you and we’ll talk. Good Shabbos”

“You too! It was a pleasure!”

And so that was how I got to meet Elie. We were to become very good friends over the next year.

Chapter Three

It was a brutal winter. It was unusually cold, and it snowed like crazy. The subways were a mess and often I didn't get home until very late. I was busy covering the Giants and the Jets, then the Knicks and the Rangers.

Winter slowly passed into spring and then in late April, Passover was celebrated throughout the neighborhood. I didn't see Elie much all winter, but one morning as I was leaving for work, I ran into him in front of the house and he accompanied me down Avenue P to the Subway.

He asked me, "Do you have a place for the Seders (the Passover festive meal)."

"I am going to my daughter's house." I told him even though I knew it wasn't true. He seemed satisfied with that answer.

"Well if something changes and you find that you need, come join my family. There is always room for you, my friend."

I smiled and thanked him, but I could not imagine spending the Seder with his family. They were so "Jewish". For myself, I probably would be more satisfied with a ham and cheese on a Matza then going to a Seder. It occurred to me that this was an odd thought. As a child, I loved the Seder. But I had drifted away into indifference to all things religious and I realized that it kind of scared me to entertain the notion of going to his home. Anyway, we parted when I reached the subway.

The weeks passed, and I was settling in well. The house was comfortable and a good place to escape from the pressures of work. I walked out in front of the house one night and looked at the patch of ground in front of my house. What should have been this dime sized lawn looked used up and ugly. The next Saturday, I drove into Staten Island and bought trays of marigolds and petunias and a bag of grass seed. I needed some small hand tools and gloves, so I bought them in a hardware store. I brought them home and put them in the garage for the next day. Opening a beer, I flipped on the TV and watched the Rangers lose another playoff game. Their season looked about done!

The next morning, I gathered up the plants and seeds and tools and set them down in front of my stoop. I surveyed the lawn and saw that the soil in my front was pebbly and hard. I needed to rake the soil. Only I didn't have a rake and it would be a waste to throw seed down without trying to at least soften the ground up a little and make it reasonably level. I stood there with my hands on my hips, looking down at the ground, when I heard behind me,

"Stan. You look perplexed." It was Elie. I slowly turned around and looked up to his porch where he was sitting calmly with a big religious book open on his lap.

"Hey Elie. I bought all this stuff to make a garden, but I forgot to buy a rake."

"What do you have to buy a rake for? I have three different kinds in the shed in the back." He got up and motioned me to follow him as we walked along his driveway to the backyard. There he had an old metal shed. He fiddled with the combination lock and the lock opened.

"Ta Da! Magic." He slid the door of the shed open and started pulling out a tire, then some boxes and a hose.

"Elie, please don't go to so much trouble."

"No bother, they are here somewhere. I just have to look. I haven't used them in years and unless my wife threw them out, they are here. Aha, found them!"

You could hear some scraping metal sounds and then sure enough, he pulled out three distinct types of rakes. One for leaves and two for grooming soil. He reached out and handed them to me.

"There you go. This should take care of things." I smiled and took them from him while he locked up the shed. We returned to the front of the house. He went back to his book and I started to break up the soil. It took me a couple of hours to get the soil smoothed out and ready to seed. It was getting hot and well, I am no longer a young man, so I stopped for a while and sat on a step, mopping my brow with my handkerchief. Elie got up and went into the house. He returned to his book shortly and I just sat recovering my strength and letting the breeze cool me down. Elie's wife Shoshana opened the screen door and asked me if I would like something cold to drink. I nodded yes and a few minutes later she returned with a glass of iced tea. It tasted so good and was perfect. I thanked her, and she went inside. I had only met Shoshana in passing a few times. She was a tall, painfully thin woman with large square glasses. She was what one would call a plain looking woman. She was the mother of 8 and grandmother of 9. She normally wore a kerchief or a snood on her head, although on the Sabbath or holiday, she wore a wig. Sneaking out from the front of her kerchief were wispy strands of red hair. Now I'll tell you; I don't get the wig thing. But all the women in the community seem to do it, although sometimes you will see a young woman wearing a baseball hat. Shoshana always seemed very reserved and I don't think I have ever seen her really smile, just a quick upturn of the creases of her mouth.

Refreshed, I decided to go back to work. Elie had gone inside for lunch, so I had no one to talk to. I went back into the house and brought out a small boom box and grabbed a bunch of tapes to play while I worked. I worked at planting the petunias and marigolds and kept stopping to change the tape to something more my liking. Finally, I found an Elvis Presley tape and slipped it into the machine and went back to work while singing along. I was listening to Blue Suede Shoes.

Another voice joined me in the singing. The voice sounded just like the tape. I turned around and got startled. Standing right behind me was Elie singing along animatedly with me. We both finished the song with some flourish. Then we both laughed and high fived each other. Elie went back up onto the porch and opened his book, but you could hear him singing in the background, not too loudly, but just enough to notice that he knew all the words to every song.

I got up and walked to the bottom of his stoop and looked up to him on his porch,

"Big Elvis fan?"

He nodded, "You might say I'm his biggest fan. I mean, I grew up in Memphis. How could I not be an Elvis fan?"

"You ever saw him in person?"

"All the time."

"What was he like?'

"Nicest guy. Seemed a bit troubled, but really nice guy"

"Yeah, he was troubled. Tragic life, tragic death. I remember, I was driving upstate on Route 17 near Monticello. Listening to the radio when they announced he had died. I got so upset at the news, I pulled over onto the shoulder and sat for a while. I can't tell you why I did that. Now, I liked his music, but I wasn't, you know, into his music, per se. I mean I was into all those folk singers and the Eagles and Fleetwood Mac. But every once in a while, I would put on this Elvis tape and sing along. Beautiful voice. Just a beautiful voice."

"I agree. Beautiful voice." Elie looked away for a moment as if in quiet reflection. "Beautiful voice."

I returned to planting and singing along and in the background, I could hear Elie singing along quietly. I was crouching down planting this marigold plant when it hit me like a thunderbolt.

I turned and looked up at Elie. This was a tall man who although not fat, was not slim. His hair was cropped short and he had side curls, pulled behind his ears. He had a long full beard which was mostly gray, but not all gray. The nose was long and straight and his eyebrows full but not bushy. When he smiled, his lips kind of curled up to the left.

Stan looked back at the marigold he had been planting, but them quickly turned his head back to Elie.

"Elie, what's your Hebrew name again, I forgot it?"

"What?" Elie looked at him quizzically.

"Elie your Hebrew name? You know what they call you when you get called to the Torah in Synagogue?"

Elie looked at him strangely, then shrugged. "Elijah Aharon ben Abraham"

"Got it. Elijah Aharon Pressler." Stan turned back to the garden. Thinking for a second, something clicked in his head Elijah Aharon … Elvis Aaron. Pressler, Presley. He caught his breath. Then he fell back from his crouch onto the concrete. He grabbed his legs, so he didn't hurt himself. With his butt flat on the ground, he took a deep look back into his memory. The light bulb went on in his head.

"My G-d,", Stan thought to himself, "He's been hiding in plain sight."

Stanley took some long deep breaths. He could hardly control himself but said nothing. Sweat was suddenly pouring down into his eyes. Eyes stinging and tearing, he tried to lift himself from the concrete without making it seem that something was wrong.

"Stan, are you alright?"

Looking hard at Elie, I tried to visualize him without the beard and much younger. I looked away. "Yeah, yeah", swiping my handkerchief across my brow, "Got a little overdone in the sun. I'm okay." I looked down at the concrete.

"You sure?"

I looked at Elie again. It was as if his face melted into the face of a younger Elvis Presley, clean shaven, long sideburns, the upturned lips. I looked away again.

Answering him, "Sure. Sure, I'm fine. I am just going inside to get some water." I went into the house and stood by the kitchen sink. Turning the faucet on, I let the water run for a minute. Dipping my hands in, I splashed my face and arms. I grabbed a glass from the cupboard and filled it. Leaning over the sink, I poured it over my head and then neck, soaking my tee shirt. Grabbing a kitchen towel, I dried off as best I could and drew a drink of the water with the glass.

Sitting down at the table, Stan took a long swallow. Head spinning, he tried to talk himself out of what was swirling around in his brain. He laughed to himself. It must be a weird coincidence.

But if it was true, it was a reporter's dream. The scoop of a lifetime. Easy street. A book, a movie, lots of green.

Stan thought to himself, "What a crazy idea." But the more he thought about it, the idea seemed to resonate with him. "I'd have to confront him on this, but what if I am wrong? How ridiculous would that be? Elvis Presley. My neighbor? But his last name is Pressler? His middle name was Aaron. Elvis could easily be turned into Elijah. Close enough, but different enough to not raise flags. And of course, he grew up in Memphis? Too easy! Got to be just coincidence. For sure, coincidence, must be!" Stan walked around his kitchen musing, "But if it's true, who else knows?

He stretched his feet onto another one of his kitchen chairs. Staring straight out into space, he imagined that he was right. Therefore, of course, Shoshana surely knows. Or maybe not. She seems so…parochial. Maybe Elie never told her. But that can't be, she's his wife. They have kids together. Heck, they have grandkids. But of course, she knows if her husband is really Elvis Presley!"

Stan went into the living room and turned on the television. He stood watching golf and drinking his water. Then he went out to finish his work. Elie had gone in. Stanley knew that was probably a good thing. He would need time to figure this all out. Stan's mind kept running all kinds of scenarios. If this was all true…! If so, who helped him pull it off? And surely there had to be more people involved?

Finally, he went back into the house and stretched out on the couch. "This is craziness", he thought to himself. Yet, he could not shake the thought that he was right, and he kept contemplating every conceivable way it could be true.

Grabbing his reporter's notebook, he started writing down every possible scenario or circumstance that might have occurred. He envisioned it, as if it were real, in his own mind. He asked himself a bunch of questions and each one that flowed from his brain was recorded in that notebook.

Putting the pieces together would either be the greatest story of his career or it could be the makings of a great novel. Either way, he married himself to the idea of putting it to paper. He hoped so badly that his suspicions were right. Stan wasn't sure he could handle the embarrassment of confronting the man and being wrong. He might have to move away just when he felt the most comfortable living here.

Besides, he had no idea how to confront the question with the man. But he ached to know. Well, being a reporter, there was only one thing to do. Arm yourself with the facts and then bring them to Elie and see what became of all that.

Stan drifted off to sleep. The next day in the office, he asked his assistant to bring him everything that the paper had in the newspaper's morgue on Elvis Presley. The mental voyage had begun. Hopefully, it wouldn't drown him.

Chapter Four

It was after dark when Stan knocked on Elie's door. Shoshana opened the door looking at him quizzically,

"Stan, is everything OK?"

"Hi Shoshana, everything's fine. Is Elie around?"

"I think he's out the back. I will go get him."

"Thanks, but I can go walk around back."

"He is not in the backyard. He's actually down in the back of the basement."

She walked to the back of the house and down the stairs into the basement. A few moments later, Ellie came up. Elie wiped his hands on the front of his pants and the two men shook hands.

"Stanley my friend. What's new?"

"All good. I have to ask you something. When I was gardening this weekend, a thought came to me. I'd like to discuss it with you if you have a few minutes."

"Sure. Come on down with me into the basement and we can sit down like Menschs in my office."

They walked down to the basement and settled into a small closeted area filled with a small desk and bookshelves teaming with Jewish religious books. There was so many they were overflowing onto stacks on the floor. Elie produced a half-filled bottle of whiskey from behind his desk with two plastic cups. He smiled at Stan. Stan laughed and shook his head. Elie poured and they both said L'Chaim and took a swallow. Elie sat down behind the desk and motioned Stanley to clear the books from the other chair in the room and sit down.

"So, my friend, what's on your mind?"

"When I was gardening Sunday, it was the first time I have ever heard you sing."

"Well you know, I am a cantor. I sing all the time. You should come to Synagogue once in a while. Even though I am retired, they let me sing pretty much whenever I want to.”

“I should.”

Elie added some whisky to both cups. They both took another swallow.

“You know Elie, you really know your Elvis songs.”

“Singing them my entire life”

“When did you get into Elvis’ music?”

“Ah, I must have been a teenager, actually, I was singing for my family when I was just a kid.”

“They all must have thought you had talent?”

“I guess”, laughing,” they kept letting me sing, especially my Mama.”

“When you sang those Elvis songs, I am telling you, it sounded so much like Elvis, I could not tell the difference”

“Lots of practice singing those songs.” He lifted the cup up at Stan and took another swallow.

“Elie, you know I am a reporter?”

“Yes”

“Elie are you hiding in plain sight?”

“I don’t understand.”

“I think you do!”

There was a pause. Elie took another swallow.

“Elijah Aaron Pressler. Born in Mississippi. Grew up in Memphis, Tennessee. It might be coincidence, but it might not be. Was Elvis your cousin?” Elie sat quietly with his hands folded together across his belly. “Elie, I mean, well, you know Pressler could easily be a replacement name for Presley. And Aharon is Hebrew for Aaron and Elijah could easily be a construct for Elvis. I mean, this may sound really stupid, but are you Elvis Presley hiding in plain sight?

Still not a word from Elie. He just sat there behind the desk. Then tears started to roll down his cheeks. He placed his finger on his lips and sighed deeply.

“I guess I always knew that someday ...!” Then he looked around as if expecting someone to pop in at any time. He motioned for Stan to swing the door closed. He took a deep breath as if trying to control his emotions. He whispered,

“Please Stanley, Shoshana and the kids do not know. You must never tell them. You must never tell anyone. Let this be our little secret.”

Stan exploded out of his chair, "Little secret? Elie, I am a reporter! This is like the biggest story a reporter could ever hope to break. My G-d, your Elvis Presley and you ain't dead!"

Stanley grabbed at the cup of whiskey. He swallowed it down in one gulp and motioned Elie for more. Elie refilled the cup. Stan motioned for him to fill it all the way up and then took a long hard swallow, again in one gulp. He wiped his lips with the back of his hand and looked at Elie. Finally, he sat back down.

"All those sighting, are they all true?" Stan got up again and tried to stretch himself but was so excited he almost fell over a stack of books. He recovered, setting some of the tumbled books back in the stack. Sitting back down, he almost knocked them over again, but quickly caught them and set them straight. He leaned over and put his head in his hands. Shaking his head back and forth, he looked up at Elie and said softly, "How can I keep this a secret?"

Elie sat there looking at him saying nothing. Tears were streaming down his cheek and he reached for a tissue from the box on the desk.

Stan sighed and looked right in Elie's eyes and said, "And the most important thing this reporter wants to know is, how did you do it? Really? How in the hell did you get away with it?"

Elie smiled weakly. Stan continued, "You can't be the only person who knows your alive. It is impossible that you just walked away from Graceland without someone knowing!"

Elie sat there motionless, just kind of slumped in his chair. Stan looked at him questioningly.

Stan leaned over the desk and pointed right at Elie. Almost screaming out loud, "Elie, do you get this? Do you get that everyone thinks you're dead, for crying out loud?"

"Shush, everyone in the house will hear you" Elie said, as he just kept crying. Shoshana yelled down if everything was alright. Stanley opened the door.

"Shoshana, it's all good. Nothing to worry about. Stan was telling me a sad story."

"Ok, if you need something?"

"We're good"

Elie looked at Stan with imploring eyes, "Stanley, my life is good here. I am happy, but I am also old and sick. I do not know how much longer I will be in this world." He stopped for a moment to wipe his eyes with a tissue, then he said, "I know you are a good man and I know that you would not want to harm my family. I will make you a deal."

Stan looked at Elie, knowing that at this moment in time, he was a broken individual. He reached for the bottle and poured some more into Elie's cup and then poured some more into his own.

"What kind of deal? Look Elie, I don't want to harm you, but how can I possibly hide this? I am a reporter. This is what a reporter lives for. The greatest story that ever will fall into my lap?"

Elie got up and stretched his legs. "I know Stan. I really do!" Sipping from his cup, he said to Stan, "I'll tell you what. Let me tell you the entire story, but you must not publish it until I die."

"Elie, that could take years!"

"Or it could be months, probably no more than three or four at the most." He sat back down and whispered to Stan, "I have Pancreatic Cancer. You are the only person other than Rabbi Kaplan who knows. I am not going to tell my family until near the end." He took a deep breath. "If you work with me on keeping this secret, the scoop, so to speak is yours. Exclusively! You can publish it as soon as I die. It will not be a secret to the world anymore and I can live in peace until my maker takes me home. Do you think you can do this for me Stanley?"

Stanley sat back down, shocked at the news of Elie's sickness. He shook his head yes and tears appeared on his cheeks. The two men got up and hugged.

"Stanley, one other thing. Any money you make from this story, you must share with my wife. A fair share! We will work out the details. Ok?"

Stanley nodded yes.

"Good, then we will start tomorrow. We can walk over to Ocean Parkway and sit on the benches and you can ask me anything. Are you good with that?

Stan shook his head and wiped his eyes. "Sure, Ok!"

Chapter Five

"I remember the day I "died" like it was yesterday."

"Now that was an interesting statement! Elie and I were sitting on his front porch in old fashioned cloth folding lawn chairs. He was drinking some soda from a large glass. He breathed heavily and then just started talking.

"Stanley, let me tell you my story. So, it went like this, believe it or not. I know it's going to sound crazy, nonetheless, I remember the day I "died" like it was yesterday. You may ask what am I talking about? However, you heard me right. I did in fact say I remember the day I "died" like it was yesterday!"

Stan looked at him quizzically. Elie saw immediately that Stan did not understand, but how could he. He was about to describe to Stanley a scenario that only crazy people could have imagined. This was the stuff of conspiracy jockeys and the National Enquirer. Soon he would be able to show, that every crazy speculation over all these years was often the truth.

"So much preparation had gone into what I'm about to tell you that when I finally did it, well ... it was so surreal. I just walked out of my life. Walked out of my life! That's right, I said that! Walking out of my life seemed so impossible. After all, how could I just go do that? I had worldwide fame. All these people worked for me, depended on me for a living. I had all these friends, these acquaintances, these wannabe friends and wannabe acquaintances. The press? They were always around. How could I just disappear into the oblivion?

It seemed impossible to me, maybe it will seem that way to you as well, but I really just walked out of my life. And then I walked into a more stable, more conventional life instead. A life of peace for me.

In the strangest way, I never really wanted any of the life I had. I just wanted to sing! I just wanted to make music. I wanted to sing for my Mama, because it made her happy to listen to me sing my heart out. But as it turned out, when the success came, I was still just a teenager. All I had was my fame and all the nonsense that went with it. Sure, there was lots of money, but there was also lots of pressure. That pressure sat right in my gut. Oh my G-d, I felt it all the time. I would wake up shaking. My chest felt full and fluttering all the time. My neck was so tight that I could barely move it. Stan, I'm telling you, I could not turn my head from side to side."

Elie looked away. He seemed to drift to a bygone place. Stanley looked at him closely, not able to understand where Elie had mentally gone off to. He coughed for a moment and went on. "Continuing," he said, but this time differently. Not the soft-spoken Elie, rather like a reborn Elvis Presley.

"Oh, that stress. It was a constant pressure! I cannot even begin to tell you. It was just too much for me. My chest always felt like it was going to burst. I can still feel it. Even now! My gosh Stanley, I feel it now as I am thinking back on it. Believe me, it was so impossible! I couldn't stand still or even sit in one place for more than a few minutes. Forget about sleep. Even when I did sleep, I woke up groggy and dazed.

As I said, my neck was so tight that I couldn't turn my head from side to side. Man, I tried massage. I worked my martial arts, but it didn't do anything to relieve the stress. I took all the muscle relaxants my doctors could give me. But nothing worked. Well the muscle relaxants worked sometimes. At first, they worked all the time, but later ... ...? Sometimes I felt that I could not breathe. Lights bothered me, so I had to wear sunglasses much of the time. My skin seemed to crawl all the time. My guts just locked up like a clogged pipe. Nothing the doctors gave me helped. When I had a clear enough mind, I would look at my world from the outside in and wondered how it had come to this.

I just needed to get away. To breathe, to live! I couldn't even take a piss without someone wanting to know where I was and what I was doing. It was way too much for me, way, way too much!

How could someone like me just walk away from everyone and disappear? Everywhere I went people followed me, even in my own home. Sometimes I wished that I could be alone without someone interrupting me with some detail they wanted me to deal with. You would think that everyone wants fame and fortune. But by now, all I wanted to be was an average Joe. From the time I was a teenager, fame was all I had. Money, well I had so much money, I couldn't figure out how to spend it all. I had cars, motorcycles, houses, ridiculous gifts, but I didn't have a home. Graceland was a big old house, but it was never a home for me. A home is where one can feel safe. I definitely didn't feel that. No siree, I never felt safe! Anywhere! I could practice Karate all day long and not feel any safer. All my guns didn't make me feel protected.

If I knew then what I know now ... Well of course it is easy to say I would never have traveled down that road. But the truth was that I was a young pup then, who just wanted to make my Mama happy. Then all of a sudden, I was an old dog trying to make everybody else happy. But I was not happy, just confused. The truth be known, I was miserable almost all the time. No one around me took me seriously, until I acted up. I am almost certain that if I had continued on this path much longer, I would have really died. So in the end, for me dying was as easy as anything else.

And I actually wanted to die! Self-abuse can lead to self-deceit and that can lead to self-hatred. Almost all of mine came from never finding my true self.

On one level, I wanted to die, but not really. I just wanted to run away. Disappear for a few days, maybe a week! Go incognito! Have a Big Mac without the entire world watching or maybe some ribs. I didn't know! Just wanted to get away from Graceland and the Colonel and my father. I'd find a cheap motel and sleep. A good sleep, not the foggy sleep that never seemed to go away. Biscuits with my eggs in the morning. It would be a breath of fresh air!

So, you see, dying was as easy as walking into the toilet. Or so it seemed to everybody else! Except I walked out of that toilet and out the door.

How could I explain this to Ginger or the Colonel or anybody! I just wanted out for a little while.

And then I met Anna Rabinowitz."

Chapter Six

Elie came back from synagogue. It was a warm summer evening, so we sat together again on the porch. His kids flitted in and out of the house, playing in the street, but they were out of earshot. Elie had a cup of tea Shoshana had just given him. She looked at him for a moment before opening the screen door and going in.

"Have you told her yet? Stan asked.

"No, I still have some time. Soon it will be obvious that I am sick."

"Do you think that's fair to her?"

Elie sighed deeply, "I don't know. Probably not, but I don't want to worry her any more than I have to. Just remember, you promised me that you would give her a fair share of the profits from this. Remember Stanley, we discussed this" He said emotionally. Tears formed in the corners of his eyes.

"I know Elie, I gave you my word and I will keep my word."

"A substantial share! She will have no other income."

"You don't have to remind me. She will be taken care of!" Stanley lifted his can of soda and touched it to Elie's teacup. He nodded acknowledgement. "So, let's continue."

He stopped for a moment to drink down some tea.

"We were playing Las Vegas. We were slipping into the hotel through the kitchen to avoid the crowds. I heard a woman's voice with a thick European accent calling out to me. "Mr. Presley! Mr. Presley! I need to talk to you. Mr. Presley!" I looked around and could see the kitchen staff running to do their tasks as we tried to move through to the elevator up to our rooms.

"Mr. Presley, please don't run away, I need to talk with you."

I focused on a very small woman, in a waitress' uniform, blocking my path. I stopped to look at her as one of my bodyguards stepped in front of me to move her. But it was something in her look, in her eyes, that told me to stop and listen.

"Hey man", I said to my bodyguard, "it's alright, leave her alone. You need to talk with me?'

"Yes, I do."

"What this about?

"It's very important", she said as she slowly raised her pointing finger at me.

"Important? What? Do you need an autograph for your grandkids?" I said smiling.

She made a face, "I don't need autographs, I need to speak with you!"

"Me? Why? Do you know who I am?" I tried thinking back to see if I had ever met her, but I didn't remember. Besides, she looked at least 60 years old. She spoke with a European accent. Maybe I had met her when I was in the Army in Germany. A maid in a hotel? A cook? She didn't look familiar!

She answered, "Of course I know who you are. I called you by name, didn't I? She leaned close to my ear to whisper, "I need to speak to you because a member of your family did a very bad thing to my family and you should know about it."

"Do I know you?"

"No!"

"You say a member of my family did something bad? Who? Who in my family are you talking about? I don't even I know you!" What are you talking about?"

"What I am talking about ... ", She looked around the room. Everyone in the kitchen was looking at her.

The Chef walked over to me," I'm sorry about this disturbance Mr. Presley", He turned to the woman and said, "Anna, get back to work! This is not the time or place. Leave him alone!"

She said to the Chef, "This is none of your business. This is between me and", then pointing at me, "him"!

I shrugged my shoulders and looked around. I really wanted to get to my room and go to sleep. It had been a hard tour and a tough show, and I was beat.

But she persisted. And then I saw it. I saw it on her forearm. The numbers! For some reason that I did not understand, I just knew I had to talk with her. I looked around at all the people in the room, then at her arm again. I had heard about it but had never seen it. The numbers, the tattoo!

"Mr. Presley, please listen to what I have to say!"

I put my hands up in mock surrender, "Okay, I'll listen, but not here". I looked at my bodyguard and told him to bring her to my room in fifteen minutes. I needed to get my head straight.

She looked at me and said in almost a whisper, "Danks Got, he will listen!"

Chapter Seven

"She sat on the corner of the couch. I was spread out in a chair opposite of her. She peered at me intently and looked around the suite. The guys were in the other room laughing and joking loudly as they ate sandwiches and drank beer. I was exhausted. Physically and mentally, I had no energy left. What was I doing letting this old woman disturb me at this hour? I didn't know!"

Stan asked, "What did she say?

"She said to me. Mr. Presley, my name is Anna Steuben Rabinowitz. Rabinowitz is my married name although I have been widowed for many years".

"How come you never remarried?" I asked her.

"That is for another time, another place".

I swallowed hard but did not say more. She continued, "I come from a small village in Europe called Skalat."

"Where is Skalat?" I asked her.

"Most people would say Hungary. It was really in the Ukraine. It doesn't matter much as we were constantly being taken over by other nations and who knew who really owned the place" My father was a doctor and we lived a comfortable life until the beginning of the War. The Second World War."

She looked around again. The boys were making a lot of noise in the next room.

"May I shut the door?"

"Sure"

She got up and closed the door; you could hear hoots and hollers from the guys, who were watching a baseball game on the television.

"It was hard for us during the war, Mr. Presley"

"I would guess it was. What was so hard?"

She looked at me ferociously, "It was war and we were Jews."

I squirmed in my seat. She continued,

"We were hated by all the sides in the war, not just the Germans.

But because my father was a town doctor, the people in town protected us from much of the bad things that were happening to our neighbors. He was lucky. Even the Doctors were killed during the pogrom. Do you understand what I am saying, Mr. Presley?

I nodded yes. I wanted to yawn but didn't. She looked into my eyes as if she didn't believe me.

"Do you really understand Mr. Presley. It is important that you do."

I nodded yes to her. Then I asked, "What's a pogrom?"

"It was an organized riot, permitted and encouraged by the Germans in which Jews were brutally murdered."

"When the German's came, they allowed the local Ukrainians to have a pogrom. We got lucky. we went into hiding with the help of some of our Polish neighbors. After the pogrom was over, they kept us hidden. They were not Jews and it was a huge risk for them to take. We hid in a farmer's hay loft and depended on him and his family to feed us. Because it was unsafe during the day, they would slip us food at night, but everyone suffered during the war, there was never enough food, only enough for one miserable meal a day, if we were lucky. The farmer was a kind-hearted man, but if he got fearful, he might not bring out food for a couple of days. Once my mother had to sneak out and knock on the farmer's window to feed us when the German troops were in the area. But we survived! As for the rest of the Jews in town, they were rounding up the remaining Jews not killed in the pogrom and shipping them to concentration camps. Not all at once, but over many weeks, people just disappeared. Many times, my father would say to my mother that we should run up into the hills to hide out, but with five children, two of whom were just babies, it was too dangerous to try. So, we stayed in our hiding place, hoping against hope that we would not be caught."

"Were you caught?"

"Yes, Mr. Presley, we were caught. It took several months, and we might not have ever gotten caught but for one man, who notified the Germans of our hiding place. The result was the farmer was arrested and probably killed and the rest of my whole family ended up in Auschwitz. Of the seven of us, only I live today."

I leaned over to her and said quietly, "What a miserable person to do that".

"Yes, a miserable person, an animal! Worse still was that he was a

Jew, just like us."

"That's just crazy!", I said, "one of your own?"

She looked down at the floor and said,

"I know! But Mr. Presley, who knows why people do the things they do. He might have been scared for himself. Or the German's might have paid him money, or he did it to escape the camps himself! Who knows and what does it matter now? Will it bring my family back?"

"No" I said and sat quietly for a moment.

Then I said to her, "Why are you telling me all of this?

She looked at me closely and leaned in and speaking softly she said to me,

"The man who turned my family in to the Germans was named Mendel Tackett. Does the name Tackett mean anything to you, Mr. Presley?

The name sounded familiar. I was not sure where I had heard it before.

"I am afraid I don't know anyone named Tackett".

Then I thought back to when my Mama talked about her Great Grandma Nancy. Grandma Nancy's married name was Tackett. Suddenly, it all seemed to make sense.

Chapter Eight

Elie and Stan sat in Elie's little basement office. Stanley had brought a flask of Scotch with him. The two of them had already drank two or three glasses and were feeling loose. Elie seemed a bit withdrawn.

"What's bothering you my friend? Stanley motioned to the bottle for a refill. Elie poured a little into Stan's glass.

"Remembering", he sighed, "Just remembering."

"What about?"

"Anna Rabinowitz. I still think about her a lot. The night she spoke with me, I could not sleep at all. I sat out on a couch and tried to escape by watching TV. It didn't help much. I thought long and hard about what she had told me. A distant cousin of mine ratted out his Jewish neighbors to the Nazis. It just made me sick to think that I could be related to a person like that. I felt sickened inside. I still do, after all these years." Elie motioned to the flask. Stan passed it over to him and watched him pour some of the brown liquid into his cup. He raised it his lips and took a good swallow.

"But I thought to myself that night. What did it have to do with me? I never knew this person and he was probably dead himself from the Nazis. Why then was this weighing me down so heavily?

When Anna left my room that night, I asked her why she told me this story. She shrugged her shoulders, but didn't say anything. I asked her if I could do anything for her. She again shrugged, but then she said, "Mr. Presley, I do not want anything from you. You are a very famous man and I am sure you are very busy. I just recently became aware of the fact that you were related to Mendel Tackett. I have been trying to find him since after the war, just to ask him why he did this terrible thing. I do not know if he even survived the war. A librarian has been helping me to look. She discovered that you were related to this man. So, when you came to sing here, I felt the need to tell you?"

"But surely there is something I can do for you? What can I do to help you?", I asked her.

"Again Mr. Presley, I don't need your help! I need nothing from you. I just wanted to tell you because you are this man's family. It is not your fault that your cousin did such a terrible thing. In truth, it is not even your burden. You seem like a nice man. I am sorry to have disturbed you". She looked up at me and shook her head. Then she looked down at the floor.

"Really I should not have come and disturbed you like this."

She started to cry, "I just needed to finish this ... for my family"

Then she was gone.

And from then on, I was a lost soul dedicated to refinding myself!"

Chapter Nine

By then, Elie and Stanley were quite drunk and quite sad. The flask was drained, and Shoshana came down to bring Elie upstairs to go to sleep. Elie walked Stanley to the front door and stepped out onto the porch with him. The two shook hands. Then, Elie sat down on one of the chairs on the porch.

"I'm not done. Stanley, sit down here next to me. "Stan looked at Shoshana and shrugged. She looked back at Elie but knew better. She closed the screen and went back inside.

"When Anna Rabinowitz blocked my path that night, something shifted in my head. It was cosmic! It was a shift that gave me a purpose and a cause. But if I didn't know it then. It would become obvious to me soon. Mendel Tackett was not me; his family was not mine. The fact that we shared a bloodline was just that. I had no relationship with any European Jew. I was just a Rock and Roll singer from Mississippi who was killing himself slowly with drink and drugs and unhappiness.

Yet this little woman had changed my whole focus and I spent many days wondering who I was, why I was the person I am. I pondered what my purpose here on earth was. Was I really supposed to be this Rock and Roll singer?

The truth of the matter was that I realized, in many ways I was Mendel Tackett. Mendel must have been a very troubled man to have turned people over to the Nazis. Either he was troubled because he had no morality, or he was just a dog trying to save himself. Either way, I could relate to all that. Despite my best efforts, my life had become this big wave and I was riding on it, like a surfer, hoping not to get swallowed up and knowing that I had.

Mama was long dead, and Daddy knew nothing about my Great Grandma in this regard. I had asked him about it, but Vernon just shrugged his shoulders and asked why I suddenly cared. I tried to explain about Anna, but he just looked at me, reaching into the refrigerator for a beer, and asked me why I was even worrying about it. "She is just some old lady. Probably wanted some money or something!"

"I don't know about that." I said back to him angrily. "She didn't want money. Just wanted me to know! I don't know why that was important to her. I guess she figured that by telling me she would clear her head. You know like a dying confession or something."

I remember grabbing the back of my neck at that point. "I sure got a damned headache. We got any aspirin around here?"

I left the room and went to lie down. I closed my eyes, but I couldn't sleep. I was going over this conversation again and again. I got up and called my lawyer and told him the story. He wanted to know why I called him about this. I told him I wanted him to hire an investigator to look into this.

"Hell Elvis, what are you trying to gain from this. It will be awfully expensive and even if it is true, what difference does it make in your life? It's just an old lady letting off steam. And you being the nice boy that you are, let her have her moment. Now, we'll just let it die a natural death and not worry much about it. It is a waste of your precious time."

"Of course, you couldn't let it go." Stan looked at Elie.

"No, I couldn't." He chuckled gently, "Of course, I hired an investigator myself and sent him off to find out the truth."

"Ellie, I am going to ask you the same question your lawyer originally asked you. Why did it matter to you then? What were you hoping to find out?"

"At the time I had no idea. I was a mess, all screwed up, a head full of drugs, my family deteriorating around me. Honest to G-d, I had no idea what I was doing. But something, deep inside me, told me that I had to find out. I just had to. So, I did."

"Did you get the answers you were looking for?"

"I'm here now."

"And what does that mean?"

"I am here now, because what I learned about Mendel Tackett ..., but not from the lawyer"

"I don't understand? What did you learn about Tackett?"

"Let's just leave that right now."

"Elie, you promised me a story?"

"And you'll get it. OK? But I'm a bit drunk right now and should go to bed. So, let's leave this to lie for the moment"

Stan shook his head, "Wow. This must have blown your mind?"

Elie nodded and got up to go into his house. As the screen door closed on his back, he reopened it. "Stan, we'll continue tomorrow. I'll knock on your door."

Chapter Ten

❝I grew up, at least in my teen years, at The Courts. The Courts was a public housing complex in Memphis. It is now known as Lauderdale Courts. We lived in Apartment # 328 from 1949 through 1953. It was a complex of three-story buildings. I remember for some odd reason, that there were 442 units. You could walk down to the Mississippi because we were a few blocks away. The place was mostly poor to lower middle-class whites. I'm told that today, it mostly rundown. It's become really dangerous. The city doesn't take very good care of it, not that they did when I lived there. But still… When I made it big, we moved to Graceland, approximately 15 miles away. Graceland was built by a doctor in 1939. I purchased it in 1957. It was my home until 1977 when I "died". I'm told it's now the biggest tourist place in Memphis."

"Ever miss it?" Stan asked.

Ellie shrugged, "Not really. Well I guess sometimes I think about it, but mostly in sadness. It's not who I am now. In truth, I wanted to show off to Mama. She loved all the glitz. I always felt kind of well…I don't know. I mean I liked living there. But the place lacked a moral compass and it dragged me down. Lots of fun, but mostly sad memories."

I went to Humes High School. I was the shy outsider who brought his guitar to school every day. I liked school but believe it or not I failed music. Never learned to read music. It's all by ear, you know.

I am a twin, born second of twins. My brother, Jesse Garon, passed away either in very early infancy, or was stillborn. Mama would never tell me exactly which. A cousin of mine once told me a story of coming to the house in Tupelo. Someone had died. I suspect it was Jesse. Everyone from the family sat on low chairs and the mirrors were covered. "It was years later," she told me that she learned, "that these were Jewish traditions."

Mama always told me I was Jewish, even though we went to

Church regularly. She was really proud of her Jewish roots. I once asked her how she knew we were Jewish. She looked at me closely. I must have been about seven or eight. Then she said to me, "Well you was born and grew up in Tupelo, Mississippi. We lived in a poor area called "The Pinch." The Pinch was what locals called the home of the "rag trade."

I asked her what that was? She said it was an industry, which up here we call the Shmatta business and as you know, it is still going strong even today, It was worked mostly by Jewish immigrants who repaired and then resold secondhand clothing.

Our family tradition goes way back to a time when Jewish immigrants, settled in the South bringing the rag trade with them. My great great maternal grandmother was a woman named Nancy Burdine. She came from a family that had traveled to America from Lithuania. They say they most likely came around the time of the American Revolution. I don't know if that's true, but Mama was most insistent about that. Nancy married a man named Abner Tackett around 1850. We always said that Abner may been Jewish himself, or at least half-Jewish. The Tackett's had two sons, Sidney and Jerome and a daughter named Martha, my great grandmother. Martha married a man named Whitey Mansell. They had a daughter, Octavia, who they nicknamed Doll. She was my Grandma. Doll married Bob Smith and had nine children; their fifth child was a girl they named Gladys Love. Gladys was my Mama.

Now my Mama was so proud of her Jewish roots. When she died, I told the stone makers that I wanted a stone which had a Star of David and a cross inscribed for her. Later when her body was moved to Graceland, they put up a stone with only a cross. I couldn't do anything about that without giving up the secret.

Getting back to Memphis, we lived in a small apartment. Above us lived a Jewish Rabbi and his family. His name was Rabbi Fried. I liked visiting with the Rabbi and his family. They always fed me. I loved chicken soup and matzah balls.

I would listen to Jewish music with the Rabbi and grew to love the wailing and crying sounds. It reminded me, in some strange way, of the Blues I heard on Beale Street. I was their Shabbos Goy. I never told them of my Jewish side, so they thought I was 100% Gentile. I would come into their apartment and do the things that were forbidden to them on Shabbos, such as lighting a stove or turning on the lights. Rabbi Fried tried to pay me doing this, but I always turned him down. I enjoyed being there so much. I somehow acquired a skull cap, which I always kept in my back pocket of my pants. I think I found it in my Mama's drawer. Not sure why she had one, but from then on, it was mine.

Mama, as I said, never made a secret about her family tree to me. I also learned that I was part Cherokee Indian and was very proud of that. But Mama always warned me not to make my Jewish stuff too well known. Anti-Semitism was a big problem in the South in the 40's. But I loved the Fried's and was glad to help out whenever I could."

Chapter Eleven

Avner Tackett was done with it. Just done! He stood in the middle of the small synagogue in Hanover in what is now Germany. The year is 1841 and Avner is 17 years old. He is an apprentice tailor. It is a job he despises along with despising everything else in his life. He hated being tucked into a traditional Orthodox Jewish life and yearned for freedom from conformity.

But this morning as he puts his phylacteries away and prepares to go work, he decides he has had enough. "No more", he thinks to himself, "I am going up north to Hamburg and sail to America. He dreams of a new life, new fortunes, free to be whatever he wants, no matter what.

Willing to leave his entire family, his entire community, and his entire legacy and going to America had been a thought Avner had been pondering for some time. He had no use for the tailoring business, but he was good at buying and selling. His patron Reb Elimelech had come to rely on the boy to choose the best quality materials when they went to the fairs to buy and he was especially good at negotiating good prices from the sellers of cloth, especially from the gypsies. Smart, with a quick wit and slight smile, he was well liked by most everyone. He came from a well thought of family of workmen. Most of the men were either carpenters or masons or merchants. Not well off, the family managed to get by.

Avner's immediate family lived on the outskirts of the Jewish section of Hanover. His father, Mordechai Tackett was a dairy merchant. His mother, Elka ran a household of seven children. Avner's older siblings were Menachem Mendel, who was 21 and married to Sara. They had a little boy Aaron. His sister Shoshana was 19. Younger than him were David, Gila, Bella, Reina and the baby Moses. Avner was the classic middle child, lost in a big family, feeling ignored and put upon.

"They won't even miss me," he thought to himself often, I am just another mouth to feed." He was a voracious reader and a brilliant student. But more and more, he was reading books that his parents would have been troubled by and he yearned to travel and get away. His father, seeing that he was such an antsy kid, set him up in an apprenticeship to tailor with a Reb Elimelech, who had a dry good and cloth store in town. He hoped this would calm his son's wayward spirit and set him on a responsible path. While Avner never outwardly showed his dissatisfaction, it was obvious to his parents that he felt restrained by life in the Jewish Quarter. They sought out a matchmaker and although he was still rather young to be married, they hoped that if they found him the right girl, that would calm the wayward spirit in him, and he would settle down.

The matchmaker had come over the last Friday and talked with his parents for a long time. On Sunday morning, his father and mother left their house dressed like it was the Sabbath. They went to the home of a local merchant, Reb Yehuda Rapoport and met with him. They met his daughter, an 18-year-old named Chana. Chana was a slightly plump girl on the throes of womanhood with a pretty face and a quick wit. She had a sarcastic and sharp tongue, but today, when she met the Tackett's, she showed only the sweetest disposition. The fathers agreed to the match and the men scheduled the engagement announcement, for the next Sunday in the Rapoport home. The whole synagogue would be notified by word of mouth and an announcement from the pulpit by the Rabbi. They shared glasses of schnapps and congratulated each other with a Mazel Tov.

The next morning the announcement was made in the synagogue to the amazement of Avner, who of course had no idea. As the men came up to him to congratulate him, he felt shaken and annoyed. He was not ready to get married and he had no idea who had been picked for him. He looked to the back of the Synagogue at his father who looked up from his book and nodded briefly at him. Avner gathered his things and brushed past his father as he departed the building. He took a long time to get home. He dressed and went to work. Reb Elimelech congratulated him and shook his hand. He grunted thanks and went to work sewing pants. As Avner looked up from his work, his patron brought over a small flask and two glasses and poured him a drink. He made a toast and the two touched glasses. Avner then returned to his work.

He stewed over this all day and when he went home, his father and mother pulled him aside and talked to him about getting married. He said nothing and shrugged when they asked what he thought. They told him the wedding would be in a month and that he would have great blessings from such a match. Her father was well to do, money would not be a problem. If he didn't want to be a tailor anymore, his father-in-law to be could bring him into his business. It would all be good, they assured him. He shook his head yes. But he said nothing.

That Sunday evening, he dressed in his Sabbath clothes and went with his family to the Rapoport home, where the formal announcement was made. He met his future wife for the first time. He looked at her, she wasn't exactly his type, but she wasn't heaven forbid, ugly. She sized him up quickly as someone she would be able to control easily. Tall, thin with dark eyes and hair, he was nice looking. In her mind he would be a quiet compliant husband. She was satisfied. They barely spoke to each other the rest of the night but stood next to each other as praises were spoken about them from the Rabbi and family members. Avner spoke a few words and then everyone mingled, had some cake, some schnapps and then it was over. Everyone went home and Avner and Chana were engaged.

Chapter Twelve

The next month flew by so fast, Avner had no chance to catch his breath. The Rapoport's sent over many fine gifts to him and his family. Reb Yehuda, as he was known, invited Avner to his office, where he spoke to him with earnestness about his daughter and the impending wedding. Avner did not speak much, nor did he have to. Reb Yehuda was most loquacious and even if Avner had wanted to speak, he couldn't get a word in anyway.

On the Sabbath before the wedding, they all gathered in the Synagogue for a celebration by the groom's family. After the service, they all shared wine and some cakes and congratulations all around. They went home and prepared for the wedding which was that Tuesday night.

Avner was caught up in this whirlwind of activities and frankly, was totally numb to what was going on around him. On Tuesday morning, he got up before dawn and ate a small breakfast, knowing that since today was his wedding day he would have to fast from sunup until after the service under the wedding canopy, the Chuppah. He slowly got ready for the morning service and left the house with his father and walked to the Synagogue.

There he is once again confronted with the thought, "I'm done with this. Just done!"

It struck him this time like a lightning bolt. "I am really done with this! This is not what I want, I am not going to do this. No. No. No! I am not going to do this!" He could not imagine that this was going to be the way his life was going to go. "No, not like this!" he thought to himself, "Not like this! I can't endure this." He gritted his teeth and sat down to get his composure. He looked backward to where his father was praying. His father seemed serene and happy. He glanced at Avner and smiled. Avner's heart sank. He looked down at the prayer book, but just saw scribbled ink on a page. Tears formed in the corner of his eyes. He was doomed. He couldn't hurt his family.

He stood under the Chuppah and watched his bride come towards him. She circled him seven times as was tradition. They drank the wine. Avner placed the ring on Chana's finger. Then he broke the glass and they were married. He danced, drank and ate all in a daze. Finally, the party was over, and he went with his new bride to their new home.

The two joined as man and wife and the next morning, Avner was gone!

Chapter Thirteen

No one initially noticed that Avner was gone. Chana thought that he had gotten up quietly to go to Synagogue. The rest of the town assumed that when Avner didn't show up there, that he was enjoying the time with his new wife. In fact, nobody seemed concerned at all until around 4:00 in the afternoon, when it became obvious that he couldn't be located. They all waited around for hours assuming, he would be back for the first night celebration, the Sheva Brochos (Seven Blessings) meal. They waited several hours. As it soon became painfully obvious that something was very wrong, the men organized a search party, but since it was dark already, they realized that they would only be able to search local buildings, but that to search the roads they would not be able to start until dawn. They could not find him in any building, so at dawn several men on horses started up the roads and found nothing.

Avner however, was long on his way to Hamburg. He had snuck out of the house as Chana slept and went to the tailor shop of Reb Elimelech. He opened the shop, went to his workbench. Under the table, he gathered up a box in which he had been gathering things for the past month that he would need to escape. He had assembled a duffel bag and some clothing and had hidden them all under his tools.

When he entered the shop, he quickly filled the duffel bag with his clothes and some rolls that he had taken from the wedding feast, locked the shop and hit the road under the cover of darkness.

He walked for several hours until a horse cart came alongside him with two horses and a heavy-set man driving the cart. The driver was clearly not Jewish, but offered him a ride. He jumped aboard.

"Where are you going?" asked the driver.

"Hamburg."

"Long way to walk."

"Yes, it is, thank you for giving me a lift."

"Not a problem for me. Do you plan to walk all the way?"

"If I have to! But I am hoping to find people driving in my direction and maybe pick up a ride or two along the way."

The driver nodded, "Your running away!"

Avner nodded.

"From what or whom?", the driver asked.

"From my wife." Avner replied. The driver laughed, "Aren't we all?"

Avner laughed as well.

"Seriously?" the driver asked. Avner nodded his head.

"You are so young to be married? How long have you been?

"I got married last night." He stopped and took a deep breath. Looking at the man, he said, "Listen, it's really a mess, I don't really want to talk about it."

The driver looked over at the young man and was silent for a moment. Then he said to Avner. "Young man, in a strange way, I understand," and shook his head and returned his gaze to the horses in front of him.

Then he reached back over his shoulder to shake the young man's hand, "Herman is my name."

"Avner", returning the handshake. "Thank you again."

"No need to thank me again. You're Jewish?" Avner shook his head yes.

"Don't worry I won't bite. This may be your lucky day, young fellow. I happen to be going to Hamburg myself to buy supplies for my shop. If you want, you can ride with me. But you have to pay for your own lodging and food. So, if you want to go with me, you can."

Avner again thanked the man. Herman shook his head and snapped the whip over the two horses. "We are going to have to put some distance between you and all the people who are going to come looking for you. Hold onto your hat my boy, because here we go."

Chapter Fourteen

vner had been in Hamburg for three days before he found a small ship which would take him. He would travel in steerage to Liverpool, England where he disembarked. Not speaking English, he nevertheless was able to find the small Jewish community there. He was put up for a few days with a family who spoke Yiddish like he did.

He explained to his new acquaintances that he wanted to go to America. They told him they knew about America. Their cousin had gone there a few years back. They told him that a good place to go was Charleston in South Carolina.

Charleston had a decent size Jewish Community and he could expect to be sent in the right direction once he got there. Many packet ships regularly crossed to Charleston and he should have no trouble finding one. Packet ships carried mail and regular supplies between England and the States. They were reliable and decent to travel in.

Avner was able to secure a place in steerage on a small packet sailing ship after a week in Liverpool. He boarded the SS Sanctity and crossed over the Atlantic, landing in Charleston. The Charleston he arrived in was a vibrant Pre-Civil War city, full of people bustling around. He found his way to the Jewish section of town and found himself directed to Kahal Kadosh Beth Elohim, which was the main synagogue in town. Although, it was Sephardic and Avner was a German Ashkenazi Jew, he was quickly taken in and a place for him to room and board was arranged. Avner soon took a job with a millinery company and quickly became well known for his ability to discern fine fabrics and to buy and sell them for a good profit. By early 1842, his English skills had become much better and despite his accent, he was becoming a successful merchant. Never telling anyone that he had been married, he became the subject of many family's attempt to fix him up with the local girls, but he demurred for the most part although there were one or two young ladies that captured his attention. He told everyone he was 21 rather than the 18 years that he really was. And although he looked so young, they took him at his word.

His employer, Mr. Simon Isaac liked the young man and soon decided that he should go to New Orleans to look for and purchase bundles of cotton cloth for the store at the very best prices. Mr. Isaac had just received a contract from the Army to make uniforms and tents and ammunition bags and the like. It was a very lucrative contract, but the South Carolina cotton was too expensive to make the contract really profitable. Also South Carolina cotton was rough and not the best quality when processed. Cotton coming into New Orleans from Texas and Egypt was much better quality and was selling for much cheaper prices. Unable to go himself, and convinced that Avner would do right by him, he sent the young man by boat to purchase cloth for him in New Orleans.

Avner was thrilled at the opportunity to go and took full advantage of the boat trip to perfect his English and to enjoy the surroundings. He ate whatever was served on board and quietly dropped all the markings of his Jewish heritage.

He renamed himself Abner and as the newly minted Abner Tackett, the first thing he did when he got to New Orleans was purchase clothing that was more in the keeping of a Southern gentleman. He thus abandoned the clothing that marked him as a Jew all his life. He didn't pretend that he was a Gentile, rather he just never mentioned his religion. When someone asked him his nationality, he told them he grew up in Germany.

He made many cloth purchases in New Orleans for Mr. Isaac and arranged for their transport back to Charleston. He stayed in the city for a few days, enjoying the restaurants and the inns and the music. Abner decided that rather than going back to Charleston by boat, he would go up the Mississippi River to Natchez and then go across overland. Boarding a steamer upriver, a few days later he landed in Natchez.

As it happened, he arrived in Natchez at an auspicious time. A year earlier, the first Jews started settling Natchez in earnest. A man named John Mayer and his wife came from New Orleans to Natchez and settled there. He worked initially as a tailor and then became a merchant successfully for many decades. Following the Mayer's a few years later, were merchants Simon Adler, Solomon Bloom, Aaron Beekman, Isaac David, and Joseph Tillman. They all came to live in Natchez and established a Jewish community. Within a few years, their businesses began to grow exponentially. Stores became famous throughout the South, such as Schatz's, producing ladies' ready-to-wear clothing. Schatz continued to sell ladies garments into the early 20th Century. By 1858, eight out of 12 Jewish businesses in Natchez traded either in clothing or dry goods. It was probably the right time for an enterprising young man from Germany to settle down and grow his own business.

Abner wrote to Mr. Isaac that he was staying in Natchez but offered to be his agent in New Orleans and make several buying trips a year. Isaac's agreed to the deal and arrangements were made with a bank in New Orleans to provide the credit, so he could make the purchases. Soon, other merchants in Charleston heard about the arrangement and contacted Abner to work as their broker to purchase supplies for their businesses as well. Soon he was buying corn, wheat, leather, dried meats, firearms for the army and whatever he felt he could get involved in safely.

By 1850, he was a very rich and very eligible man. He was 28 and had purchased a large house and owned several slaves to take care of him and the home. He traveled throughout Mississippi, Tennessee and Alabama, scouting out new opportunities. On one of those trips, he went to a small town in Mississippi called Tupelo. There he met a beautiful Jewish girl name Nancy Burdine. Nancy's family had originally come from Lithuania and they all spoke fluent Yiddish, so he again able to speak in his mother tongue. They fell in love in short order and he married her. Unbeknownst to her, he was still married back in Germany. But he said nothing, and no one was the wiser. In 1851, Nancy gave birth to Sidney and then in 1853 the couple had Jerome. A daughter named Martha, came in 1857. By then inklings of war were becoming louder and louder. Abner continued to prosper, and the couple hoped that their good fortunes would continue.

Chapter Fifteen

eanwhile, back in Hanover, all hell had broken loose. Nobody knew what had happened to Avner. Nor did anyone know what to think about his disappearance. Initially, the local Jews thought that something terrible must have happened to him. He must have been kidnapped. But no ransom letter was ever sent. Or he could have gotten sick. Possibly, he had lost his mind and wandered off alone, without knowing who or where he was. G-d forbid he might have even been killed by some locals or some wild animal. They looked everywhere and found not a trace. Not even a clue. They sent letters to the surrounding towns and to relatives as far away as Bohemia and France. It never occurred to them that he had just left, because it seemed an unbelievable thought to them. Why would he, after all he had just gotten married. The Rapoport's and the Tackett's were at first both in shock and fearful. Then as time passed by, it became obvious that Avner was not returning any time soon. He may simply have died somewhere and was lost to them.

Chana, having spent only one night with her husband was now a trapped woman. She was neither a widow nor a divorcee. She could not remarry under Jewish law, even if she wanted to. Her initial response to Avner's disappearance was actually a kind of bemused concern. No crying or histrionics from her. She was far too cynical than that. She suspected that he had simply run away. She never said that to anyone. And of course, she was right.

But she was unconcerned about it for the moment. The spotlight was on her. She proceeded to go through the motions of the stricken young wife, but that ran thin for her after a short time. Soon, she just wanted to go away and think for herself about what to do and plan how she would now live. She was young and pretty. Hopefully, Avner would soon be found and she would divorce him and move on with her life. All that might have been possible, but she missed her period during that first month after the wedding. She kept silent about that for the month. Then another month passed with no period and then a third. It was obvious she was pregnant. She had returned to her father's home right after Avner had disappeared. Now she came downstairs, gathered her parents together and told them the news. They were stricken. Reb Yehuda listened carefully to the news, felt a sharp pain in his chest and collapsed from his chair. He was dead before he hit the floor.

She would give birth six months later to a son she named Yehuda in memory of her father. She would never hear from Avner again and she remained in limbo until she died of consumption when she was fifty.

Yehuda would grow up to be a Rabbi. He would marry a woman named Fruma in 1860 and they would have five girls and a boy named Boruch. The son would grow up to be a merchant and would move to Bohemia and marry twice. His first wife Sara would die in childbirth after delivering a son Moses in 1882. His second wife Rebecca would have five boys and three girls. By 1900, Moses was a strapping young man who married Lina and had a son they named Mendel.

They moved to the Austro-Hungarian Empire into a town in what had once been considered part of the Ukraine. The town was called Skalat. Mendel grew up to be a lawyer. He was living there just as the Second World War started around him.

Chapter Sixteen

It was a warm humid evening to sit out on the porch, but Elie preferred to sit out rather than go into the air-conditioned house. He would not say it, but the cancer made him feel cold all the time. The summer heat seemed to revive him in contrast to Stan who sat there sweating profusely.

Stanley went back into his house for some cold beers and gave one to Elie. He smiled at the beer and though he knew that he shouldn't have it, he reached greedily for the bottle opener that Stan handed him. Elie popped the top and brought the bottle to his lips and drank joyously.

"L'Chaim to you Stanley."

"You too my friend."

Stan sat down, and Elie continued his tale.

"So, when last we spoke, I was telling you about Rabbi Fried. Yes, my dear friend Rabbi Fried. I loved that man. We would sit sometimes and listen to records of these old time Cantors on the Victrola. Great Voices. There was this one guy, Yoselle Rosenblatt. I tried to imitate his voice and did a pretty good job at it. Rabbi Fried was impressed. Told me if I were Jewish, I would make a good cantor." He chuckled, "He would have never guessed that someday, I would be one." He thought about that quietly for a moment.

"Of course, I don't think he ever envisioned that I would become a rock and roll singer either. But you know, later on when I was such a big star, we met in the street one day. He gave me a big hug and a kiss and shook his head saying, "My Elvis, my little Elvis. Look at you now. Such a success!" Then he grabbed both of my shoulders and looked me right in the eye very carefully. I tried to look away, but his grip was too strong. He said to me,

"Elvis are you happy?"

Stan asked, "What did you say to him?"

"I looked away. I felt sheepish. He was like a father to me and he was asking a question a father would ask his son.

"Am I happy?" I teared up behind my sunglasses. He saw the tears running down my cheek."

The Rabbi said to me, "I see you're not so. You miss your Mama and all the money in the world cannot replace her. Elvis, you have such a gentle soul and you are so lost. I can see it."

"I told him he was right. He told me, "Of course." He could see that I was not right. That I was not happy."

"Elvis", he said to me, "You can always call on me. I'm still in the same place. You know that. Don't be afraid to …"

"I never really expected to see him again, but you know, life is never what you expect it to be."

Stan interrupted. "What do you mean?"

"Let's just say that the hand of G-d plays out in mysterious ways and with the most unusual people."

"I don't understand. Did Rabbi Fried have anything to do with your great escape?"

Elie smiled and looked at Stanley. "Maybe he was the escape!"

"What? I don't understand."

Elie just smiled.

Chapter Seventeen

"It would be ten years or so before I saw Rabbi Fried again. I never sought him out in all that time. He never really expected to hear from me again and was surprised when I just showed up at his door early one evening, all by myself. By then Priscilla and I had divorced, and I was coming apart in every which way. I was studying all this eastern religion stuff, trying to find meaning in my life. It wasn't helping but was so interesting.

I just couldn't focus on anything. I was doing all this Karate and meditation, but none of it made any difference. My head was always hurting. And I was on the road constantly trying to support this big Elvis machine that needed endless dollars to keep everyone working. My big television special had returned my career to star status and now the Colonel wanted me to tour as much as possible to make as much money as possible in the shortest time imaginable. I really don't know how I did it, but in the end, it cost me my marriage and my daughter Lisa Marie.

I was never home and when I was home, I was constantly working on the next tour or the next special. It was no life and now I was alone with a house full of people dependent on me for their living. I started dating again about six months after Priscilla left. She was a beauty queen named Linda Thompson. She was my companion for over 4 years. I was not good to her. I was drugged most of the time. She tried really hard, but she had to compete for me with my "Memphis Mafia" as they were called. There were six of us, mostly boyhood friends, Sonny West, Red West, Billy Smith, Marty Lacker and Lamar Fike and myself. We hung together. We drank together. They loved me like brothers and some of them really did try to look out for me. But man, I was so hard to deal with.

One evening, I took a drive all by myself. I went back to the old neighborhood. I had disguised myself, so no one would recognize me and kind of skirted around the building so no one would see me.

I went up to the Fried apartment. I wasn't sure they still lived there or whether the old Rabbi was even still alive. I nervously knocked on the door and saw someone look out the peephole in the door. There was some hesitation on the other side, and I heard Mrs. Fried call out, "Who is it?"

I steeled myself for a moment and then said, "Mrs. Fried, is that you?"

She repeated, "Who is it?" and I clearly recognized her voice. I whispered, "Mrs. Fried, this is Elvis. Elvis Presley." I waited for what seemed like a long moment, then I heard the door chain being removed and the door unlocked. She opened the door a crack and look out at me. Then she recognized me and opened the door wide. She smiled at me then gave me a big hug. From the hallway Rabbi Fried came over. He was wearing slippers and a red sweater over a white tee shirt and black pants. His skullcap was perched on the top of his head and his reading glasses were at the tip of his nose. He smiled broadly and shook my hand. He had grown very old and frail looking. She didn't look worse for wear, but he really looked tired and worn.

"Mamale, please make Elvis a cup of tea. Elvis, come into the living room and sit on the couch. What brings you here?"

He looked at me closely and could see that I was a real mess. I had grown so fat and my face was pasty white. He could tell that I was not well.

Mrs. Fried brought in some tea and put it on the coffee table in front of me. She also brought a plate of cookies that she remembered I liked as a kid. She looked at the Rabbi as if to ask whether she should sit with us. He just looked up at her in that unspoken way in which long time couples communicate, and she retreated to the kitchen leaving the Rabbi and I alone to speak.

"Son, you look terrible"

"I know sir"

"Trouble?"

"I am afraid so sir."

"What kind of trouble son?"

I started to cry. He sat there quietly as I cried for a long time. Here I was this big star bawling on the couch in the little apartment in the projects where I grew up. I could not believe that I was even there, and I was not sure why I even came. But I have come to believe that

G-d sent me to him that night and that through him would be my saving.

"Elvis, you want to tell me what's going on with you? I don't know if I can help you, but I can certainly listen."

"Rabbi. I am just a mess. My life is a disaster and I am just so confused as to what I need to do." I stopped and tried to gather myself together. "I need help sorting it all out. It is so complicated, and I do not know where to turn." I started to cry uncontrollably again.

Rabbi Fried got up and put his hand on my shoulder. He sat down next to me on the couch.

"Son take a breath first. I am here to listen. But you need to take a breath and gather yourself together. Whatever it is, it can only be solved calmly."

I tried to control myself and stop crying but couldn't. I was coming completely apart right in front of him.

"Miriam dear, please bring me a glass of whiskey," the Rabbi called out to his wife. She came in a few moments later with a glass of ice and a bottle of Canadian Club. The Rabbi poured a little into the glass and handed it to me.

"Here, take some sips."

I slowly sipped on the liquid, a little at a time. Rabbi Fried just sat there saying nothing, motioning me to take another sip every few minutes. I started to feel a little more in control. I yawned loudly. The Rabbi went into the kitchen and I could hear them having a quiet conversation, although I couldn't hear what they were saying.

The Rabbi and his wife asked me if I had eaten anything recently. I shook my head no. They brought into the kitchen and she made me a turkey sandwich with potato chips and some seltzer. They watched as I ate.

She said to him, "I see some color coming back into his face."

The Rabbi looked over at me and nodded agreement. Then he spoke,

"Elvis, we are going to put you up tonight and maybe for a few days. My wife will put some healthy food into you, and you can rest and get your head straight. That is, if you wish. We can talk and maybe map out a plan to get you some help. That's all I can do. The rest is up to you. Call your home and tell them that you are taking a few days away. Please don't tell them you are here. I don't want a whole circus of people trying to reach you here. It would disturb my wife too much. Let's take a day or two to help you figure this out. Agreed?"

I felt like a great weight was lifted from my chest. I agreed, but my car was parked in front of the building. The Rabbi made a telephone call. A young man from the Yeshiva came over about an hour later. He took my car keys and told me he would park the car in his home garage, so no one would see it. When I wanted it back the Rabbi would call him, and he would bring it back. He was a young man in a black suit with a black fedora hat. He told me, I could rest assured that he would tell no one, not even his wife. "She never goes in the garage anyway and even if she did, she doesn't know who you are Mr. Presley."

Elie looked at Stan, "You have a question?"

"So, you just disappeared for a few days and no one came looking for you?"

"Oh, I wish that it were that easy, No, there was a bit of excitement at Graceland. The Colonel apparently got all mad and talked about sending out private investigators to look for me. But Red convinced him that I was just exhausted and wherever I was, it would only be few days before I was home rested and ready to work. The Colonel had calmed down but told Red that if I wasn't back in three days, he would send the investigators out looking for me."

"How long did you stay with the Frieds?"

"About a week."

"And did the Colonel do what he said he would do?

"No, I called him and told him I was in California and that I would be back in a few days. He got all sore with me and was yelling and everything. I told him I was holed up with some girl and that he should leave me alone. I guess he decided that was alright, because when I came back to Graceland, he was all nice, joking with me about my "good time" in California."

"Amazing, you got away with it."

"Yes, it was. It was amazing that I got away with it, but I also learned something. For the first time since I was a boy, I could get away and hide if I wanted to. I really figured that out from spending the week away from Graceland. And it was the beginning of a plan in my head. Oddly enough, however, it was Rabbi Fried who would help me to make it happen."

"What?", Stanley almost screamed, "A Rabbi helped you escape?"

Elie smiled and nodded. "No," he said, "Not him alone, actually there were two Rabbis who helped me!"

"Two? Who else helped you pull this off?"

"Not so fast! I haven't told you how we did it. Tomorrow is a new day. That's for tomorrow's conversation."

With that, Elie got up from his chair and went into his house.

Chapter Eighteen

Stanley had something to stew on as he tried to get to sleep that night. Ever since figuring out that Elie was, in fact Elvis Presley, he had wondered how the whole escapade had been pulled off.

In Stanley's head, he remembered that on the day Elvis "died", there was a body found in Graceland. So, he reasoned that clearly, there was a conspiracy of some kind to get Elvis out of Memphis and to safety. This place of safety had to be a place where no one would really suspect him to be this huge international star. There had been supposed Elvis sightings for years. Additionally, there developed a vast Elvis disappearance conspiracy theory. In speaking to Elie, Stan now had to consider that instead of these being crank sightings, some of them may very well have been real. It now was evident that real people had actually seen Elvis and, in the end, talked themselves out of it.

He laughed to himself as he got into bed. If true, how did Elie pull it off. One side of Stan's thoughts centered on a very small group of people, who knew what was going on and helped him pull it off. These must have been people like the Memphis Mafia who could be trusted to keep the silence. But now 35 years had passed and seeing how Graceland and all the Elvis paraphernalia had become so profitable, it would be natural to assume that someone would have talked by now and tried to cash in. As so many years had passed without a peep from Elvis' close companions, Stan had to discount that group of people.

A second stream of thought Stan reasoned that Elie would have gone back to Priscilla, reasoning that he had the history with her, and they shared a child. Giving it some thought however, he quickly discounted that. He recognized that after the "death"; Priscilla had turned the whole Elvis enterprise into an enormous money-making machine. It just didn't figure into his equation; she had been the grieving ex-wife with a young daughter who would never again see her father. Well then again, Stan thought to himself, "Maybe Lisa Marie was told years later and had contact with her father?" Stan sat up in the bed. He thought to himself that didn't make sense either. Lisa Marie had been married to Michael Jackson. He was a big self-promoter. Would he have kept the secret if he had been told?" He reasoned not! No, Priscilla couldn't have been a part of this. Surely not!

A third stream of thought for Stan went like this. Maybe Linda Thompson knew. After all, she had been with him for more than 4 years. She loved him and had tried so hard to take care of him. Interesting possibility! After she left Elvis, she married former Olympian Bruce Jenner in 1981 and had two sons with him. They divorced him in 1986. She then married David Foster, the composer, in 1991 and was married to him for almost fifteen years until they divorced in 2005.

"No" he thought to himself, "too much baggage to carry around for so long, No way!" It became clear to Stan that the more people involved or interacting with other people, the more likely the story would have gotten out." For those reasons, he dismissed the notion of Linda Thompson being a participant.

He immediately dismissed Ginger Alden, the fiancée. Getting up and going over to his computer, He looked up Ginger Alden. As he read the various articles, his thoughts became muddled. "Ginger was just a kid. 20 years old! Elvis was 42 at the time. She was also disliked by almost everyone around Elvis." But then he thought to himself that it was Ginger who had found the body. "She had to have known", was a passing thought. But why would she have been so willing to give him up after she had agreed to marry him? Maybe that's the missing piece. She might have gone along because, she saw how miserable he was and how she would never belong in the Graceland world." Somehow, that thought stuck in Stan's head, but it seemed to be full of holes conceptually. In the end, he realized it was all mindless speculation on his part. He shook himself straight.

"I really need Elie to tell me how he did it," he said out loud to himself.

Chapter Nineteen

Rabbi Fried sat at the kitchen table sipping on a cup of tea. Elvis had been sleeping for at least 12 hours. He got up and woke him.

Elvis shuffled into the Fried's kitchen clutching at his head. Miriam Fried seeing this, reached into a cupboard and handed him a bottle of aspirin. He looked at it for a moment, then opened it and shook out three. She handed him a glass of water. He swallowed down the medicine and sat down at the table. Then turning to the stove, she fried three eggs. She made some toast and buttered it before placing it in front of him silently. He looked up and quietly thanked her and began eating quietly with his head down looking at the plate. Rabbi Fried watched as Elvis ate the eggs and toast. Mrs. Fried placed a cup of tea by Elvis and he drank it up greedily.

"Would you like another tea Elvis?'

Looking up at her, he weakly smiled, "Yes ma'am, that would be nice."

She made him another tea and he slowly sipped on it. "Would you like more eggs?"

"No ma'am, but some more toast would be nice."

She placed two more pieces of bread into the toaster and pushed down on the lever. A few moments later the bread popped up and she buttered the bread and gave it to Elvis.

"Thank you ma'am."

"That's no problem Elvis. Last night when you came here, we were really worried about you. I will leave you and the Rabbi to talk. If you need anything, just ask." With that she quickly wiped the counter with a towel and left to the living room.

Elvis looked up at Rabbi Fried, "Really, I am so sorry to have bothered you. I'll finish up and get out of your hair."

"Where are you running to son?" Rabbi Fried asked. "Where do you have to go that's so important right now?"

"Well sir, I have rehearsals and I have to get ready for my next tour."

"If you missed today, would it make any difference?

"I suppose…., well probably not."

"Then where are you running. You're safe here. Why go looking for trouble? I am really frightened for you my boy. How old are you now?

"Almost 42"

"Almost 42! And look at you. Is this the way you want to live your life? Well maybe it is, but you seem so sad. The Holy Book, the Mishna says that he who doesn't take the time to learn in wealth will not take the time to learn in poverty. You see Elvis, life is one big circle. Sometimes you are on top of the circle and other times, you are on the bottom. Those times are clear to a person. But as you ascend the circle, life seems wonderous, but you don't understand why. As you descend the circle, you really do know why, but refuse to accept it until you are at the bottom. It seems to me; you are on the descending side of the circle. But you don't have to go to the bottom and even if you do it doesn't have to be for very long. But you have to acknowledge where you are at and try to change the things that are dragging you down. Do you understand that?"

"I think so."

"Well clearly you came here because you know what is dragging you down. What you don't know, is how to fix it. So, Elvis, why are you so distraught right now?"

Elvis told the Rabbi about his encounter with Anna Steuben Rabinowitz in the hotel kitchen and in his room later.

The Rabbi's brow furrowed. "You said her name was Steuben?"

"No, Rabinowitz"

"That was her married name. it must have been her maiden name that was Steuben. My wife had cousins named Steuben back in Europe. Where did you say she lived?"

"She said it was town named Skal…. I can't remember it exactly."

"You must mean Skalat. Did she say she was from the Ukraine?"

"She said Hungary or Ukraine. She said the borders kept changing."

"I know about Skalat. I grew up in the next town over, which was called Grzymalow. She said you had a relative named Mendel Tackett. It must mean you have some Jewish relatives in your family tree."

"Well actually, Rabbi, I think I am Jewish. Mama always told me I was."

"How so? I remember you and your mother always going out to Church on Sunday mornings."

"I know. But Mama always talked about my Great, Great Grandma Nancy Burdine. She was Jewish from Europe. She married a guy named Abner Tackett, who came from Germany.

"Abner Tackett must be how you are related to Mendel?"

"I suppose."

"But that was a long time ago, how did your Mama think she was Jewish? For that to happen all of the women in your family line had to be Jews as well."

"Well Nancy had a daughter Martha, my great grandmother. Martha married a man named Whitey Mansell. Their daughter was Octavia. Everyone called her Doll. She was my Grandma. Doll married Bob Smith and their fifth child was a girl they named Gladys Love. Gladys was my Mama.

Rabbi Fried sat kind of stunned. "Well Elvis, if all that's true, you are Jewish! 100%. That's amazing."

He got up and walked into the other room. Elvis heard some murmuring between the Rabbi and his wife. They came back into the kitchen together. She sat down at the table and looked at Elvis sadly. She took his two hands in her own.

"Elvis, Is it true? You're one of us?", then she looked seriously at him. She turned to her husband and shook her head, pursing her lips, "Of course it's true! David, just look at him. Look at him carefully." The Rabbi just shrugged. He was not so sure. She sat down on a chair and looked at Elvis.

"Elvis, I grew up in Skalat. I knew Anna Steuben. She is a distant cousin. I am so glad to hear she is still alive. You must tell me where she works, so I can get in touch with her. We were childhood friends as well. I also knew of your relative Mendel Tackett."

She looked at sadly at Elvis. She took a deep breath and sighed out loud. "It's such a sad story. Skalat! Elvis, I can tell you the story of Skalat. Maybe it will give you a better understanding as to why it was so important for Anna to speak with you. Tell me, do you want to know? Because I can tell you. But only if you wish to hear, it brings back many hard memories."

He shrugged, then looked at her. There was some intensity he had never seen in her eyes before. He remembered her as she was when he grew up. Always smiling, always welcoming, she would sit him down, feed him and schmooze. She was so vibrant then, now she seemed just old and tired from life. Sitting in this small apartment that had been her life after Europe, he could not possibly know what she had gone through or what her life had been like before Memphis.

"If you think it is important."

She shook her head. "Elvis, it is not a pretty story. Anna didn't tell you all of what went on and she told you her story alone. Clearly, it has affected you badly. What I will tell you will shock you even more deeply. Are you really sure you want to hear this?"

Elvis looked at her and nodded. She got up and poured a glass of water and sat down again at the table.

"It was 1939. Of the approximately 8,000 inhabitants in my town of Skalat, some sixty percent were Jews. Most of us lived in the center of town. We consisted of some craftsmen, businessmen, some small traders, a few professionals. Some of us Jews were minor local officials. There were also a few Yeshiva students, learning the Torah. We, of course, had some full-time beggars and the ordinary unemployed, reluctant to work. We also had a high rate of unemployed Jews, whose circumstances amounted to that they simply unable to find a decent job to support themselves and their families. In all respects, Skalat was no different than any other typical shtetl. Jews started settling there as early as the 1500's or even earlier, making it one of the oldest Jewish shtetls in the part of Europe known as Galicia. Jewish life thrived in Skalat. Jewish organizations and participated actively in the town's social, cultural, religious and political activities. On the surface, Skalat was an orthodox, for the most part a Chassidic town, the younger generation often strayed from those values and more often than not they pursued a secular education in addition to their religious instructions. All of the politics of the day, from the extreme left to the extreme right, exerted their influence on the young Jewish people in the town. Modern clothing, modern music, modern mores and values started to infiltrate the minds and the lifestyle of the young people. Otherwise, our Shtetl life was not very different from other Eastern European towns and villages. The people of Skalat occupied themselves in the constant daily struggle for existence and human dignity.

In 1941, the Germans occupied my town. It came with tragic, terrible consequences. When the Soviet Russians returned ultimately in 1944, the town was without a Jewish population.

Germany attacked the Soviet Union, on June 22,1941. The war had been going on for two years with the Russians and the Nazis carving up Poland. Skalat had been under the control of Poland for a long time. Now as a result of the war and the dividing up of Poland, Soviet Russia took power in Skalat. The Soviets presence introduced a certain calm and order throughout their 22-month rule of Galicia. Life in Skalat was more or less ordinary and normal. Day to day activities went on much as they had always. Life did not significantly change for the townspeople. The Poles, who formerly controlled the land, now were defeated and divided. The Ukrainians, who had for centuries dreamed of again ruling this land, now saw their dreams again dashed. They're response to the Soviet rule was virulent hatred. But outwardly, they appeared to accept the Soviet regime.

Soviet rule in Skalat put the Jewish population in a very precarious position. At first, they adjusted to the new regime, but they feared how their Gentile neighbors would view this adjustment. For many generations, quiet but powerful Anti-Semitism had been engrained into the souls of their non-Jewish neighbors. With the Soviet in power it would seem that this Anti-Semitism would start to break out into the open having found a fertile soil to flourish in as the Soviets were no friends of the Jews either. With the coming of the Soviets the fires of the Jew-Haters had the fuel to erupt into the open, but in quiet ways. The term "Commie Yids", was an old slogan in Polish politics. Now the Jews were perceived as being chummy with their old buddies, the Bolsheviks. The Ukrainian nationalists now used this for their Anti-Semitic rationalizations.

Under the Soviets, everyone could find work. Despite that, everyday life could be both good and bad. In a strange way, the Soviets in charge of Galicia trusted their Jewish population more than the local Ukrainians. Because the Jews had survived over so many centuries of political upheavals, it was quite understandable that the Jews were able to adjust more easily to the new regime than their Gentile neighbors. The Jews, therefore, the workers, artisans and the working intelligentsia, were able to take on leading roles in the economic and social life of the town. Many held important posts in the cooperatives as well as in communal and public institutions. For the Jews, it would seem that no other group could have adjusted better to the Soviet occupation than they did.

This was a radical change in the social and economic structure that had previously left a great deal of the Jews without a way to earn a living. Amongst them were businessmen, small traders and craftsmen. There was also now opportunity to work for the formerly chronically unemployed. In our typical provincial town, Skalat, the number of prosperous Jews was very small. Jews were desperate to obtain formal positions because one of the clear distinctions of the new order was: *One who does not work does not eat*. Additionally, the middle class, the former house owners and traders, made sure that they found find employment in order to obtain a work-card. This protected a person from being deemed "non-productive" thereby exposing themselves to various troubles. These could include exile to Siberia, which no one obviously wanted to have occur. Whether it was out of necessity or simply as a ruse, the previously non-working Jewish population made every effort to work and be productive. The changing social standing seemed to take place overnight. This trend, undoubtably, had some positive value in the social, egalitarian restructuring of the Skalat Jewish day to day existence.

For the local Ukrainian populace and the Poles, who mostly lived as farmers on land of their own, they did not experience a noticeable disturbance in their lifestyles. As they already were "productive". they had no reason to find new employment or other sources of income. Peasants did not stop being peasants.

They also had seen regime changes many times over their history. "Our people left; our people will return" was a familiar, meaning-filled folk-saying among them. The particular tragedy for them was of an ideological, nationalistic and certainly a territorial quality. Peacefully living, waiting for better times and hoping for better conditions, their lives were essentially static. With a Soviet power in place, the Ukrainians and Poles were weak and powerless. This did not bode well for the Jews as powerlessness brings out hatreds bred over centuries. The result was a spreading of the Anti-Semitic poison. This sowed the soil for the eventual slaughter.

And when it came, it would be quite powerful and almost obliterating. Despite their Gentile neighbors own national tragedy, germs of envy, mixed with ancient hatreds and traditional Anti-Semitism grew into such a powerful force that it confused the minds and consciousness of both the masses and their leaders.

So, in that, the local populace could hardly wait for the inevitable German invading forces to arrive. Amongst the Poles the thought was "better the Germans than the Soviets. The Ukrainians flatly loved Hitler and saw in him a savior, one who would help them create an independent Ukraine. Almost from the first days of battling in Europe, Skalat was gripped by a rough, edgy and raw mood. It was as if instinct told them that momentous events were soon to occur. Radio broadcasts kept bringing alarming reports: A German force under General Von Runstedt was successfully advancing through Galicia and Wolin. Soviet authorities knowing that soon they would have to retreat, tried maintaining the calm of the civilian population, even as they themselves prepared to evacuate the region. During the early days of July 1941, an orderly withdrawal of the Soviets from the town began.

But they didn't go alone. Foreseeing disaster, they were accompanied by some 200 Jews, mostly workers, craftsmen and some who simply had good sense and could see the writing on the proverbial wall. My father was one of them who could see the writing, but he was talked out of it by his friends. Where we should have gone with the Soviets, we didn't. We learned the hard way. That in itself was another type of trial for us for we were in danger either way. Russia was not much better and was enduring a terrible beating by the Germans that summer. If the truth be told there were very few of the town's Jews who fully understood the danger that awaited them by staying. No matter how fatally foolish it may now appear, there were some Jews, mainly amongst the more affluent, who thought that it might be easier living with the Germans than with the Russians. And again, where could they run to? Russia proper was being devastated by the war. So, that was how some Jews assessed their situation. The reality was, in war most thought, "How can we leave our homes and go off into exile? And where to go?

Again, that questioned loomed heavily. So many Jews left their fate in the hands of God and hoped for the best in the future.

On the 3rd of July, the Soviet civil administration, police and the armed detachments left Skalat for good. With only a few soldiers remaining behind to carry out specific assignments. The town was left without a government. The town became a scene of chaos and disruption. The underworld of the town and various peasants from the neighborhood took advantage of the many new opportunities for robbery and other acts of disruptions.

As it became obvious that the German war machine was approaching Skalat people could see the seeds of agitation and turmoil beginning, even before German jackboots began their march into town. It started with a peasant named Hilko saying to some Jews," Wait. Just wait, you kikes. Hitler's coming soon, and we'll slaughter you all like chickens!" A Soviet soldier, hearing of the incident, got outraged at such talk and tracked down the peasant. He caught him and dragged him off into the fields, leaving him there dead. The executed peasant was venerated a "holy martyr" by a local priest. This action only infuriated the already animated peasants and served as a pretense for the peasants to carry out an act of vengeance on a few Jewish families living nearby. Murdering them all in a horrific way, they blamed Hilko's death on the Jews.

Now the peasants in town were all stirred up. They prepared their knives for the inevitable slaughter that would come when the Nazis took over the town. By midnight on Friday, July 4th, the continuous sound of machine guns could be heard as well as those of exploding grenades. At 2:00 AM the first German patrol arrived on motorcycles. They looked over the neighborhood. Then they called out over loudspeakers, "All of you, our Ukrainian brothers, awaken!" The Ukrainians, however, were already wide awake and fully ready to help the Germans. The Jews were already fleeing for their lives in all directions. By Saturday, July 5th, the regular German troops finally arrived and encamped. The Ukrainians were delighted. They got dressed in all of their holiday clothing some fully decorated with ribbons in the blue and yellow of their Ukrainian national colors. Ukrainian flags and Red swastika flags were draped in front of their houses. Bearing flowers and gifts, singing loudly, the Ukrainians came to greet their German liberators. They danced in the streets, kissing and hugging each other like it was a party.

Since it was the Sabbath morning, some Jews walked openly and unhesitatingly to services. They carried their prayer shawls, as though nothing had happened. There were others, very few, who went off to look at and admire the German military equipment. Some of the local Jews were convinced that the Germans, such a cultured society would not harm any of them. Others believed that in fact, now they would be more secure. While before there had been danger from the enraged townspeople, many Jews now thought the Germans would impose some law and order. Looking at that from today's perspective, it seems incomprehensible.

And at first, they were right. The German military harmed nobody. In fact, they were friendly to the Jews, boasting of their swift heroic deeds against the Soviets. While some Jews remained frightened and alarmed by the German presence, this group of Jews who had interacted with the soldiers later argued with the others saying, "Fools, what are you hiding for? Are they harming anyone?" Some of the affluent Jews, though not all, naively thought that even if the worst were to occur, it would not affect them but only the impoverished amongst them who couldn't buy their way out. They reasoned that the Germans themselves knew that the prosperous were also victims of the Soviets. Maybe the new rulers would return their land and their confiscated wealth and maybe even their nationalized houses. Such was the reasoning of the deluded. They were to quickly learn otherwise, but for the moment such foolish optimism clouded their minds.

At around 10:00 in the morning, several battalions came to a halt in the Shetl. Other German troops continued their "triumphal march" eastward. The Commander of this SS brigade gave the order: "Tzen minuten shlachten Juden!" *(Ten minutes for killing Jews),* so that his troops might "have some fun," Passing the order on to each other, the troops quickly jumped from their automobiles, tanks and other armored vehicles and ran to the very center of town. Like animals, these troopers ran about like wild wolves, firing their guns. Initially, they simply assaulted any Jews they came upon in the streets. The first victim was Mendel Dienstock, whose beard they cut off along with part of his face. Miraculously, the bullets they fired at him missed. The German troopers were in such a hurry, they left their victim, who simply fainted, onto the ground.

Some of the peasant children ran after the Troopers, pointing out, "Jude! Jude! (Jew! Jew!)." The whole of Skalat was in turmoil and the Jews were gripped by panic. The Germans ran after the fleeing Jews, shooting at them continuously. One man, Mordechai Wolf (the milkman) and his wife were chased down to the riverbank and then the driven into the water. They fired at both of them until their bodies sank, leaving only red stains on the surface. Then some Germans, led by some Ukrainian peasant children, started running among the houses, shooting at each Jew the children pointed out. Other soldiers broke into homes on the pretense that they were searching for weapons and hidden Communists. They robbed, defaced and destroyed the contents of these homes in the most outrageous way. At the end of allotted ten minutes, Skalat been turned upside down. Twenty Jews were killed and an equal number wounded. Some slightly wounded and others much more seriously. The Jews sought hiding places wherever they could. Their homes, now left open and unguarded, were ransacked by Ukrainian peasants and the Polish town hoodlums. They rioted for hours afterwards. They stole whatever they could. They beat, without mercy, any Jew that they found out and about.

But this was only the prologue to the slaughter which would follow the next day. This event was organized and perpetrated completely under the direction of the newly appointed Ukrainian "administrators."

Wołyń Voivodeship
Tarnopol
Voivodeship
(1939)
Stojanów
RADZIECHÓW
Chołojów
Łopatyn
STYR
Stanisławczyk
Toporów
BRODY
KAMIONKA STRUMIŁOWA
Sapieżanka
Busk
Olesko
Podhorce
Podkamień
Bug
Sasów
Białokamień
Załoźce
Krasne
ZŁOCZÓW
Olejów
Gołogóry
ZBARAŻ
N. Sioło
Tokica
ZBORÓW
Jezierna
PRZEMYŚLANY
Dunajów
Pomorzany
Kozłów
Berezowica
TARNOPOL
Borki Wk.
Płotycza
SKAŁAT
USSR
PRZEMYŚLANY
Kozowa
BRZEŻANY
Mikulińce
Struśów
Łoszniów
Grzymałów
Podhajce
wysokie
Potutory
Strypa
Złotniki
TREMBOWLA
Zbrucz
PODHAJCE
Złota Lipa
Janów
Chorostków
Wiśniowczyk
Budzanów
Husiatyn
Monasterzyska
Jabłonów
Jazłowiec
BUCZACZ
Wygnanka
KOPYCZYŃCE
Barysz
Czortk.
CZORTKÓW
Probużna
Koropiec
Jazłowiec
Jagielnica
Wielka
Potok Złoty
Terebin
Wagłów
Tłuste
Biłcze
Skała
BORSZCZÓW
Stanisławów Voivodeship
ZALESZCZYKI
Krzywcze
Iwanie
Uście
Romania

POLAND (1939)

Chapter Twenty

Mrs. Fried looked at Elvis. He seemed in shock by what he was listening to. She asked him, "Should I go on or this too much for you to handle right now?

He looked up slowly at her. There was a look of shock on his face, but he nodded for her to continue.

"As strange as it might seem Elvis, the Ukrainians, the Poles and the Jews had lived together in Skalat for centuries in relative peace. Over the generations, the Ukrainian part of town and the Jewish shtetl had relatively friendly contacts. After all, why would the Jews want any conflict? They had no territorial designs in the area. The Ukrainians had suffered almost as much as the Jews had under the Polish rulers. Oddly enough, this tended to bring the two groups together in what was a common struggle for minority rights and also for the ability to the preserve their national identities. Often, the leaders of the Ukrainian folk movements spoke out in sympathy with their Jewish brethren. In elections to the Polish Sejm, (the Polish Parliamentary body) in some districts, the Jews and Ukrainians often ran jointly. In other districts, the Ukrainian press, would at times, urge its readers to vote for the Jewish slates.

So, who would have predicted that these same Ukrainians, who had lived in peace with their Jewish neighbors for centuries, would turn so savagely against them. How could this have happened? Well, these hideous deeds were carried out, not by unenlightened individuals among the Ukrainians. Nor were they carried out by some fascist terror groups. Rather, these acts from hell were the work of none other than the UNDO, (Ukrainian Nationalist Democratic Organization), the main Ukrainian political organization in Galicia and its official representative for many years.

The UNDO organized, controlled and coordinated the first pogroms in almost every town and village in Galicia. They involved almost the entire Ukrainian community in these massive, bloodstained events. With few exceptions, most notably a small group among the older generation, which found this savage behavior of their children to be disgusting, the balance of the Ukrainian population of that time shared the full burden of guilt for destroying Galician Jewry.

It was the Ukrainians for the most part, not the Germans, who became the murderers of their age-old neighbors. Without a doubt, the Germans permitted it and let the savage behavior run wild. But the established facts and copious documents and the multitudes of eyewitness testimony prove, undoubtably, that the hands of death were wielded by the Ukrainians. If one was to make a chronological review of events in this single shtetl of Skalat, it stands as a testimony and reveals similar behaviors of the Ukrainians in other Galician towns. Wherever Jews were killed, it was the Ukrainians who actually carried out the mass murders. The same criminal hand was at work in all of these places throughout the Ukraine."

She looked down for a few moments, needing to catch her breath or her thoughts. Her mind was obviously spinning. These memories were so painful that she needed to stop long enough to regain her composure. Rabbi Fried seeing her in distress, got up and made her a cup of tea. He poured a little whisky into the teacup and stirred the contents for her. She took a sip and sat back in her chair. Reinforced, so to speak, she continued.

"Already on that Friday evening, (although some say it was after the Sabbath evening), the Ukrainians in Skalat had held a secret meeting to consider their new situation, now that Hitler's troops were in the town. This meeting was attended by all the elite of the local Ukrainian townsfolk. Every segment of the Ukrainian population was represented from the priest down to the peasant. They opened the meeting with the singing of the Ukrainian national anthem, "Shehe Ne Vmerla Ukraina," (*The Ukraine is alive)*. The conversation quickly turned to matters of state. They discussed organizing a Ukrainian militia as well as choosing persons for public positions and institutions. Opinions were expressed about what would be the nature of their work, and how they looked forward to the fulfillment of their aspirations in the future. Those thoughts were a return to a Ukrainian State. They discussed how the Ukrainians should treat the Polish population in the town. After all, there was real enmity between them and the Poles.

But the most important question was what to do with the Jews? One person after another took the floor, quoting whole pages from

Hitler's <u>Mein Kampf</u> and from Alfred Zweigberg. They concluded that the Germans were to be given their total support, because only they were the true liberators. Words were spoken like, "We must gain the Germans' confidence," "Hitler is right. The Jews are a menace to the world." "They are like a bone in our throats as well, so let there be an end to them!"

Voting, a majority of the assembled supported a proposal to bring a pogrom against the town Jewry. Understanding however, that they would need permission from the Germans to act on this proposal, a three-man delegation was chosen to go to the Military Command in order to obtain permission. They all agreed that it would be a slaughter of the Jews for a 24-hour period. They believed that this one full day period would result in the end of the Jewish presence in Skalat.

The main spokesmen at the meeting was a well-known personality in town. His name was Canon Onuferko, the Greek Catholic priest. He had a long history with the town Jews, having been involved in many business matters with them. He boasted of having been a Judeophile all his life. He spoke Yiddish fluently. Local Jews would say of him, "A hen that crows and a priest who speaks Yiddish should both be sent to the chopping block." This folk expression was quite on point. In addition to the priest and his wife, others at the meeting were Judge Politila, a Maruszszuk (a blacksmith), a Bilyk, a and fellow notables Jaromiszyn, Chruszcz, and Wilczynski. All of these were unofficial leaders of the Ukrainian community and were well-known people in Skalat and its local nearby towns.

On the following day, the three-man Ukrainian delegation led by Canon Onuferko went before the German General Staff. They carried a signed petition. This petition requested permission to carry out an anti-Jewish pogrom. They were seen by the commander, an aged general who considered their demand. But he had other considerations in his head. He agreed that the Jews should be murdered, but he felt it should be done in a planned and orderly way. His first thought had been that he could use their physical labor. This would be useful to his military machine. But after some thought, the general gave permission for a pogrom. He did not agree to a full day of killing, limiting it to only eight hours in duration. He specified that all of the women and children should be spared. The entire delegation thanked him, bowed deeply, and went home.

The Ukrainians immediately called a general meeting of all their community activists. This included their newly organized militia. They decided to make the necessary preparations to execute the pogrom.

The General sent a report to Berlin, enclosing documents which showed a "justified" local hatred of the Jews. That petition was later released to the press by the German ministry of propaganda, along with hundreds of similar petitions from Ukrainians in various other cities and villages. This was to show the world, that it was not the Germans who were slaughtering Jews, rather local populations were demanding the right to carry out their own slaughters.

On Sunday, July 6, 1941, at about 11:00 AM, the pogrom in Skalat began.

Ukrainian organized gangs set about moving through the town. The new militia armed with rifles, as well as civilians carrying sticks, went house to house calling Jewish men and youths to come out to work. While German soldiers stood and watched the scene, these gangs of militia and townspeople cursed, shouted at, slapped and pushed these men into the streets. The wailing of women and the cries of children could be heard from Jewish homes.

These Jews, having been drawn out, were forced to perform sadistic and fruitless tasks. The first group was ordered to uproot some small trees with their bare hands. Since they could not successfully do that, they were beaten to death. Another group was ordered to crawl on all fours and gather stones in their mouths. Then they were to crawl further and place the stones into pots. Others were forced to clean outhouses with their bare hands. Another group was forced to sweep streets with their hats and to perform other senseless tasks. All this time, they were tortured by the gangs. Scores of Jews were further tortured and then put to death. Some of the Jews were assigned to the German military units, where they worked while being beaten about the head with rifle butts. One Jew, Chaim Kaczer, who had already been badly beaten, was thrown to the ground and run over by a truck, which crushed his bones. Writhing in pain, he was finally shot through the heart by a soldier.

At the water-pump in the marketplace, some Ukrainians forced the spout of the water pipe into a Jew's mouth and kept pumping the water until he drowned. Another Jew, Levy Cohen, an imposing man, who was tall and handsome with a silver-grey beard, had his legs broken by assassins wielding iron rods and then was placed under the pump for a "cold shower," as his attackers laughed. Levy pointed to his heart, as he could no longer speak, pleaded to be shot to end his suffering. Wild, crazed bystanders laughingly egged on his killers to let him live a little longer, so he could suffer more. The mob then attacked him, ripping his hairs, one by one, from his beard. Near dead, he was again placed under the waterspout. They pried his mouth open and pumped water into him until he drowned.

The Rabbi Judah Wolowicz was tied behind a horse. Germans, Ukrainians and other peasants, standing on the sidewalks, whipped the horse into a gallop. The Rabbi at first tried to run, but soon he fell down and was dragged as far as the towers. Bloodied and tortured, he died there. At the tower, his body was tossed onto a growing pile of corpses. Similarly, was the fate of a Jonah Steuben (son-in-law of a tinsmith from Grzymalow), who was tied behind a car and was dragged through the streets until his body became unrecognizable. Dr. Leonard Simon was dragged to the public outhouse near the bathhouse where he was ordered into the cesspool and shot. Many Jews shot by Ukrainians had their clothing and shoes and other personal effects taken off their bodies. While this was going on, village peasants roamed the streets of the Jewish sections, ransacking and robbing houses.

In the center of town stood the four old towers that were part of the old Skalat Palace. It was there that the worst of the bloodbaths occurred. The Ukrainian police led Jews, in groups of thirty or forty, to the tops of the towers. They were ordered to jump. While falling they were shot at with automatic weapons. The men died in pain and many crying the Shema Yisroel as they fell. While this was going on the Germans photographed the slaughter, and the photos, captioned, were later sent on to Berlin to prove that it had been the Ukrainians who were killing the Jews. They wouldn't have wanted it said that Germans had killed anyone. All told at the towers, more than three hundred people were brutally murdered, including some thirty children and youths.

At the cemetery, new horrors! Groups of Jews were forced to bring the dead to the cemetery and bury them. As soon as they finished their work, they were shot to death themselves. A story told of Isaac Lerner, son of Zvi-Nuty Lerner, a butcher, that among other corpses he had to bury was his own father. While reciting the

Kaddish for his father, he was cut down by a bullet, falling on top of the just-filled grave. Approximately 150 people were destroyed at the cemetery alone. By 3:00 PM, the total death toll in the town had reached five hundred. We can only speculate about how many more victims there would have been that day. But right in the middle of all this killing, Soviet bombers attacked Skalat from the air. This caused the killers to scatter across the fields. Had it not been for the attack, the synagogue would have been attacked by the mob. The bombing caused a break in the murdering.

For the next few hours, it was quiet. Soon however, the mob came back to finish what it had started. Even though the permitted eight hours was over, the killing went on another two days, but on a smaller scale. Despite that, additional scores of Jews fell as the Ukrainians let blood. Wednesday morning, Ukrainian militiamen dragged out the three Klastorin brothers and Loma Goldman and shot all four claiming that they were Communists.

All of the remaining slaughtered Jews were still lying around the towers where they had fallen. The Ukrainians dragged more Jews out of their hiding places. They were ordered to take the unburied corpses to the cemetery. Using horse carts, the Jews carried these corpses, wrapped in blood stained sheets and prayer shawls. Blood dripped the entire length of the road route to the cemetery.

A very deep sorrow now permeated the town. The remaining Jews tried to observe Shiva. The surviving Rabbi proclaimed a community day of fasting and ordered the wearing of sackcloth and ashes as a sign of mourning for the martyred dead. Surviving Jews sent a delegation to the German commander. He promised to restore the calm. Military authorities issued an order for the population to return all stolen items. Of course, nothing was returned, nor could the five hundred lives lost in the pogrom possibly be returned.

Meanwhile, similar tragic reports began to be heard from the surrounding areas. The Ukrainians had conducted a pogrom in the neighboring shtetl of Grzymalow. That is where my husband was from. Luckily, he had left the town, having been conscripted by the Red Army. In his town, some five hundred men, women and children had been driven into the river and all were machine-gunned to death. For days, the river ran red with Jewish blood. In the village of Chmielisko, the Ukrainian peasants buried alive some thirty of their long-time neighbors. In the village of Turowka, the local

Jewish doctor had his legs broken and was then impaled on the tines of pitchforks. In Tluste, a smaller town near Skalat, the Ukrainians slaughtered all of the Jews.

The Rape of Skalat was finished. But the great tragedy of my town had just begun. Many of us hid in the forests, many tried escaping into Russia. Over the next year or so, we were rounded up by the Germans and sent to work camps and finally to concentration camps. When the Soviets returned in 1944, there were hardly a Jew left in town."

She stopped speaking and looked silently at Elvis. Tears streamed down his cheeks. He reached for a napkin to wipe his face. She looked at him, "That is why Anna Steuben wanted to speak to you. Her father was the Jonah Steuben who was dragged behind a car to his death. But he had already gotten the rest of the family to safety. He had befriended a Polish farmer and this farmer agreed to hide his family. On the day, the pogrom started, Jonah went back into town to try to collect some foodstuffs and clothing to take back to the farm. The Ukrainians caught him in the street."

The Towers of the Old Skalat Palace

The Old Ruined Cemetery of Skalat

Chapter Twenty-One

After the pogrom ended, the Skalat shtetl was in complete shock. Jews simply could not recover after such unspeakable horrors. The Germans let the Ukrainians become the masters of the town. Their brutal behavior terrified the Jewish population daily. Each new day, hundreds of Jews were dragged off to perform hard labor and throughout this process they were beaten mercilessly and degraded.

Amazingly and somewhat naively, the Ukrainians believed that this was their time. They had somehow won and the "liberation" they sought had come to pass. Under the protective wings of the German forces, young and old rushed to join the militia and other administrative offices of what they perceived to be the beginnings of the future free Ukraine. Once established in their new positions, each tried to outdo the others in patriotism. They expressed this in an active and thorough hatred of the town's Jews, and through public beating and kicking of the Jews, their neighbors and former friends. In this way they hoped to gain favorable status in the eyes of their German "liberators."

Nikolaj Bilyk was chosen from among the local Ukrainian activists to rule over the Jews. Two weeks after the pogrom he authorized a former cattle dealer, Leibisz Degen (to whom he had a business relationship) to form a provisional committee. This temporary body consisted of twelve members. Bilyk would come to the local leader, Leibisz Degen and demand a designated number of Jews to be assigned for forced labor. The required number of workers would assemble early each morning at the marketplace to await their assignments. Jewish men and women were chosen to sweep streets, clean toilets and wash floors in various government offices. Some were assigned to local farms in the surrounding villages. Additionally, a special store was established in the marketplace for Jews to obtain goods.

Four weeks after the pogrom, an order arrived from the German Security Service (SD) in Tarnopol, to establish a Judenrat (Jewish Council) to serve as the liaison between the German authorities and the Jews. The Ukrainians asked Jacob Weiderman to undertake the task of establishing the Judenrat in Skalat. He absolutely refused. No one amongst the professional intelligentsia would accept the "honor". After a number of days of indecision, Mendel Tackett, the local lawyer was placed at the head of the Judenrat."

"So, you see Elvis, I knew Mendel Tackett. At least I knew who he was."

Elvis got animated at the mention of Tackett's name." You knew him? What was he like?"

"I was a young girl at the time. The adults knew him better. He didn't have either a good or bad reputation at that time. He had survived the Pogrom by escaping into the forest during the night when the Germans first entered town. Where he went and how he survived, nobody could say. He showed up back in town a few days after the pogrom was over. He seemed to avoid most of the trouble with the Germans and the Ukrainians that the rest of the Jews had encountered. Other than that, he sort of fell into line with what was happening to all the town Jews. As the head of the Judenrat, he was extended a certain amount of protection from the Germans. But I can tell you, your cousin soon became a very terrible man. I am sorry to say that to you, but it is the truth.

Elvis seemed a little shocked but said nothing. He was having trouble processing all that he was hearing. Mrs. Fried got up and went out of the room. She returned shortly with a photograph of group of young girls. When the picture was taken, they were all dressed for school and were sitting outside. It was a bright sunny day. It looked like any picture, taken anywhere, of young people with their whole lives ahead of them. She showed it to Elvis while standing behind his chair.

She pointed at one of the girls, "That was me. We were twelve at the time." Then she pointed to another girl who was standing behind her but to the left of her. "That's Anna Steuben."

Elvis lifted the picture up closer to his eyes. He looked closely at Anna. "That's amazing! I recognize her. She still has those eyes and that pointy chin. My gosh, how old is this picture?"

"This picture was taken in the spring of 1941. A month or so before the Germans marched into town and the troubles began. Anna was a sweet girl. Very shy. We were friends. I mean, she was in the same group of girls that shared classes together in school. I slept over by her once. She came by occasionally when she was near my house to say hello. We were not, what you would call close, but we were friends. I always wondered what had happened to her. I wondered about a lot of the girls. Some I knew never made it past the war. But I never knew about her. I just assumed…" She became quiet for a moment and looked up at the ceiling.

"Then again, I always thought that I was the only one of us to survive. It is nice to know she lived through this as well. I hope she is well."

Elvis answered her. "What I can tell you was that she was working as a waitress, so I assume she was healthy enough to do that. It is hard work. But I can't tell you more than that. She was thin, and she looked so tired. But that might have been because of what she had to say to me. Tremendous burden to bear. And I did not even understand it until now. And I'm not sure that I even understand it all. It is so unbelievable to listen to. It blows my mind."

They sat in silence for a moment. Elvis looked at the picture again then gave it back to her. He took a deep breath. "Tell me more about Mendel Tackett. How did he become such a terrible man?"

She sighed long and hard. "Are you so sure you want to know?"

Elvis shrugged.

There is a lot I can tell you about him. What a chazer (pig)! I will tell you a lot more about what happened in Skalat after he took over the Judenrat."

He looked over at her as she sat back down at the table.

"Go ahead."

Chapter Twenty-Two

At first, it seemed to some, that it might be possible to live with some sort of relative normalcy. For the most part, the Jews were allowed to take care of their own affairs. Some Jews dared to joke that, "We have a small Jewish Republic, here under the sheltering wing of the Germans." It was impossible to imagine that soon the Judenrat would become a tool of the German regime.

The Judenrat's main function in its early days consisted of providing between 200 to 300 workers every day to the German and Ukrainian authorities. They also had to provide food to the Jewish population. They did this by use of a bakery that was made available to them. They organized the activities of all of the newly established administrative functions to keep the "peace" with the Germans and Ukrainians. They were also required to provide "gifts" for the Germans who made it a daily activity to extort money and property from the Jews. Soon, they found it necessary to set up a storehouse for items to be handed over to the Germans on demand. This storehouse quickly filled up with clothing, furniture and tableware collected, often not without a fight from the Jewish population, by members of the Judenrat. Soon a sort of resignation fell over the population.

Orders came from Tarnopol on Saturday, July 19, that a ransom of 600,000 rubles must be paid by the Jewish population of Skalat by Thursday, the 24th which was five days later. Tragic consequences would result if they failed to meet this demand. All Jewish affairs in Tarnopol were then under the control of a German named Faulfinger. The Judenrat was summoned to the Regional Command Office where they received this harsh order in Faulfinger's name that the Judenrat was to provide, by the same deadline, lodgings for twelve Germans. These lodgings were to be completely equipped with pots and pans, furniture, linens, and anything else the German's might need or want.

Faced with all of this, the Judenrat created a large committee to make it happen. First of all they needed to raise a large sum of money. That would not be easy, but Jewish tradition requires the "rescuing of souls". Often times in Jewish history, that was enough to overcome the impossibility of the situation. The committee chose to tax those who were rich amongst them and between them and the ordinary Jewish citizenry, they hoped to succeed. Working feverishly, day and night and in consideration of the danger the community now faced, the Jews accomplished this goal. Tackett, as the chairman of the *Judenrat*, worked tirelessly to organize and bring the effort to success. When the appointed day arrived, the required sum, as well as a surplus amount, had been raised.

The delegation took the funds to Tarnopol, but the surplus amount was kept, serving as a reserve in the Judenrat treasury. The lodgings for the twelve Germans, fully equipped as per the order, were also provided."

Elvis looked at Mrs. Fried, "He does not seem so bad from what you just told me." She took a breath and looked up again at the ceiling. She looked at him, made a face and continued.

"During the same period, on July 16, the Germans ordered the Jews to wear white armbands marked with the Star of David on their right arms. The members of the Judenrat however were to print the word JUDENRAT in large letters on their armbands. The Jewish *Ordinungsdienst* (Jewish Police) were ordered to wear yellow armbands marked as such.

Additionally, Jewish houses were required to show Star of David signs. The Judenrat was required to pay a high fee from the Germans to obtain them for each house. After that was in place, life in the shtetl became somewhat routine. With the exception of some minor changes, life continued this way until the beginning of the Autumn.

A few days before the start of the High Holy Days, the *Judenrat* made an announcement that all the town Jews were to report to the marketplace at 9:00 the next morning. No one seemed to know why they were ordered to gather. Tackett came forward. He explained to all of us gathered there that we had no reason to worry, simply a certain number of Jews would be taken away for labor. The German Kommandant of the Skalat *Schupo* (Security Forces), a man named Schneider, designated 200 young people they were sent off to Maksymowka to perform heavy labor on the rail line. The conditions there were brutal. Most of these young people returned by the end of the month because they were ransomed from the Germans for a large sum of money.

The Germans also established a camp for Russian prisoners of war in the nearby village of Borki Wielkie. These inmates were worked extremely hard. Their subsistence was a single daily ration of watery soup. Their treatment from the Germans was subhuman. The Russian POW's in the camp were broken in spirit and exhausted. Every day more and more of these men died. The Jews feeling sorry for them would help them as much as possible. In secret, they would toss them pieces of bread and food and cigarettes. When these actions were discovered by the Germans, those Jews were punished by beatings and occasionally by shooting. These prisoners, unfortunately were systematically starved to death. When the workforce got too small due to all of the POWs dying, the Germans filled their ranks with transports of Jews from Lwow and Stanislawow. The Skalat Jewish labor office was also forced to supply Borki-Wielkie with 200 Jewish workers each day. These workers were returned home by train in the evening.

On Christmas Eve 1941, the Germans murdered all of the remaining Russian prisoners. That is when they established the forced labor camp exclusively for us Jews. Starting that day, the 200 Jews from Skalat no longer returned to their homes. They became prisoners of the new Borki Camp.

Seeing the situation in Borki-Wielkie, the *Judenrat* in Skalat organized a Women's Committee. Their task was to bring aid to the Jews in the work camp. Every other day, the women would travel there to bring food. This food consisted of mainly bread. During the winter of 1942, it was extremely cold. The Women's Committee also tried to supply warm clothes, gloves and even straw to serve as fill for shoes to serve as insulation against frostbite.

By early 1942, a camp in Kamionki was established. This camp was filled with Jews from Czortkow, Kopyczince, Trembowle, Mikulince, Chorostkow and Grzymalow. New camps were soon started in Stupka and Romanowka. Food packages were also now being sent to the Jewish inmates there through the connections of the Skalat *Judenrat*. So as the camps around Skalat took so many lives, it became the duty of each city in the Tarnopol area to supply a monthly quota of men, primarily youths, to replace the ranks of workers who were dying.

There were people in town, who talked to the Germans. The various Judenrats from towns and villages around the Tarnopol district, connected through these peoples to conduct transactions such as ransoming of people. Often and unfortunately, this meant trading poorer inmates for wealthier ones. The Germans found a way to financially gain from all that was happening.

Over time, the Skalat *Judenrat* became the main point in the trade of human lives, and thus they began to sink deeper and deeper into a vicious swamp of lies and deceit. While the leadership was trying to be of help to the population, it was faced with hard choices and soon became an arbiter over life and death. In its attempt to help the local life, a home for the elderly and a soup kitchen for workers was put in place. Whenever possible, children received extra food rations, even if it was just some extra milk and cereal. Officially, the ration per person was supposed to be 100 grams of bread, a few hundred grams of grain and a couple of kilos of potatoes. Believe me, these were starvation rations. If you had money, you could purchase more food on the black market. Some families, in that way, were even able to manage some small reserves. If you were poor, however, you suffered. Deprivation, hunger and starvation became the normal way of life for those without money. The main sources of food were bartered with the village peasants, who took advantage of the situation when they traded with the Jews for clothing and other goods. The Judenrat social aid group helped out as much as they could, but their financial resources were extremely limited. Collections of various goods and funds were regularly imposed on the population, but you know, you cannot draw blood from a stone. They had very limited success in accomplishing this goal.

Just when things seemed as bleak as possible, the Tarnopol SD issued an order in January of 1942, for the Jews to turn in all fur coats they might own. They had three days to comply under pain of death. By the deadline, the warehouses were filled. The higher German functionaries took the best coats. A few days later, two wagons were loaded with furs for the "Winterhilfswerk". This was a campaign to provide warm clothing for German troops inside Russia during the winter of 1941-1942. Specifically they were designated for the German troops fighting deep inside Russia. Some of the Jews burned their furs, rather than give them up to the Germans. Many turned in the fur collars of their winter clothes. Thus, these Jews' outer garments were left with collars of raw buckram. They looked ridiculous. As crazy as it might seem, an ordinance that the collars be covered with dark cloth was instituted by the Judenrat because of their concern with the appearance of the people in these coats.

February and March of 1942 were quiet in Skalat. Then in April, the Jews were ordered to evacuate their homes on the main streets of the town. Their homes were assigned to selected Ukrainian families. Over the next eight days, scores of Jewish homes were emptied and turned over to these Ukrainian peasants. The expelled Jews moved in with people in the back streets of Skalat.

Then in Tarnopol, in May, their occurred the first 'action'. This consisted of a quota of the aged and sick, rounded-up for extermination in Belzec. These victims were predominately people from the hospital, the old-age home, and some of children from the orphanage. This dreadful news from Tarnopol brought panic to our shtetl. It was clear to everyone that disaster was close at hand.

Chapter Twenty-Three

"

We were getting near the planting time. All of the villages and rural estates nearby needed farmhands to help with the crops. The Judenrat's labor office was assigned a daily quota to provide five to six hundred Jewish workers to these farms. They left town to their workplaces guarded by the Jewish Ordinungsdienst (Security force). When the Jews began to receive authorized work-passes with German and Ukrainian signatures, those bearing the documents thought that they were in some way protected against eventual dangers.

These passes were arranged through the *Judenrat*: These working papers became like gold. Because soon they also became available to those who did not work, at high prices for those who could pay. The rush to get these passes gripped the entire Jewish population in Skalat in a fevered way. We assumed that by possessing a pass, our very existence was assured. But everyone was running around like chickens with their head's cut off. The passes were only good for about two weeks. After that they were worthless. Anyone could and would be shipped off to the work camp at Borki Wielkie at any time.

Then in July of 1942, the Judenrat was called on to supply thirty girls a day to the tobacco plantations at Jagielnice. These young women worked under atrocious conditions. It took a while, but eventually, most of their parents were able to ransom them home. This was a miracle in itself as a few days later, 400 other girls were brutally shot to death there.

So, life went on in Skalat during these so-called "calm" days from July of 1941 to August of 1942. Contrasting what was to come shortly thereafter, that period could almost be called the "Golden Age", as if that were possible, under the German regime in Skalat.

Elvis asked Mrs. Fried a question. "How did Mendel Tackett fit into all of this? It would seem that he was trying to work in terrible conditions and had to make difficult choices. You could hardly blame him in having to make choices like that. They could have just as easily killed him."

Rabbi Fried interrupted to answer, "Son, it is true what you are saying. I had escaped from the Red Army and returned home. I unfortunately, lived through the bloodbaths in the Tarnopol district. Having come home, I saw with my own eyes. that as sometimes happens, the people who are trying to keep the situation under control simply break. Then they become much like their captors, sometimes they become much worse. They take on the airs of their captors. What starts out as a survival technique, now becomes a terrible habit for them. They come to love their petty powers and they come to believe that their captors will not turn on them in the end. They become horrible murdering people themselves, willing to sell souls to protect themselves. Cowards really! The German's cultivated those people. Many of the capos in the Concentration Camps were Jews themselves and often were much, much worse that the German soldiers."

Mrs. Fried continued. "I know that I have told you a lot of terrible things but there is much more to this story, my dear Elvis. Do you want to hear the rest?" She stopped for a moment and looked him directly in the eyes. He seemed weary and tired. She worried that this was too much for him. Finally, she said, "I think you know that you should hear the whole thing. I can promise you that it will give some of the answers you seek. But it will bring you no peace. That I can assure you of. It will bring you only pain and you will not like it. Should I go on?"

Elvis got up and walked around the table with his hand on his forehead. He paced for a few moments. The Fried's looked at each other curiously. The Rabbi motioned to his wife that she should leave and just as she rose from her chair, Elvis sat back down.

"By G-d, he was my relative, I should at least know the story." He put his head down on the table for a moment to get his composure. Then he looked up at her, "Go on!"

Chapter Twenty-Four

❝It had been a year since the first pogrom of July 6, 1941, but the wounds had not healed. During the year, under profoundly difficult circumstances, our lives were controlled by the Judenrat. Tisha B'Av came, the saddest day on the Jewish calendar, when both the temples in Jerusalem were destroyed. It is a very difficult day even in the best of times. In our circumstances, it was almost unbearable. Afterward, the Judenrat leadership seemed to become particularly dejected. They announced to us, "Fellow Jews, things are bad. There is an evil hanging over us and may G-d be merciful." This sadness spread quickly throughout the Shtetl. For many, there were sleepless nights. People were depressed and despondent with the lack of control over their future security. Every day, a new fear permeated them. What was about to happen? When?

The Judenrat held daily meetings, racking their brains, looking for a way out of this crisis, knowing that as long as the Germans were in charge, nothing would change.

For lack of any other real possibilities, it was decided to raise a large fund of money. Its purpose was to bribe the Germans, hopefully averting the obvious imminent jeopardy. The Jews contributed whatever belongings they still had.

Within two days, the Leaders had gathered two valises filled with cash, gold and silver jewelry and implements, and any other valuables they could think of. The Committee chose a delegation, headed by Tackett, to promptly go Tarnopol and meet with the Gestapo. How much of the treasure was actually given to the Gestapo is not known, but the delegation returned seemingly encouraged and satisfied. The encounter was somewhat traumatic for the delegation. Tackett was missing a few teeth and the other delegates were badly bruised by the SS.

The delegates believed, nevertheless, that they had accomplished something for the common good. They came back saying to the crowd, "It was worth it. We have saved the town." They believed in some magical way that having met with the Germans in Tarnopol, they had accomplished much. They truly believed, that going forward, no further evil would befall Skalat. In their imaginations, they believed that the gift to the SS was so successful that this delegation had saved the day.

Now hearing these tales of wonders and miracles helped to calm the nervous Shtetl, which wanted so badly to believe all this was true. But wishful thinking, as it can be, is just that. These leaders, these "protectors of the community" soon began to doubt the success of their mission. They held secret meetings every day. No one understood why they were constantly meeting, but eventually the whole story came out. In truth, to the dismay of the Judenrat, the Germans had intended to carry out an 'action' against the sickly and the old. The bribe had been worthless.

The Judenrat delegation to Tarnopol tried to deal with the matter themselves, telling the Germans, "You need not come to Skalat." They pleaded with the SS. "We will carry out the 'action' ourselves. Just set the quota for us." The chief of the Tarnopol Gestapo, an Obersturmbannfuhrer Muller, agreed to let the Judenrat pick the five hundred souls to be delivered on August 31, 1942.

So, on August 30, 1942, the residents of the Skalat Shtetl, strolled about the town with no thoughts of any ill winds. At 5:00 PM, the Judenrat set out in pairs carrying prepared lists of names and accompanied by the Jewish policemen. They entered scattered houses and dragged out aged grandfathers and grandmothers, elderly parents, orphans and other children considered to be sickly. They also captured the so-called "useless" Jews, the relief cases. All of the people who had been gathered were led to the synagogue. There the designated unfortunates were gathered at this collection point. These khapers (catchers) deceived their victims, saying to them that there was nothing to fear, they were simply coming to a meeting at the synagogue. They told them it was a matter of state. For those who resisted, they told them, "Would you rather have the Germans drag you there?"

Frankly, it was useless to cry or protest. One had to go! Those who refused to go peacefully were taken forcibly by the militia. Unable to walk? You were carried. Unbelievably heart-rending scenes took place when the sick were brought out of the hospital."

She stopped for a minute and got up to take a tissue from the box on the counter. She rubbed her eyes as the tears flowed copiously from her eyes. Elvis reached over and placed his hand on her arm. She gathered herself together and with a will of steel continued,

"It is difficult for me to talk about all the awful scenes that took place that evening. In the end, the Judenrat was successful.

With Mendel Tackett in the lead, the Judenrat members went around all night looking for even more people, even searching in holes. They looked in cellars and attics, forcing the aged and sick to the Synagogue. By then, everyone knew what was going on. Very few of the victims succeeded in their attempt to hide. This was because when a calamity comes unexpectedly, hiding is useless. The 'catchers' were determined to fill their quotas. If a designated person could not be found, another family member took their place. Every 'catcher' had to meet his quota. The Germans had successfully taught them discipline and order.

Those not directly affected by this misfortune, were saddened and confused. Hadn't they been assured that they would be safe? Exactly what was happening here? Unfortunately, people react strangely to tragedy. A small segment of the Shtetl thought that if people had to be sent to their deaths, maybe it was better the aged were picked. After all, they had already lived out their years. This thinking, though wrong and morally crazy, helped influenced the supporters of the Judenrat. In their minds, these men were doing their best they could, on behalf of the community, in a terrible situation."

She stopped again, stood up and bent over the sink sobbing. Rabbi Fried stood up to comfort her, but she motioned him away. Elvis stood up as well, but she told him to sit. He did without a word. Soon she reached for a towel, wet it in the sink and wiped her eyes and face. She sat down again at the table.

"I always wondered, thinking back, how such a twisted idea could have arisen from the *Judenrat* members and their supporters. I can only think that their minds had become warped by the tremendous pressure they were under. In some cases, they had smothered their thought processes to mimic the Germans. The overwhelming majority of us were too weak to resist and powerless to do anything about it. All we could all do was watch the bloody happenings with horror.

By 9:00 that evening, most of the victims had been gathered in the Synagogue. The building was now surrounded with an enlarged guard of the Jewish police to prevent any escapes. They were most concerned about escapes during the night when the new victims were brought in.

After all of this, incredibly, the Judenrat members came together to review the day's 'accomplishments'. Liquor and cake were brought out and these Jews amazingly congratulated each other, believing they had rescued the town. They believed that 'if not by us, it would have been done by the Germans'. In their minds they rationalized that if the Germans had made the arrests, much more blood would have been spilled. I heard that one of the council-members Meyer Leopold was given a cash prize from the Judenrat for being the first to bring in all the people on his list. This payment was authorized by the Chairman Mendel Tackett himself.

After they were finished celebrating, they telephoned the Gestapo in Tarnopol reporting that the job had been completed. The Gestapo came the next day to take over the transport.

All of this may seem hard to believe, but the surviving witnesses know it to be true and reported it. No matter how painful the truth, it really happened that way. My mother, who was in the Synagogue on that tragic day, took the place of her mother, my grandmother, whom she wanted to save. Miraculously, she escaped in the confusion of the next day. But she told me, and I will always remember her eyewitness account. She told me and I quote, 'On the tragic day of 31 August, I was able to hide my mother, Freida Perel Kaczer, age 87. My mother was a treasure. She was well-read in the Tzenereneh ("Let's Go and See" a book of prayers written in Yiddish and read mostly by women.) and other books of Torah. She had borne five sons and three daughters. Some 30 years earlier, three of the sons went to America, and from them, she received regular support until war broke out. In Skalat and in Tarnopol, she had two daughters and a son, whose families included some twenty-five grandchildren and great-grandchildren. On Sabbath days, the old woman was always trying to decide which child or grandchild she should visit first. Almost every year, one of the American sons would come to visit her and see to her needs.

On that fatal day, we said to her, "Come, Mama. We will hide you. We won't let you go to the hangman's hands!" She trembled like a leaf. Mama still wanted to live. "My dearest children don't leave me," she said and went into the hiding place on unsteady legs.

The *Judenrat* officials ran about looking for her everywhere. They were furious asking how could it be that the old Kaczer woman had not been crossed off the list as of yet? In their warped mind they justified their anger by saying outright, "Can you imagine the gall of such a conscience-less family, to hide away such a broken old woman? No, they won't get away with it!" The militia came to Mother with an ultimatum demanding: 'Are you turning over your old mother or not?' 'I don't know where she is,' She replied.

Then they shouted "If you will not hand her over, then you must come with us... You will bring harm to all of us! We must have the total number of people - don't you understand?" No. She did not understand. She felt it was better to go herself than to deliver an aged mother to her death. She screamed, went faint, cried, then fought with these awful men, refusing to go. But it was to no avail: they dragged her off to the Synagogue as a hostage.

The Synagogue was crowded and suffocating. There was screaming, then sobs. Old people sighed, or coughed, made a fuss or just fainted. Not even a drop of water in the heat. The Judenrat figured we were all dead anyway the next day, why waste time providing food or water. A few of the aged and sick, lacking stamina, had already died.

One of the old timers, Hersh Solomon stood at the pulpit and recited Psalms in a tearful voice. A teacher, he had become penniless and was supported by communal funds. So, he ended up on the list of the 'useless' and, as such. he, his wife, and his three children were dragged to the Synagogue

The time passed, and hours flew by. Nothing is heard, nothing is seen. The night comes, and no rescuers appear. New victims are brought in regularly. They are surrounded, being asked what is happening in town. Faith in any kind of rescue becomes ever weaker. Fear of death assaults one's thoughts. What a night the other Jews and my mother spent there! I cannot imagine that a night in hell could be worse. When the dawn arrived, the red, blue and green panes of the tall *Synagogue* windows let in the daylight which revealed the frightening reality.

Fearfully, everyone awaited whatever the coming hours would bring. My mother had lost hope and no longer believed she would be rescued. Meanwhile my old grandmother had found out what had happened. She experienced the ultimate dilemma. How could she permit her own daughter to be lost? She wove together the strands of Fate and Divine Providence. G-d must know what He is doing! She did not sleep all night and barely survived until morning to be able to ransom her daughter from the murdering hands. "My daughter. I have come!" Mother surprisingly heard her mother's voice in the background. "You will not die, I, alone, will be the sacrifice for the family. Go back home. You are younger than I and I have lived a long life," She said to me. Into her hand she pressed a gold coin, worth $20.00, and whispered in her ear, "Maybe you will be able to ransom me." She looked at her with a small smile, "You never know?"

My mother did not want to go. Tears choked her as both of them, mother and daughter, stood there frozen and mute. Finally, my grandmother pushed her away, "Go, my daughter. Before it is too late!" My heroic 87-year-old grandmother warned. "But try... to remember me. Perhaps you may yet be able to ransom me." She still so wanted to live. They embraced for a very long time. A policeman led Mother outside. She was barely able to walk. My dear old grandmother remained in the Synagogue!"

At 4:00 PM on Monday, a group of the SS came to get the victims. Led by Obersturmbannfuhrer Muller, they arrived from Tarnopol with eight empty trucks to transport this "live contingent." After the first truck stopped at the gate of the Synagogue, the Chairman of the Judenrat, Mendel Tackett and his cohorts appeared before the SS. They were servile and obsequious at the feet of the Germans

"How many have you gathered here, you sh---y Jews?" Mendel Tackett waved his hands about and managed to stammer out a few words. This enraged the German who replied with a wild shout, "What? So few? Damn you! Another hundred Jews in a half hour or we will shoot you down like dogs!" There were supposed to have been 500 people. Miraculously, there were only 480 people in the building.

Somehow twenty people had disappeared. One of them was my grandmother. It was said that one of the policemen had permitted that number of people to ransom themselves and had let them out through the back door during the night. He had figured that if the Judenrat could let people ransom themselves or replace their relatives with other people, why couldn't he do the same?

A few Germans and the Jewish police spread out across the town. They grabbed anyone they could. In that half-hour chase another eighty souls were added to the "live contingent."

Obersturmbannfuhrer Muller checked his watch and waved his hand to indicate that had enough people. The hour was getting late. The doors of the Synagogue were opened and everyone inside was loaded onto the trucks by the Germans and the Police as if they were handling freight. People were packed in tightly to accomplish the fullest load. All this occurring while the Germans cracked their whips overhead. The old people were carried and loaded with significant effort as they could barely move.

"Move them out!" the *Obersturmbannfuhrer* shouted, and the trucks began to move, to the sound of sobs and wailing. The 560 victims were taken to Tarnopol, and then, from there, some to work camps, but most on to an extermination camp. One of those victims was Anna Steuben. I never expected to hear she was still alive. I guess she was one of the victims that ended up in a concentration camp.' That was the story my mother told me when she got home, and I have never spoken about this until today."

Elvis looked at her, unable to say anything.

Chapter Twenty-Five

Stanley looked over at Elie who had stopped talking and was quietly weeping. Stan asked him, "that's a remarkable story, how could you remember it all so well?"

Elie looked up at him as he dried his eyes with a handkerchief. "When Mrs. Fried told me this story, it was if I became a part of it. I felt this all so vividly. I was a part of it, not because of my cousin's presence in these terrible events, but because I felt that in some measure, I was one of those victims whose life was dust. I was one who was being destroyed, in part because my cousin was a wicked coward and also because at the time the story was told to me, I was also a coward. Now, I may have never killed anyone, but I wreaked havoc over people's life and did it with wanton disregard. This was not who I wanted to be and if I was to continue doing the same things, well… I would still be the worst piece of crap. I finally knew my truth and could not look at myself in the mirror. Both inwardly and outwardly I despised who I had become. Simply, I could not be Elvis Presley anymore!"

With that said, Elie got up and went in to go to sleep.

Chapter Twenty-Six

Stan and Elie reconvened the next day on the porch. Elie looked tired and pale. When Stan asked him if he was up to it, he just started talking like he had a mission to get his story out.

"So, you see, I stayed with the Fried's for several more days. I gave Mrs. Fried what information I had on Anna Rabinowitz. Working like a detective, she quickly found Anna and got her on the telephone. They spoke for hours, it seemed. Mrs. Fried cried almost the entire time she was on the phone. At one point, she handed the phone to me. Now, I really had no idea what to say to Anna. But Anna made it easy for me.

"Mr. Presley, thank you for not forgetting me. Thank you!"

"Anna, how are you? Since we spoke last in Vegas, I have never stopped thinking about you."

"Really, Why?"

"Something got turned on in my head. I could not put my finger on it while we talked in my hotel room. You were talking about my cousin as a horrible person. Even though I had never heard of him and really, I mean, I felt nothing to connect him to me, nevertheless, I felt very lost after speaking with you about him. My first thought was, in fact, that if he was a relation of mine, he couldn't have been so bad. But Anna, I was really wrong about that. Really wrong! I apologize for what he did to you and your family. I don't know if that will do any good, but I am so sorry for the way he treated you."

Anna was silent on the other end of the line. It was an awkward silence. I was just about to hand the phone back to the Rabbi's wife when she said to me, "Elvis, you are not Mendel Tackett and I never wanted you to think that. I only wanted you to know about him. It would seem that Miriam told you far more about your distant cousin than I did. For that matter, more than I ever could. It was a horrible thing that happened to the Jews of Skalat. Miriam and I were lucky to have been able to survive and come to this country."

"What happened to you after you left Skalat?" Elvis asked her.

He heard a deep sigh on the other end of the line. "It was very difficult. We arrived at a work camp by truck. That is, those of us who survived the trip. Those who were healthy enough to work were sent to farms to work all day away from the camp. The work was back breaking. Eventually, after the harvest was over, we were returned to the camp. One day, trucks came and took all of us who were still healthy enough to work, to a railway station. We were herded into boxcars, like cattle, but much worse. There was no room to move, no food, no water. People vomited continuously. There was no privacy, no place to take care of your bodily needs except in a couple of buckets. We could not see light except from the crack of the doors. We traveled for many days. There were many who died on the trip and two women actually gave birth on the train. Then the train came to a stop. The door was thrown open. We were at Auschwitz."

Chapter Twenty-Seven

"Stanley, after I got home to Graceland, I was very depressed. I knew what had to be done in my life, but I was afraid to do it.

Life kind of returned to what had been normal before I went to the Fried's. The Colonel was booking tour locations and I was back on the road. Las Vegas was a particularly good place to play because there were a million distractions and I kind of settled back into my numbness that had existed before.

But I had this powerful feeling continue to stick with me. My stomach was a mess and I couldn't sleep. Visions of Skalat continued to haunt me. Finally, I had my assistant go to the local library and get me any and all information, she could find about Skalat. The librarian she spoke with contacted the Library of Congress and within a few weeks, I received a large box filled with eyewitness reports from the Germans and the Jews of the events that Miriam Fried had described. The Germans were crazy. They took take pictures of everything, as if they could rewrite history when they won the war. I saw for the first time, pictures of Skalat from the earliest days of the 20th Century through the present. Skalat had cleaned itself up pretty well. From the look of it now, they had become another pretty European village, like in Germany, when I was in the Army. Kind of like a sanitized version of themselves. I saw pictures of the four towers where all the killings had taken place. It was deceptive, as they looked to be nothing special. I could not imagine what it must have looked like the night of the first pogrom."

Stan interrupted, "Elie, stepping back for a moment. Did you go back and see Anna again when you were in Vegas?"

"No, actually not."

"How come? She obviously had forced you to look differently at your life. Weren't you at least curious what had happened to her?"

Elie stopped for a while to think. " Stanley, I really don't know why I didn't reach out to her. I wish I could tell you that Vegas caused me to go into a mental fog. That would be such an easy excuse." He looked up at Stan with a blank look. Then he got up and went inside. He was inside for a long time. Stan got concerned and knocked on the door. Shoshana answered it.

"No, I don't know where he went. Hold on, I will go down to the basement and see if he's there." She went looking for him and soon returned. "Elie wants you to come downstairs." I opened the door and came in. I walked to the cellar door and went down into the basement. He was not in his office, but in the corner of the basement was a closet where he kept some bottles of whisky and liquor. Behind that was a false wall that Elie was trying to remove but didn't have the energy to get it moved. I helped him remove all the liquor bottles and watched as he popped the wall out of position. Behind that wall was a large box. I helped him bring it out and together, we brought it into his office. We replaced the wall in the closet and returned the bottles to their place.

The two of us went back into Elie's office. He opened the box and took out pictures and papers all about Skalat. Digging through the box, he would grab a picture or a document and hand it to me to look at. I looked at them for quite a while. My blood ran cold as I read through some of the documents. The pictures the Germans took were frightening and unnerving."

Stanley sat down in front of the desk and took a deep breath. "Elie, somehow I don't understand all this. Sometimes, I think I do. But not really. Why is this Skalat stuff so important to you? Really my friend, what has any of this got to do with you leaving Graceland and coming to live here?"

Now Elie sat down. He leaned forward and said "Stanley, my dear friend, this is me! It is because of all this, that I decided to give up my whole life as Elvis Presley. This may be hard to understand, but I left my old life to make amends and the only way I could do it was to return to my real roots as a Jew and start a new life to make things right."

"Elie, make amends for what? All this has nothing to do with you, yet you cling to it as if you lived through it yourself. To whom were you able to make amends? Anna? Mrs. Fried?"

He leaned back in his chair and played with his beard. Refusing to look directly at Stanley, Elie said again quietly, "I needed to make amends."

Again, Stan asked, "Amends for what? For what Mendel Tackett did to all those people?

Elie said in a whisper, "Maybe?"

"Elie, do you realize how absurd that sounds? Is this life you have led for the past 35 years brought you that peace you so desired?"

He looked at Stanley with an intensity that he had never shown him before. "My life now is a blessing. I have a wonderful wife; a terrific family and I get to say Kaddish every day for all the people who died because my cousin was such a coward that he was willing to sacrifice all their lives. Hundreds of lives, thousands actually. I get to make those amends and when I meet them in heaven, they will know, and the Master of the Universe will know, I tried to right a wrongful legacy of my family. It may not be enough, but it is something. I will be able to rest in peace with that thought."

Chapter Twenty-Eight

Vernon walked behind Elvis and swatted his head, "Boy, what the hell is wrong with you?

"Huh? What are you talking about?"

"Man, ever since you came back from California, you've been moping and yelling and just acting like a total A-hole."

"I have not!"

"Yes, you have! Ask anyone around here. Hell, you shot out another T.V. the other day. What the hell is wrong with you? Give me that gun. You are scaring the heck out of everyone around here, especially the help."

Elvis reached for the back of his neck. He rubbed at it hard. He looked down at the table and shook his head. Then he slammed his fist on the table, knocking over the salt and pepper and the bottle of ketchup. Vernon's cup of coffee, which was sitting across from Elvis, spilled all over the place.

Vernon yelled at him again. "Have you gone crazy boy? Look at the mess you just made. Geez!" He went to the sink and grabbed a towel to clean up the spilled coffee. Then he sat down at the table and looked at his son.

"What the hell happened in California? You came back a different person. Come on boy, what is going on with you. Did some broad screw you over?"

"I wish!"

"Well what is it Elvis? There are lots of people depending on you and you are acting like a damned crazy man. So, what gives?" Vernon reached into his shirt pocket and took out a pack of cigarettes. He shook one up and drew it out with his lips. He grabbed a match and lit the cigarette. He drew deeply and blew the smoke out into the air above him. Elvis watched the smoke curl above Vernon as if it were a cloud changing shapes in the sky.

"Daddy, I didn't go to California."

"You didn't? Then where the hell were you?"

"Here in Memphis."

"The whole time?"

"Yeah"

"You are full of --it. You expect me to believe that you hid out in "this" town. The minute you walked onto the street or if anyone saw that big old Cadillac of yours, everyone would have known who you were. Come on boy, if you weren't in California, where the hell were you?"

"Really Daddy, I was in Memphis."

"Yeah? Tell me where?"

"I went back to the old neighborhood. To the Courts."

"To the Courts? That place is a --ithole. Why would you go back there and where the hell could you hide in that G-d forsaken place?"

"Rabbi Fried still lives there. Same apartment and everything. I stayed with them."

"Rabbi Fried? You mean the couple who lived upstairs from us? They're still alive? He wasn't so young when you were growing up there. How old can they be?"

"In their 80s, I suppose."

"And they remembered you?"

He nodded yes.

"And why would you go to see them? Did they know you were coming?"

"No. When I went to the building, I wasn't even sure if they still lived there. But they were there, and they took me in for the week."

"I don't understand Elvis."

"I had run into them about ten years ago. The Rabbi had followed my career for some odd reason. I guess they really liked me. I mean, you know I was their Shabbos Goy."

"Their what?"

"Their Sabbath Gentile. I took care of the things they were not allowed to do on their Sabbath. Lighting lamps, turning on the fire, adjusting the thermostat. You know Jews can't do those things on Saturday."

Vernon shook his head, "Crazy. I didn't know that. You did that for them all the time?"

"No, just on their Sabbath and Holidays."

"That explains why we couldn't find you on the weekends. So, you went back there?"

"He said to me when we met back then, that if I ever needed help from them, well I knew where they lived."

"So, you went over there, not knowing if they even were still there? Because you needed help? And how were they going to be able to help you? Explain that to me?"

Elvis looked down and rubbed his scalp.

Vernon just looked at him in amazement, "You could have gotten help from any of us here. And what kind of help exactly did you need? Because I got to tell you, Whatever the help they gave you, well, you came back a bigger mess than before you left here."

"I know Daddy, it seems like that. But they really did help me. I hate this life. It doesn't work for me at all. It is killing me, just killing me."

"How can you say that? Look around you. You grew up in a dump in Mississippi. Then we moved to those damned projects here in Memphis. We couldn't rub two nickels together for anything. And now look at how you live. Man, this is luxury. Luxury, G-d damn it! What could be better than this? What are you on drugs? Well get a damned doctor and get yourself straight. Whatever it takes. Get yourself straight."

Vernon stopped for a moment to compose himself. He sat down at the table looking at his son. His early adult life flashed across his eyes.

"I know you hated doing those stupid movies, but they paid the bills. Those concerts pay the damned bills around here. They pay your alimony to Priscilla and the child support for Lisa Marie."

"I know. I know."

"Yeah maybe! What are you going to do anyway, just run away somewhere?"

Elvis just looked up at him. Vernon looked at him in disgust.

"You do want to run away! My gosh, you are one stupid ... Agh! You must have jello for brains boy. Where in the hell are you gonna run to anyway? Where? Your Elvis Presley! Where in this whole damned world could you hide? Do you think no one would come look for you? Where? You dumbass, where? You think you could just disappear somewhere, and that Colonel wouldn't have an army of private eyes looking all over for you? They'd drag you back here so fast, you wouldn't know what hit you. We have contracts. That's right, contracts. Contracts that have to be fulfilled or we will lose everything. You don't think they would take us to court. You don't think those boys in Vegas wouldn't want to get a piece of you if you didn't show up at their hotels. These are not nice guys Elvis. Definitely not nice guys. I'll tell you, they'd leave you for dead and they'd take everything. The house, the cars, the money. Everything. You'd be better off dead. Wake the f—k up, you stupid spoiled baby. You would end up on a street corner with nothing. Nothing I tell you!" Vernon was screaming on the top of his lungs. He ran out onto the porch slamming the door loudly.

Elvis groaned loudly. The maid came in and asked if everything was alright. He nodded to her that he was fine. He got up and took a drink of water from the sink with his hands. Then he went upstairs, took some sleeping pills and went to bed.

Chapter Twenty-Nine

" "Vernon was really pissed off at you, huh?" Stan looked at Elie.

Elie chuckled a bit at the thought, but then said, "he sure was, but I can't blame him. Daddy had a hard life and now he was living it up, Mama was gone. She died of a heart attack on August 14, 1958. She was just 46. I was heartbroken. She was my everything. Vernon married two years after Mama's death. He married a younger woman named Davada Stanley. He called her Dee. I hated her. They stayed married 17 years. They divorced right before I "died". Miserable woman! But with Mama gone, he had his freedom. Nice cars, all the booze he could drink and all the cigarettes he could smoke. Everywhere we went, he could find a woman because he was Elvis' father. And so, he found her. It was a good life for a man who had nothing growing up and had gone to prison as an adult. But that's a side issue.

Getting back to Vernon… while I was growing up! How we kept the family together then was a miracle in itself. And that Mama took him back? Well, she did it for me, so I would have a Daddy in the house. He was impossible, but she was so strong willed that he just buckled under to her. I can see it now. At the time, I was just happy to have him home. Vernon was in many ways a complex man."

"How so? Stan asked.

"Well he always was difficult."

"Tell me about your Dad, Elie. What was life like growing up with him?'

"Stanley, do you know anything about him?"

"Not really too much. I couldn't find very much about him when researching your family."

"Really? Well we were very close. He could be impossible, but he was a really great guy. You will see that without him, I wouldn't be sitting with you today."

"How is that Elie? Are you telling me that Vernon helped you escape?"

Elie grinned for a moment and then continued, "we're getting way ahead of ourselves right now. First let me tell you about him."

Stan got up from his chair and walked around for a second, "I knew it. I couldn't figure it out, but of course, Vernon would be the one to help you. I just knew it! I looked at all the possibilities, Priscilla, Linda Thompson, Ginger Alden, the Memphis Mafia. But the thought that kept coming into my head – Vernon. I'm right Elie? Am I not?

"Stan, I said we are getting way ahead of ourselves. Let me tell you about Vernon and maybe then you can figure it out."

"You mean it wasn't Vernon?"

"Stan, let me tell the story!"

"Ok, Ok, talk." Stan sat back down.

"As I said, Vernon was a complicated fellow. He was born in Fulton, Mississippi on April 10, 1916. My grandparents were Jesse and Minnie Mae. His full name was Vernon Elvis. I ended up with Elvis as part of my name. When he was around 16 or 17, he met my mama Gladys at church. She was five years older than him, but somehow, they got together and fell in love. Since he was 17 and Mama was 22, they couldn't get a marriage license and they would not have been allowed to marry. But when they filled out the papers, they switched their ages and were married in Verona by the Pontotoc County Clerk on June 17, 1933. Daddy, his brother Vester and his father Jesse built a little house for Mama and Vernon to live in. It was really a two-room shack. Mama gave birth to me and my twin brother Jessie who died, in the house. That was January 8, 1935.

My father worked at whatever job he could get. It was the Depression and work was not so easy to get. Daddy worked manual labor and whatever odd jobs he could get, but we barely got by. We were a loving family and would sit around an old piano we had acquired and sing together. Mostly gospel songs, you know.

Daddy got into trouble with the law when I was 3 years old. Daddy had sold a pig to our landlord, a man named Orville Bean. They had argued over the price of the pig and finally Orville told him to take or leave it. Needing the money, he took the check. But he was very angry. He always had trouble keeping a job, most likely because he drank so much. Anyway, he altered the check and got caught. He served 9 months in Parchman for forgery. When he left, he told me to take care of Mama. I remember crying and crying. But he was gone to prison.

Things got much worse during that time for Mama and me. We lost the house and had to move in with relatives. I was so upset by all this that I started to sleepwalk, scaring Mama half to death. Mr. Bean felt sorry for us and he spoke with the Judge and somehow got Daddy released after 9 months. Mama wasn't so glad to see him, and Daddy took a lot of stuff from his family for having gotten into trouble. It was not a good time for us. We moved from place to place. Sometimes, we lived with relatives for a while, then we were out looking for places to live again. Food was always a problem. There was never enough. We were always one step ahead of the creditors. Daddy worked some odd jobs, then he started running moonshine. He could never make enough money to take care of us and he could never seem to stay with one job more than a little while.

I remember after Daddy got home from Parchman. I must have been about four years old. Daddy gave me a spanking for doing something. I don't even remember for what. Anyway, I decided that was enough for me and I was going to run away from home. I packed up a couple of sandwiches for myself and slipped out the door as soon as Mama and Daddy went to bed. I was scared. It was dark and cold, but I was going to teach my folks a lesson. So, I kept walking down the dark road. Oh, it must have been fifteen or twenty minutes later, I hear a car coming by. I moved to the side of the road, so no one would see me. A truck pulls alongside me and stops. It was Daddy's truck. He scooped me up into the truck. I was hungry, so I ate one of the sandwiches and gave the other one to Daddy, who laughed when he saw it. He took it though and ate on the short ride home. Mama was waiting for us outside, nervously playing with her apron. "Thank G-d your home safe," she said to me and looked up at Daddy. I got spanked again but, this time. I hugged and kissed my folks and promised not to do it again. Now Daddy was not afraid to use the strap on me when I misbehaved. Here is a funny story, now looking back at it as an old man. The very first time I remember committing a sin, I must have been four or five at the time. I stole two empty cola bottles from our neighbor, the Harris' porch. When Mama asked me about the bottles, I told her where I took them from. She asked me if I had asked their permission. I said no, them being empty bottles and all. I figured no one would care. But back then, you would buy the bottles and pay a penny deposit. So, in reality, I wasn't just filching a couple of bottles, I was costing them the deposit money. A penny went a long way during the Depression. Well Mama was so mad that she took me by the hand and dragged me back to the Harris' house. I was so ashamed to return the bottles. I said I was sorry to Mrs. Harris. She smiled weakly at Mama and then told me I was forgiven. She closed the door and we went home. She told Daddy later that night and then told me that I would have to confess my sin at Church the next Sunday. She was going to teach me a lesson about stealing that I would never forget. Well when Sunday came around, I pretended to be sick. I suddenly got better when Daddy showed me his strap. When we got to Church, Mama pushed me up to the front of the Church and ordered me to confess in front of the entire congregation. Crying and looking down at the ground, I whispered my sin and then ran out of the Church, crying. But I never again took anything without permission. Hard lesson for a hard time!

Daddy was away a lot and Mama and I got close. I learned to be the man of the house. I sometimes called my parents "my babies" because I did everything, and Mama could always count on me.

I learned to really love music in Church. We might have been dirt poor, but we still went to church. In our case, the Assembly of God church in Tupelo. They were Pentecostals and if you know anything about Pentecostals, they love to sing. Our Preacher especially. Boy would he sing, banging away on the piano and getting sweaty and hoarse, but letting it all hang out. There was no dancing in our church, but singing? Let me tell you, you could hear us out in the street, swaying and singing with a choir and all that commotion. I loved it!

Oddly enough, my musical talent was first recognized by my fifth-grade teacher, a Mrs. Oleta Grimes. Mrs. Grimes was the daughter of Orville Bean, who had caused so much trouble for us when I was a young one. She heard me sing this sad old ballad called "Old Shep" and was so moved by the way I sang it, that she told my school principal. He listened to me sing it to him and decided to enter me into a talent contest at the Mississippi-Alabama Fair and Dairy Show. I wore a cowboy suit and stood on a chair. Without a guitar or a piano to sing along with, I just sang this sad old song about a boy's love for his dog. It was great, and I won second place. The prize was a free pass to ride all the rides at the fair.

I wanted a bicycle really badly, but there was never money for anything so special as a bike. Shortly after the fair, I asked again. Mama always said no because she was afraid, I'd fall and get hurt or maybe get hit by a car. The real reason though was we had no money. But she arranged to buy me a second-hand guitar. The preacher from Church and some of my family and some of Mama's friends pitched in and gave me informal guitar lessons. I got good really quickly and soon I was learning to play the piano as well. When I started 7th grade, I brought my guitar to school every day and during recess, I would practice and play it.

Getting back to Vernon, we lived a hand to mouth existence in Tupelo, because he couldn't keep a job. It was hard to keep moving about and not have a steady place to live.

Soon after I started High School, in November 1948, Daddy moved us from Tupelo to Memphis, Tennessee. We left in the middle of the night with all our belongings tied to the top of our car. That is except the furniture. Daddy figured he would have a better chance at a steady job in Memphis, which was a real city not an overgrown town that Tupelo was then. We found an apartment in the Courts and I was enrolled at L.C. Humes High School or as it was known around Memphis as Humes High School. I did ok as a student for the most part, but never really fit in because I was so shy. When I became a Junior, I decided to mix things up and see if that would make me feel better. I let my hair grow out and grew long sideburns. I found the wildest, most flashy clothing in all kind of weird stores. I wore dress pants and would wear a scarf like an ascot. I wanted to look like a movie star. People thought I was really weird, but I loved it. I figured that if I couldn't fit in, I would stand out.

In my Senior year, I took a job at the MARL Metal Products furniture makers. I worked from 3 to 11 pm. We needed the money and I thought I could help after school. But it was too much, I would fall asleep in class and Mama was afraid that my grades would suffer, so she made me quit. The money was nice, but I was getting totally burned out.

Later that year, I appeared in a school talent show. I sang a song called "Til I Waltz Again with You". After that performance, boy did I become popular. My crazy looks became cool, not weird.

I graduated from Humes on June 3, 1953. Now what to do with my life.

I called Daddy into my room one afternoon soon after graduation and told him, "I want to be an entertainer." Daddy said to me "Well, you know I don't know much about that sort of thing, but you've been dealing with quite a few people in the business. Why don't you talk to some of them to see what you got to do to get into it, you know." I was most interested in singing gospel, quartet singing. I tried out for two or three different young groups, hoping to get in with one of them. They were either full or didn't think I had what it took to sing Gospel. Ain't that crazy Stan? They didn't think I was good enough to sing Gospel. Ha! They did me the biggest favor not letting me sing with them. I would blow by all of these groups in no time flat. But at the time I was so disappointed. I went back to Daddy for some advice. He told me to go record a song. I was afraid to do that. I had once recorded a song for Mama at Sun Records, but that was for her. I had been singing with some groups doing gigs in local places, but you know, you never really have the confidence in yourself at the beginning. By late summer, I finally got up the nerve to go down to the Memphis Recording Service where I recorded two songs, "My Happiness" and "That's Where Your Heartaches Begin" I don't know what happened, but it was a success for me. Then after I made this record, quite a few of the quartet groups wanted me to join them. I talked with Daddy again about what to do. I said to him, "I can get into the quartet singing now, the gospel field." Daddy's reaction was, "I wouldn't do it. I'd just keep what you got. Because you tried that before, and they wouldn't take you in." He said it again to me, "If it were me, I'd just stick to what you got." So, I did just that, and it was the best advice about my singing career that I ever got from anybody.

Then in 1956, I went to New York and the rest is history. But I realized then and still recognize it today, after Daddy has been gone all these years, that although he might not have been the brightest fellow when it came to be working like plain folks, he was a downright genius when it came to my music career."

Chapter Thirty

After listening to Elie talking about his father Vernon, Stan started to suspect that the real mover and shaker in Elvis's life was his old man. What he was trying to figure out, was whether Vernon had been involved in the escape to Brooklyn or not. Vernon had a lot to lose if Elvis "died". So, the odds of him doing something to facilitate this process began to seem remote in Stan's eyes. Vernon had died less than 2 years after Elvis's "death". He had a long-time heart condition and he died of cardiac arrest at the age of 63 in Memphis. He was remembered for crying bitterly at his son's death. It seemed to be a genuine shock to him that Elvis was dead. Stan just didn't think that Vernon could have had a part in spiriting Elvis away from Graceland to a new life. Besides, Vernon was the executor of the will. But that was a wrinkle that Stan would have to chew over in his head, because in a strange way, it reopened the possibility that Vernon might be involved in some way.

Stanley's mind still kept turning back to Priscilla or even to Ginger Alden. In his mind, Priscilla became a more viable suspect. She had joined the Church of Scientology and was an active member. Because of her fame, the Church of Scientology could be assumed to have a financial interest in the Presley family. Besides, Scientology was a very secretive organization, employing drastic tactics to keep their member's quiet about Church going-ons. In many respects, they would be the perfect vehicle to pull this off. In fact, they could have successfully spirited Elvis out of the country until the furor died down and then help him set up somewhere else.

To Stanley's way of thinking, "it had to be Priscilla! Maybe Vernon as the executor also was a part of this? Who knew? Elie was the only one who would be able to confirm any of that. If any of those thoughts turned out to be true. After all, Elie might have pulled it off in some completely unique way. He did hint that two Rabbis were involved. But how could two Rabbis pull something like this off?"

Stan thought again about that," Two Rabbis? That's ridiculous! There was a dead body found! Ginger found a dead "Elvis!" There had been an autopsy, a toxicology report and everything. How big could this conspiracy have gone? What Rabbi would have gotten involved in that?"

Stan started to worry at the breadth of all this. The only one who knew all the details was Elie. And he was dying. Stan hoped to be able to get the whole story from him in time. Elie still looked alright, but Pancreatic cancer kills quickly, and he might just miss the opportunity to get the whole story pieced together. He was going to have to push Elie to move the story along. How he would do that was anyone's guess.

Stan thought to himself that if all else fails, he could try to talk with Priscilla directly. He knew that the chances of her coming clean after all these years would be practically nill. Having built the Elvis brand into a major moneymaker, she would be risking way too much in exposing her own role. No, he would have to push Elie to get to the meat of the story, as soon as possible, or the whole thing might just go up in flames with no story to tell. That was not a thought he wanted to ponder. He had to act. Elie loved to talk and talk. And he had allowed it because, he was fascinated by the whole thing. Stanley was amazed that he had discovered this great secret and that he was sitting everyday talking with the great "King of Rock and Roll." But now Stan was going to have to be the old tough beat reporter and not the glassy-eyed fan. It was the only way to get this story at all. There were too many variables to make sense out of.

Stan tried to piece together several potential conspiracy theories to press Elie on. The Priscilla angle! The Ginger angle! Maybe the Memphis Mafia was in on it all the time? Vernon? It was conceivable that Elie went back to Linda Thompson for help. But for some reason, that did not resonate with him. He wasn't sure why? But it didn't.

Stanley sat at his kitchen table, drinking some coffee and looking at his notes. The more he thought about it, the more questions came to mind. He knew for sure that Elie had pulled off the great escape. He was also certain that he could not be the only one who knew about it. Soon, hopefully, if Elie lived long enough, he would know how and who helped him. The bigger question in his mind then became, how did Elie get to Brooklyn. More important than even that was the question of how did he manage to live in plain sight for all these years without someone else, anybody else, putting 2 + 2 together? This enflamed Stan's mind, Elie had lived for 35 years in relative obscurity in Brooklyn. He married, had a family and sat on his damned porch every day and not one person had guessed that Elvis Presley lived amongst them?"

Stan rubbed his eyes. His head was hurting. Tomorrow was another day and he needed to clear his head, so he could go to work in the morning. He turned on the television and watched the Mets lose another one.

Chapter Thirty-One

"Ok Elie, how in the hell did you do it?" Stan blurted out the next evening as they sat on the porch to talk.

"Do what?" Elie replied.

"Come on now Elie, stop playing around. How did you pull off the great escape? I couldn't sleep last night, running possible scenarios on how you pulled it off. I've guessed at hints from you. I've speculated about the people in your life who could have helped you. Any one of these scenarios, in my mind, is possible. Let may say it better, they are all plausible, but only you know the truth."

Elie laughed out loud, "How do you think I did it, Stanley? Since your mind seems to be running wild, what are your ideas?"

Stanley shifted uncomfortably in his chair. "Don't play that game with me. I could envision a hundred different ways you pulled it off and still be wrong. You know my friend, and I am going to be perfectly straight with you. You're dying! And you know it. You might be feeling sort of alright now, but tomorrow, it could change in an instant. You could wake up much worse and go quickly. Then Elie, your story never gets told. Your wife and kids will never know that you were once this great world-famous person. Any monies that can be made from this story would be lost and your family would suffer, so stop kidding around and spill it!"

Elie just sat in his chair, stroking his beard and looking out onto the street. Some boys were riding their bicycles in front of his house. He sighed loudly.

Stan looked at him, "Unless, you really don't want to have your story told? Maybe you really want to take it to the grave. Is that what you want Elie?

Elie continued stroking his beard and looking out at the boys in front of him. "I sure wish I had a bicycle at that age. I never really learned to ride one, even after I grew up and could afford them. I learned to ride a motorcycle, for sure. And that was great fun. A real rush. Just loved it. I'd take a girl on a ride. Great fun." He laughed and turned to Stan, "Almost, a guarantee, I would get … well you know. I would end up in bed with her. But gee, I would have loved to have a bike. Ride around Tupelo wherever I wanted. That would have been real freedom for a kid like me. A guitar for a bicycle. I know Mama was always worried I'd get hurt. But as much as I loved that guitar… Ah, a bike. She was right about the guitar. She knew the music was in my blood. But really Stanley, a bike! Did you have one as a kid?"

"Sure. At least until it got stolen when I was about ten. Remember I grew up in Brownsville. That was a tough neighborhood."

Elie smiled. "So, you understand"

Stan nodded, "I guess so. It did give me a sense of freedom to come and go as I pleased."

"Exactly! You see Stan, for me running away from Graceland and all that it meant was kind of like a little boy exploring his world on a bike. No one to bother me. Time was all mine. I could wander and be free. Getting there took a lot of time. Now I have all this." Waving his arm at the front window of his little house. "It's certainly not Graceland, but it is more a home to me than Graceland could ever be. In many ways, I never stopped being the little boy in my Daddy's two room shack in Tupelo, Mississippi. This is certainly no shack, but its small and intimate. When the kids were young and crawling all over the place, I would stand in the foyer in amazement and think to myself how they would never be able to understand Graceland. It was an entirely different world. So abstract, so crazy. My little sixteen-foot-wide house with two little bathrooms and hardly any room to move, means more to me than Graceland ever could.

I gave up all those beautiful, sexy women for my sweet Shoshana. Now you have to admit Stan that she is no beauty."

"I wouldn't say that, Elie"

"I know you wouldn't. But what I mean is that compared to Ann Margaret or Cybil Shepard or even Priscilla, Shoshana is no match to them physically. Shoshie is so thin and pale and so quiet. Sometimes, we can sit together for hours and not say a thing. And you know, it's alright. It really is! I mean, she would never get on the back of a motorcycle and ride with me."

"Are you so sure Elie? Maybe deep inside her is a burst of

adventure that you don't know is lurking there. Maybe she is just living the life she was expected to by her parents and family. Maybe, she wanted more. Maybe, she might have wanted to know that she is the one, not Ann Margaret, or Cybil Shepard or even Priscilla who managed to tame the great Elvis Presley. You think that's possible?"

Elie shifted uncomfortably in his chair. He stopped for a moment, pursing his lips and stroking his beard. A tear slowly rolled down his cheek. He brushed it away with his hand.

"You could be right. But it's too late now. I cannot upset the apple cart now. It would be too much of a shock and I will soon be gone. Can't do it to her. Love her too much!"

Elie got up and went into the house. He came out a few minutes later with his wedding album. He opened it and started to explain every picture. After he had left Graceland, he had lost a tremendous amount of weight. Except for the beard and his now very short hair, it was clear to Stan that the man in the pictures was Elvis Presley. Shoshana was in a white wedding dress typical of Orthodox Jewish brides. High necked and long sleeved with a simple crown and veil, Shoshana had a beautiful countenance that was belied in her everyday existence. Thin and tall with red hair and a gaunt face, makeup had made her face look more full and beautiful. Elie was obviously somewhat older than her in those pictures, but he looked genuinely happy. She looked happy but had a somewhat worried look that remained with her through all the years of marriage. Now, Elie was more filled in as age and married life tends to make a man fuller in the body. But Elie was now clearly showing the signs that a disease was working its way through his body. His hair was thinned out and he had a widow's peak. His beard was long and almost all white. His paunch was smaller than when Stan first met him. The cancer was starting to show how it ravages one's body in small but definitive ways.

"I can't do it to her Stanley. I can't tell her about all this, and I won't. I will tell you." He said with a strength in his voice. "So that you can tell her."

"Me?"

"Yes. Promise me you will tell her everything before you publish this book. She should have no surprises."

"Don't you think she will be surprised if I tell her. I think she'd be damned mad at me and even more so, she would be hurt terribly that you shared a life with her without telling her your secret. I can't do that Elie. That's not fair!"

Elie took a deep breath. "Yes, you are right. I am a chicken about this." He looked out at the street again. The streetlights were just starting to come on. There was a weird glow around him. He sighed and shook his head. "I am sorry, but I can't tell her about all this. I may be a coward about it, but I would rather it be a story from the grave, then to face her with it. Stan, this is a very big deal. This is a very long and complicated story. I did things to live this life that I am not proud of. The help I got from people were entrusted with this secret and they kept their word not to spill the truth. For all of them, I am deeply grateful, but they kept an oath to me, and I kept an oath to them. Stanley, in the Torah, when Joseph's brother sold him to the Egyptians, they made an oath to keep the secret from Jacob. For twenty-three years, they kept that secret. Even Isaac knew about it and kept the oath from his son. Joseph himself, long after he became the viceroy and could have easily let his father know he was alive, even he kept the oath and did not reveal he was alive until the moment the oath was ready to be revealed. I made an oath with the people who helped me. They have kept the oath. When some of them died, they took my secret to the grave with them. Who am I to break that oath? An oath is an oath and I must keep it until I die. Heck, I would not even have ever told you, except you figured it out. I realized that it would be better to tell you than have it leak out from you in speculation. But I thought long and hard about doing that. I determined that you are a good and truthful man. You've respected my wishes to keep the secret hidden until after I die. So now I ask you to understand that it must be you who tells my wife before the story becomes public. Can you do that for me?"

Stanley was moved but didn't know what to say. He got up from his chair, went into his house and closed the door.

Chapter Thirty-Two

The next morning before he went to work, Stanley knocked on Elie's door. When the door opened, he saw Shoshana trying to usher the kid's out the door to the school bus that was pulling up in front of the house.

"Hi Stanley," as he opened the door and the kids ran out waving at their mother. She threw them air kisses and turned back to Stan.

"Hi Shoshana. Is Elie around?"

"He's at Synagogue." Then looking at her watch she said, "But he should be home in a few minutes. Do you want me to give him a message?"

"No. How long do you think he'll be?"

"Probably another 5 minutes or so."

"I'll wait then." He sat down on one of the chairs on the porch.

"You're sure?" He nodded yes to her. She shrugged, Ok. Would you like something to drink? A coffee or something?"

Stan smiled, "No, No, it's alright. I'm fine. Thank you for asking? I'll just wait."

"She smiled back, "Ok." Then she closed the door.

Stan looked down the street and soon saw the lumbering shape of Elie coming towards the house. He walked up the first step to the house and looked up at the chair. He stopped for a moment.

"I see your point Elie. I don't agree with you, but I see your point."

Elie took a deep breath and nodded. He took his hat off and climbed the remaining steps to the porch. He sat down next to Stan. They sat for a spell, not saying anything. Finally, Elie reached over and placed his hand on Stan's shoulder and whispered, "Thank you."

They shook hands. Stanley got up and walked down the street towards the subway. Elie looked around, took a breath and shook his head. He got up and gently knocked on the door. The screen door opened and Shoshana let him into the house and then shut the front light.

$$\text{Chapter Thirty-Three}$$

Chapter Thirty-Three

Vernon sat on his bed smoking a cigarette. As he blew smoke into the air, he thought to himself, "That boy really wants to run away somewhere. Incredible, all that talent and no common sense. He's not stupid. Either he really is a spoiled selfish man, or something is really eating him to the point where he has gotten so out of control. I wish, I could figure which?"

He got up and went to the bathroom and looked into the mirror. "He'd never be able to run away. And why would he want to? He has the pick of any woman he would want. And there's so much money. Heck, he is a virtual money machine."

He looked in the mirror carefully. The reflection he saw was a younger Vernon. The man who could not sit still in any place very long. He was a man attracted to his vices. But deep inside, he knew that he always longed to be a more stable man. Managing his son's life had given him a sense that he was a responsible adult. And he was proud of how he had changed. He was a man of some substance now.

Vernon frowned in the mirror. He could also see that with his becoming responsible, there was a dark side. For one thing, he had finally gotten rid of that damned woman Dee. He thought to himself, "I should never have married her." She was just a big anchor around his neck. Elvis was right about her. She was just mean. Her three boys were decent though and I always treated them like they were my own. Elvis treated them like brothers for the most part. But really, she was just a mean bitter woman. Don't know how we lasted for 17 years, but I am so glad to be rid of her."

He walked back into the bedroom and snuffed out the cigarette in an ash tray. He reached for the pack to take another one and thought better of it when he lifted it up. He tossed the pack on his bed and went downstairs. The boys were playing pool and drinking. He walked past everyone and went outside and got into one of the cars.

He had no particular plan in mind and drove aimlessly for some time. At some point, he realized he was heading to the Courts. Vernon had not intended to go there when he started, but now he realized that providence was taking him there, for whatever reason that might be. He parked his car and went up to the old apartment. He looked around at the dingy hallways and was disgusted. But he was disgusted because it really wasn't that different than when he and Gladys had lived there. It was only older and less well kept. He was saddened that there was a time in his life that this was the best he could do for his family. They barely were able to make it. Living on government support and working when he could find something decent, they had managed to make it. But Elvis was why they were able to break out of this. Without Elvis, he probably would still be living here. Maybe? Or dead already. Maybe that would have been the end of the story.

But Elvis had been successful. Beyond their wildest dreams. Their lives were turned around so quickly that they never had a chance to savor it. Hell, Gladys wouldn't make it to her 47th birthday. All so fast! One day singing in some club in Memphis, then on Ed Sullivan, then the Army. It was too much for her. Her heart couldn't take it.

His thoughts turned to a familiar conversation that he played in his head. "Well, I tried my best to keep Elvis on the ground. With all the success, he was flying so high, that one could never know what he was doing? Priscilla! How I allowed that to go on was just crazy. She was a little girl for G-d sakes. What was I thinking? I was still the boy's father. I should have put a stop to that immediately. But I was riding the Elvis rollercoaster as well. The lights were too bright. The noise too loud. The women too pretty and the booze flowed freely."

He pondered it all as he turned around and looked at the hallway. "And now look at him. My son is a lost man! A drugged out overweight 41-year-old man-child. I've never been able to help him with any of that. Maybe now? Maybe now?"

He took a breath, found the Fried's apartment and knocked on the door.

Chapter Thirty-Four

When Vernon returned from the Courts late that night, whatever thoughts he had about his son were profoundly changed. He had sat at the Fried's table and let them talk about Elvis. He came to realize that he really never understood his son. What drove his son to succeed and what was driving him to his inevitable breakdown and failure was now somewhat clearer. He learned a lot listening to the Fried's talk. It was not normal for a man to shoot out televisions and Elvis did it out of boredom and frustration. He let himself go physically out of severe discontent and his search for some meaning in his life. He tried to get a grasp of it through Karate and eastern mysticism. But that gave him no relief, because his actual existence was the complete opposite of what they espoused.

Vernon of course understood none of this inherently. He only understood, and now grasped deeply that his son was searching for a way to survive. That Vernon knew about, searching to survive. But it had always been about having a job and enough money. For Elvis, it transcended money, because there was so much money around because of his talent. Giving Cadillacs to strangers was just the way he acted out to find acceptance. This was the world in his head. In his mind he couldn't accept his life as it was. For Elvis, there was only the numbing of his brain through drugs and alcohol. This was how he coped because he saw no other way out.

Vernon walked out of the Fried's apartment determined to find a way to help his son out. He saw that time was not on his side and that Elvis would self-destruct like an Atomic Bomb going off. While Elvis was hoping to just run away, Vernon's concern was about the contracts and losing everything. That made sense for him. He grew up poor and spent most of his adult life perilously close to being unable to take care of his family. His thoughts turned to packing up in the middle of the night and moving to Memphis. He had no job and they had not a stick of furniture. All that was left in Tupelo. They had packed everything and tied it to the top of the Plymouth and drove all night, not knowing where they would live or how they would manage.

He feared returning to that kind of existence. He was too old for that. But that was going to happen, in some form, if he didn't get Elvis some help, some way to get his life back on track.

As the car rolled along the road back to Graceland, he thought about all this. He reached into his shirt pocket and pulled out a cigarette. He pushed in the car's lighter and waited for it to pop. Touching it to his cigarette, he took a deep drag and held it deeply in his chest. He blew the smoke out of the window and continued to drive. He watched the faint red glow dangling from his lip as he looked through the windshield. By the time he pulled into Graceland, he knew what he must do.

Chapter Thirty-Five

For the second time in two days, Stan asked the question, "So Elie, How the hell did you do it?"

Elie laughed, "Seems like we've been down this road once before."

"I guess we have," Stan laughed as well, "But I think I have a better understanding now of what you need for me to do with your story. I don't necessarily agree, of course. But I get it! I guess I am just as afraid as you are to break the news to Shoshana and your family."

"I know it will be hard for you, but I know you will do fine. I trust you more than you know my friend. Maybe, I shouldn't trust so much since I've known you for such a short time. But on the other hand, I've floated through this life for 35 years. I never really expected to get away with it for so long. When the doctor gave me the news about the cancer, I was scared and then somewhat relieved. The story would go to the grave with me. But somewhere in my head and even in my heart, I did not want to die without having had the chance to tell how my new life had been put together. During the last 35 years, I've looked over my shoulder a lot. I always feared that I would run into someone from my past life on the street. They would recognize me, and the gig would be up. I imagined the headlines, "ELVIS IS ALIVE". Crowds of people showing up at my door, scaring Shoshie and the kids. All that I loved would be wiped out. I would never have a real place to hide again. People would want me to sing in public again and it isn't who I am anymore.

When you discovered that I was Elvis. I already knew I was not long for this world. Somehow, I felt safe with you. That you were a person who would respect my privacy. But more important to me was that you weren't just some stranger who had come upon this and would blab it all over the internet or to the papers. You are a journalist and I had read your column for years before I met you. I always sensed a great integrity in you. And you have shown me that. You could have run with the story and the last days of my life would have been a media circus. Now I know, my story will be told with respect and kindness, because it is not a kind tale, my friend. To get to the here and now, took great deception and I am not proud of that. Great people helped me, and they had to make choices in that pursuit that must have taxed their moral compass very greatly. I believe, they chose a greater good, because they saw the greater good in me."

He shifted in his chair, so he could look me fully in the eye. He stopped twirling the hairs on his beard with his hands and placed them squarely on the armrests of his chair. "Stan, there are people who helped me who are still alive. People you will be surprised were involved. Please respect their privacy when you tell my story. Most are now dead. There are some you will be able to talk about by name. They might even be willing to talk to you in person if you approach them in the right way. Other's ..., Please respect their reputations even though they are gone. They have families' who would be shocked. Change the names and muddy the story up enough so that they may rest in peace. Everyone who helped me did so because in some way, they loved me. They helped a helpless man to build a whole new life, totally separated from my previous existence. Some never met me, some barely knew who I was. Some simply helped me because I was a fellow Jew in trouble. I left a lot of very good and close people behind when I did this, so remember this Stanley. Remember this for me, in my memory, when you tell the story."

He looked up. A bird was flying overhead. He followed the bird with his head as it flew from one tree to perch on the tree in front of his house. He grimaced slightly and turned back to Stan.

"So how the heck did I pull this off, exactly?" He smiled warily, chuckled slightly and lifted his hands off the chair and placed them out in front of him with his palms cupped upward. "Master of the Universe, I knew there would be a time when you would command me to tell this secret. I am willing now, but I am afraid. Guide me, place the right words in my mouth. Let me be truthful and let me be fair to everyone who will soon come to know my truth. It is your truth and it must always come out either in this world or the world to come. I am ready, help me to be ready. Help me my Master!"

Stan whispered "Amen"

Stan looked at Elie, "That was pretty dramatic!"

"Would you expect anything else my friend. I am, after all, Elvis Presley!"

Chapter Thirty-Six

““It would be easy, Stanley, to think that I know exactly how we pulled this all off. The truth is. Like a true military operation, not all the players understand their role in the plan. As the man that needed to be moved, I probable know the least, believe it or not. I suppose that was because I was so messed up with drugs, that my friends were afraid to let me know too much, for fear that I would screw it up. And Stanley, I made huge mistakes that almost blew my cover several times. It is truly a miracle that we got away with it. I nearly blew it years after I was already settled here in Brooklyn. Luckily, it flew under the radar due to the help of someone you would never expect to have been involved.”

“Stanley yawned, “Elie, all that is very tantalizing, but come on man, tell me the story.”

Elie stared at Stan for a moment. “It may sound strange Stan, but I am not really sure where to start.”

“Elie, it’s not like it’s a murder mystery? Just say what happened. Unless it is a murder mystery? Is that why you’re so reluctant to tell me.”

Elie laughed, “No, No. Nothing like that!”

“Well Elie, look at it from my point of view. There was a body and there was an autopsy. And you are sitting here in front of me, so you can understand why I might ask?”

“We can thank Daddy for that!”

“What, Vernon killed somebody?”

“No! Of course not! But anyone who thought that my old man was a dumb country bumpkin would be sorely surprised.”

“How so?”

“Because without Vernon, no Elie.”

“Yes!” Stanley jumped out of his seat and turned to Elie, “I got it right that your father was involved. I just knew it.” Stan almost couldn’t contain himself. He shot a fist into the air and shook his head. “Damned, I knew it. I just knew it!”

"You mean, you guessed it."

Stan sat back down. "Yeah! You know what I meant."

"I get that!"

Stan tried to relax in his chair as Elie continued, "Why are you surprised? I mean, he was my Daddy."

"Oh, I am not surprised at all. But how was he involved and more importantly Elie, why? In a sense, he had a lot to lose."

"Darned right. He may have had the most to lose of anyone, even the Colonel."

"Huh? What has the Colonel got to do with any of this? Did the Colonel help you?"

"If the Colonel had known, he would have tied me to chair and kept me locked up until right before each performance. Then he would have locked me up again until the next one. Heck no, the Colonel was the one person, Daddy and I had to hide it from most of all."

"So, what gives Elie? Spit the damned story out already."

Elie took a breath. "Well on some level you got it right. Without Vernon, none of this would have worked. Daddy worked some real magic for me."

"But why Elie? How did you convince him?"

"Didn't have to!"

"What? You didn't have to convince him? How could that be?"

"He was my Daddy. He knew that if I continued like this, I would be dead very soon. He was the one who convinced me!"

Chapter Thirty-Seven

When Vernon pulled into the drive at Graceland, he had already figured it all out. Now the hardest thing would be to convince Elvis. He knew his son was a drug addict. He knew that Elvis also was someone who had a need for immediate gratification. This was going to take some time. He had to make Elvis understand that. But his son had a volatile personality.

He thought to himself "Damn it, Gladys spoiled the boy. Even if we didn't have some money for something he wanted, she'd give him food or something else. She could quiet his temper, but he never learned to control himself for anything he wanted. Anytime I tried to teach the boy some patience, she would yell at me and immediately give him what he wanted or give him something to shut him up. Those two, they were as close as thieves. They shared stuff I never ever knew about. G-d, I let her turn him into a big Mama's boy. I should have never let that happen. And he's still a big Mama's boy, but his appetite for things is not just for a banana or peanut butter or some pancakes. Now, it's ...whatever, he can get his hands on. Man, now I got to live with it."

Despite those thoughts, Vernon genuinely saw the pain his son was going through. And he had a plan. It was a crazy plan, even to him. But Vernon was far smarter than anyone thought he was. And he knew that this kind of crazy might just work. But he had to pull all the pieces together. As he had sat across from Rabbi Fried and his wife this evening, the ideas had started to pop in his head. They told him the story they told Elvis. He looked at the older couple and came to realize that they were probably the only people in the world that Elvis inherently trusted. The only skin they had in the game was seeing Elvis happy. They could care less about his money. And they had a track record with him. He had disappeared from Graceland successfully into their tiny little apartment. Vernon saw their fondness for his son and he now understood Elvis' attraction to the couple. He got in his head why Elvis hung out in their apartment as a teenager and he could understand why in Elvis' deepest moments of confusion, already as a grown man, he had returned to them to seek their advice and help.

Vernon sat down at the kitchen table with a cup of coffee and lit a cigarette. He drew in deeply and stretched out his legs in front of him. It was late, and it was quiet in the kitchen. His mind was turning over many different scenarios, but one plan continued to stay in forefront of his mind. There was only one glitch that he couldn't find a way around. For this plan to work, Elvis had to "die". If he "died", there would be no one coming after the estate. The income stream would only dry up from the touring. Elvis records would still produce monies. The Colonel would have to pack up his operation and leave. The hangers-on would all go. The boys would all disperse to someplace else where they could make a living. For this to work, the world had to be convinced that his son was dead. Now that would take some real effort. But if it worked, Elvis could have a new life, but only if he could clean himself up. And most important if he really wanted it!

Chapter Thirty-Eight

"Now you see, Daddy had a plan," he said to Stan as he tipped a bottle of scotch into his friend's glass. They were in Elie's little office in the basement and the door was closed. Stan lifted his glass and said, "L'Chaim," and then took a healthy sip.

They had adjourned down there because, it had started raining heavily outside. Also the basement office allowed for some privacy. What Elie was about to describe would surprise both men. Stanley would be shocked because of the sheer audacity of it. Elie, even now after all these years would remain surprised because he still couldn't believe that it had actually worked.

Elie took a sip from his glass and sat down behind the desk. "Gosh darn Stan, my Daddy was a genius. If he had only gone to school..., well that's another story. What he figured out in his head, well, no General in the Army could have. This was more like a CIA operation than anything. Really, one man's claim to fame would forever have to be secret. But Daddy was OK with that. He really loved me, and I would have never cleaned up my act without him. He passed only a couple years after that and of course, I couldn't go to the funeral. Couldn't even say Kaddish for him as he was not even Jewish. But I sort of sat Shiva for him. Miss him badly, even now! After Mama died and he married Dee, I thought I was totally abandoned by my family. But no matter what, and despite the woeful woman he was married to, he always was available to me."

Elie poured himself a little more scotch and pointed the bottle at Stan. He lifted his glass to Elie while he poured a little into the glass. They stopped to take a drink, both of them kind of sadly looked at each other. Elie then sighed!

"I was really beaten up at that point, both physically and emotionally, I started a tour in the middle of March in 1976. We all toured almost continually until the end of June in 1977. Crazy, but in less than 16 months, the boys and I spent a total of 141 days touring the country. And that didn't include performances for 10 days in Lake Tahoe and another 11 days in Vegas. Brutal!

Throughout the spring and the summer of 1976, I worked a punishing tour schedule. We only had occasional breaks. I was sick and exhausted and ingesting pills to help me sleep. More pills to help me wake up. Whatever breaks we took were far too short to get me back to full health. My weight which had been getting bad, well forget about it. I got so fat that I couldn't fit into my outfits. I didn't want to be on tour, my voice was a mess and really, I could care less. Thousands of people were paying good money to see me sing and I tried to get off the stage as quickly as I could. Not every night, mind you, but a whole lot of nights. I was physically present, but not there in any other real way. The drugs were so bad, I barely could be understood by anyone. I mumbled to the audience, forgot words to songs, I had been singing for years. It was obvious to everyone, especially the press, who were pitiless in their reviews. Looking back, they were right. I had no business being on stage."

Stanley asked, "Where was Colonel Parker during this time?? He must have seen his meal ticket self-destructing?"

"Well in all fairness to the Colonel, he was well aware of what was going on with my health and emotional stability. He tried to enlist Daddy and the boys to get me some help. But I was my worst enemy. I pushed them away. There was really nothing the Colonel could do but try to shield what my true condition was from the press in the best way he could. After an appearance in Charlotte, a reporter wrote a story and told his readers that I had a touch of the flu and my fans shouldn't worry. I would be alright for years to come.

My health did not get better, but I continued to take the stage, sapped of all my energy during performances. The night after Charlotte, we went to Baton Rouge. I couldn't go on. I was so sick. We had to cancel sold out shows in Mobile, Macon, and Jacksonville. On April 1st, I came back to Memphis and was checked into Memphis Baptist Hospital. I was obviously exhausted and whacked out on drugs. They sent me home four days later. By April 21, the Colonel had me back on the road for shows in 11 cities over the next 12 days.

At my last concerts in May and June 1977, I was a disheveled, uninterested person trying to survive my nightly ordeal on stage. It wasn't fun for me and I am sure the fans were not happy, giving the boos I was getting when I left the stage early and couldn't perform. What I needed to do was to stop touring. I needed to concentrate on regaining my physical strength and get some help for my mental state. But I was my own worst enemy. I did it to myself. I wouldn't quit, even knowing it was killing me. Daddy thought I was doing it deliberately, hoping to die. I am not so sure about that. I don't think I wanted to die; I just think it was a scream for help. On June 26, 1977, I played my last concert at the Market Square Arena in Indianapolis. The concert officially was scheduled to begin at 8:30 p.m., but I didn't perform until 10 p.m. We had warm-up acts of brass bands, some soul singers and a comedian before I went on. I sang for about an hour and a half. Amongst the songs I sang were my classic tunes like "Jailhouse Rock" and "Hound Dog," to rev up the crowd. I sang some slow and sad songs like "Hurt" and then I did a cover of Simon & Garfunkel's "Bridge over Troubled Water." I closed with "Can't Help Falling in Love with You," one of my favorite ballads.

I was exhausted by that time. I told the crowd, "We'll meet you again, G-d bless, adios" and then left the stage. The crowd was very happy and seemed to enjoy themselves. I felt that performance was one of the better ones, I had in a while. Now I had six weeks off before I had to start touring all over again.

It would be Daddy who would finally have that big conversation about how I would go forward."

"Elie, I am not clear on what exactly happened here. What did Vernon talk with you about? Who dreamed up the idea that you should fake your own death?"

"Well it sure wasn't me. And to be fair to Daddy, I don't know where that idea came to him. I just wanted to get away for a while and try to figure out my life. That February, I went to Hawaii with Ginger and her sisters, thinking by going away, I would get my head straight. Instead, we brought 30 people and it was one big pajama party. Drinking and swimming and playing football. It was the same thing as Graceland, only better weather. A total waste!"

"Why didn't you rent some private place and go away alone or with Ginger? She seemed to really care about you?"

"Oh, sure she did. She was a great kid. But that was part of the problem, she was a kid. And I was also a kid. You know a 41-year-old big kid. And anywhere we went, the press would follow. The photographers always snapping pictures of you when you least expected it. We had no real peace.

Although I wanted to marry her, and I really meant to, it was obvious to me that we were doomed as a couple. And it was probably better for her that way. I could have never given her all of myself in that environment. Not in the way, I gave myself over to Shoshie and the kids. I needed someone who was older and kind of wiser to help me figure this out. The Colonel was all business. Couldn't talk to him. As it turned out the older, wiser voice of reason was Daddy."

Chapter Thirty-Nine

Elvis had been home for just a day or two when Vernon pulled him aside in the kitchen late one night. The house was quiet, and Vernon felt he could talk freely.

"That Tackett story, wow, that was a hellacious thing."

"What are you talking about Daddy?

"Tackett, you know. That whole story about Skalat."

"What?" Elvis looked up at his Daddy as Vernon poured himself a coffee. He sat down at the table across from Elvis. "The last time we sat here like this, you told me about how you disappeared to the Fried's for a week. Son, no one knew where in the hell you went. It was just craziness around here. When you told the Colonel, you were in California with some girl, heck, I didn't believe it for a moment. I just had no idea where you could be. Anyway, you told me of your troubles and how the Fried's seemed to have helped. I went driving a few nights ago. Just driving kind of randomly. No particular place to go but thinking how you wanted to run away and trying to figure out why and how.

Almost like it was the hand of G-d directing me, I found myself back at the Courts. I hadn't been there since we left. I hated the place. Lot of bad memories. Lots of troubles trying to make ends meet. You get that son. Don't you?

Elvis nodded. Vernon pulled a smoke from the pack in his shirt pocket and lit it. He sipped on the coffee and reached for the ashtray to put down the smoke. "You see Elvis, seeing you in such pain hurts me, I guess almost as much as it hurts you on some level"

Elvis looked at him quizzically, but Vernon continued. "I may not have been such a good father..." Elvis interrupted, "You did just fine Daddy." Vernon shook his head, "No I was a real crappy father. Never could quite get it right. Hell, your mother had to get a job in the cotton fields when you were a baby, just to get us to make ends meet. She would take you into the fields wrapped up in a bundle.

She would carry you down the rows of cotton while she was picking. When you cried, she'd sit and feed you and then get up and continue picking. She was a tough lady and a good mother. I was not such a good husband to her. Wish I could have been better. It got much easier after you started making all that money, but then she was gone. So young. Way too young." He looked away and wiped at his eyes with a handkerchief. Elvis also got teary.

They sat at the table very quietly for a while. "My son," Vernon said to him, "I know you hate this life. I do actually get it. There ain't enough money in the world to bring you happiness if what you do makes you sad. There is something I don't really understand. You always loved your music. One would... I guess one would think that if you loved your music and were successful at it, then everything would be alright. But that's not true for you. I see that it's also not true for a lot of performers. Don't know why, but it sure seems true. Vernon shook his head and reached for the cigarette in front of him. He took two drags in quick succession, then stubbed it out. Sipping from his coffee, he continued talking. "It's been real tough for you my boy. And I know you want out. At least I think you want that. Is it what you want?"

Elvis took a deep breath, then reached over and took Vernon's coffee cup and took a sip. "I don't know! Really, I have no idea other than I want to go somewhere by myself, where no one knows me and live like a regular Joe. Get a job. A nice simple life. A wife, some kids and no one would be any wiser."

Vernon looked at him and jokingly said, "Looks like you want to be in the Witness Protection Program. You know disappear into middle America, get a new name, a new life?"

They both laughed, and Elvis said, "Yeah, wouldn't that be great? Sure, wish I could figure out a way to do that. That would be swell Daddy. That would sure be swell."

Vernon took out another cigarette and lit it. He leaned back in his chair and blew out the smoke towards the ceiling. He smiled deeply and took another drag. "Well son, I think I can make that happen!"

"Are you crazy? How could you do something like that? No way! You couldn't do no such thing."

Vernon smiled broadly, "Want to bet on that?"

Elvis leaned back in his chair and looked directly into Vernon's eyes. "Seriously?" Vernon looked back at him and smiled wryly, "Seriously!"

Chapter Forty

Vernon left Graceland on the morning of July 6, 1977. In the trunk of his car was a large suitcase stuffed with cash. Vernon had always stashed cash away. He didn't trust banks. The depression had taught him that the only money you could trust was the money you had hidden in a safe place. Banks are known to fail periodically. He'd been there. He knew.

Not to say that valise contained all of Vernon's money. Heck no. He had a nice size bank account thanks to his son. And his stash of cash was spread out in a number of places. In truth the valise in the trunk represented but a small percentage of the cash he had acquired during Elvis's successful years.

He drove south of Memphis and picked up US 78 by Olive Branch, after he had crossed into Mississippi. He cruised past Byhalia, Red Banks and Holly Springs, heading through the Holly Springs National Forest. He zoomed past Hickory Flat and Myrtle before stopping in New Albany to fill his gas tank, buy some cigarettes and some snacks. He continued down past Blue Springs and Sherman until he reached Tupelo. He drove down North Broadway and parked in front of the County Offices. He opened the trunk and lifted the valise out and carried it into the building.

When Vernon hit the road back to Graceland, he had two large manila envelopes with him. In one he had an original birth certificate along with a new driver's license and Social Security Card with a new number all in the name of Elliot Polk. In the other envelope, he had similar new documents, only these were in the name of Elijah Pressler. This second envelope, he would hold onto until Elvis was settled into his new life. The first envelope would carry the documents Elvis would need to escape. He put them into the now empty valise and placed them in the trunk before he traveled home. He took another route going back to Memphis. He traveled west on US 278, stopping at Oxford. He found a motel and grabbed an early dinner at The Gin, a local bar and restaurant. He drank a few beers, ate a good meal and went back to his room to sleep.

In the morning, he traveled west to Batesville and turned north onto Interstate 55, all the way back to Memphis.

Vernon was to make another trip into Mississippi before Elvis's departure. Elvis would never know the nature of this trip, even after he was safely ensconced in his new life. This was a secret Vernon would take to his grave.

On August 15, Vernon told his son that he was to go to the office of his Dentist that night. Elvis was to complain loudly about a toothache and make a big fuss about calling the Dentist to take him immediately, even though it was already night time. When he got there, a young woman took three vials of blood from his arm. She placed them into a small ice chest and handed them back to Elvis, telling him that he should give them to Vernon when he got home. One of the last photographs of Elvis "alive" is of him driving into Graceland that night, returning from his Dental appointment.

While this was all going on, Vernon took another drive south into Mississippi. He drove to the capital city, Jackson. He had another valise filled with money in the trunk. He pulled up after dark at the University Medical Center. When he left, he had an empty valise and a cadaver in a body bag filled with ice, which he put into his trunk.

Chapter Forty-One

"Daddy had me go to the Dentist on the night of August 15th. I took a bunch of pills and slept most of the day. When I woke me around 3:30, I sat with Vernon and he told me to start complaining around 9 PM about having a bad toothache, to everyone in the house. I was to make a big ruckus and insist that the Dentist take me immediately. I asked him why I was going there. He said to just shut up and do what I was being told to do. He handed me a little ice chest; you know the little ones you put a few beers in to take to the park. Daddy told me to give it to the Dentist and then bring it home and only give it to him. I went back to sleep for a while. When Red woke me up at 9, I complained loudly about my tooth. I told him it hurt like hell and that I was going to call the Dentist and get in to see him that night. The dentist called and said that he could take me after 11 PM.

Vernon had left to go somewhere and called from a payphone on the road, to make sure I actually went to the Dentist."

Stanley and Elie were sitting on the porch as the sun was going down around them. The kids were wrapping up their playing in the street and would soon head into the house and leave us alone to talk.

"What was the big deal about going to the Dentist in the middle of the night?" Stan asked.

"Well, Daddy had a meticulous plan. He knew I would be starting the new tour on August 17th. He had decided to help me to escape, but he wouldn't tell me the plans and made me agree to do whatever he told me to do. There were going to be people who would help, and I was to follow their directions absolutely. Otherwise he would not help me. But if I did agree, he would get me to a new life. But I couldn't ask any questions at all! I didn't understand exactly, but I had confidence in Daddy, so I agreed. He also told me that after I went, we could never communicate again. This made me sad to hear, but I knew it was for the best. He also told me that I could never try to get in touch with anyone from my life now. That included Priscilla and Lisa Marie. Vernon knew that was going to be the toughest thing for me to do. But you know, I kept my word, even up to this day. And there were many times, I wanted to break that word, but when I saw what Daddy did to give me a new life, even his death, could not force me to change my vow.

I didn't know why he wanted me to go to the Dentist in the middle of the night. But I did what he told me to do."

"So, what happened when you got to your Dentist's office?" Stan asked.

Elie looked at him, "When I got there, there was a young woman. I think she was a Filipino woman. She was a nurse of some kind. Anyway, she sat me down and told me to roll up my sleeves. She gave me a shot in my right arm and had me lie down on the Dentist's chair. I soon fell asleep. A couple of hours later, I woke up feeling a little groggy. She handed me a cup of coffee. As I sat drinking the coffee, I saw a bandage on my left arm on the inside part of my elbow, you know the crease. I asked her what that was from. She told me she had drawn three vials of blood. The blood was on ice in the little cooler. I was to take it home and give it directly to my father. After a little while, I felt better, collected the cooler and drove home.

I drove back to Graceland arriving, I don't know, around 1 AM, maybe a little earlier, a little later. Not sure really. I went to Daddy's room and gave him the cooler. He had just gotten in and was busy working on some papers. I was going to ask him why he needed my blood but thought better of it. I guess I really didn't want to know. What was going to happen to me was in Daddy's hand and the less I knew, the less likely, I could screw it up.

I went downstairs and sat with some of the boys and their girlfriends. I felt good. We talked about the upcoming tour. I told them that this tour was going to be different. I was excited about it and raring to go. Portland, Maine was the next stop on August 17th. I was ready."

"Elie, why would say that to the boys? You knew Vernon was planning to get you out of there."

"Yeah, well, I thought so, but I didn't know how or when. I just assumed that at some point on the tour, Daddy would arrange for me to just "disappear". That seemed easier and more logical to me."

"That's not what happened."

"Heck no and in retrospect, it made more sense for him to have me "die" at Graceland. He could control it better there. Besides, he knew everyone locally, so…"

Stan nodded, as he understood what Elie was saying. Vernon would need to control everything from the finding of the body to the autopsy through to the burial to make it all work. Vernon was going to need a lot of valises of money and a lot of cooperation.

"I went to sleep around 2:30 AM or so but didn't sleep very long. I was edgy and bored. So at about 3:30, I dressed and called Billy Smith and asked him and his wife Jo to play racquetball with Ginger and me. I had this official DEA Jogging suit that I had been given when I met President Nixon. I was wearing it that night. Yeah that's right, a DEA jogging suit. Kind of a strange irony! While we were playing, I swung at a ball and missed. I wacked myself really hard on the shin. I raised a bump immediately, so we stopped while Jo went to the kitchen to get an ice pack."

Elie laughed out loud for a second. "What's so funny?" Stan asked. Still laughing, Elie said, "When the autopsy results were revealed later, it never mentioned the bruise and man it was a big bruise. It turned blue despite all the ice I put on it and it hurt like hell!

So, we sat around in the lounge area of the racquetball building. I sat at the piano and we all sang songs until around 6 AM, when Ginger and I went up to my bedroom to read and watch some television. Around 8, I told Ginger I was going into the bathroom lounge area to read. Now this where it will get interesting for you Stanley.

"Why will I find it interesting?"

"Well that bathroom had its own back entrance. That entrance lead downstairs."

Stan made a puzzled look. Elie said to him. "Stay with me on this. This is going to be one of the keys to my escape.

Shortly after I went into the bathroom, my Daddy came into the room through that back entrance. He sat down and explains to me that today was D-Day. I was going to "die" today, and my new life was about to start. He asked me if I was ready to go?"

Chapter Forty-Two

" "Are you ready to go?"

Elvis looked stunned by the breadth of Vernon's plan. He couldn't imagine that certain people were going to help him pull it off. Vernon didn't tell him about the cadaver and ultimately never would. In fact, Vernon would take most of the details of the escape to his grave, without his son ever knowing them. Vernon was a bottom-line man. Get his son safely out of Graceland and the rest would come easy. At least, that's what he hoped for. Because the only one who could screw this up in his own mind, was his son himself.

Vernon got up from his chair and walked over to his son's face. He pulled back the eyelid on his right eye and looked carefully at it. Elvis looked bloodshot. He had a big blue bruise on his leg showing out from his bathrobe.

"How in the hell did you get that bruise?"

"I was playing racquetball with Ginger and the Smiths"

Vernon just shook his head and thought, "Why did he have to go play racquetball in the middle of the night?" Hopefully, nobody else knew about the mark except for Ginger and the Smiths. He worried about the autopsy results.

Elvis was very edgy. He needed to sleep badly. Vernon told Elvis to call Dr. Nichopolous at his office and ask for some sleeping pills. The doctor was not there, but he spoke with the nurse. She prepared a few pills in a small envelope and told her husband, who had just brought her to work, to bring them outside to be given to Elvis' aunt who would drive by soon.

At 9:30, Elvis left the bathroom area and went downstairs, A special delivery letter was delivered to the house. Elvis answered the door and signed for it. He went into the kitchen and ate some breakfast. His aunt arrived with the sleeping pills. Before she could give them to him, Vernon came in to the kitchen and snatched them away from her.

"You'll need these for later", he said to his son. At 10 AM, Elvis went to the porch and brought in his newspaper. It would be the last time anyone would see him "alive"!

"As soon as I walked into the kitchen with the paper, my father took me into the basement. He sat me down on a chair and put a towel around my neck, like a barber does when you get a haircut. I started to ask him what he was doing, but he told me to shut up and trust him. Then he asked me again if I was really ready to change my life? He said that he didn't want to waste his time here, so if I weren't really ready to go through with it, I should get up now and he'd call the whole damn thing off..."

Chapter Forty-Three

Vernon had arranged a big bath towel around Elvis's neck and shirt, like a barber. He walked in front of his son again and said to him, "Now listen boy. Here's your chance. It's the only chance you are going to get. I'm with you and I'll help you. There are a lot of people who are going to help you along the way. None of them know what the other is doing except for just a couple of us. If you follow directions, you will get a whole new life. If you F--k it up, a lot of people, including myself will get into a whole lot of trouble. Do you understand?

"I think so."

"Thinking so ain't good enough Elvis! It just ain't good enough! You're a big star. This ain't no lonely housewife disappearing or some husband running away from his responsibility and finding a nice cool beach in Mexico where he can spend his days drinking Margaritas and bedding the local honeys. This is serious s--t boy! You are going to disappear! You are going to become Elliot Polk for one year and then when you are safe where I send you, I am going to send you a whole other set of papers and you will become that person for the rest of your life. If you have a good life, you'll get married, have a family and you'll die an old man. If you mess this up, you'll just be..." He paused and pointed to his son's robust belly, "this"! A mess, a total f--king mess and just like things are now, it will be much worse. Because who will know how long you are going to live! And if you live, it will be the same old unhappiness, just the same old nonsense.

My boy, I didn't want to do this. But I saw your future and you ain't going anywhere except down a bottomless pit. I see how messed up you are. I can't clean you up or make you happy. I know that. That's on you. And only you! So, I am doing what you asked and all you got to do is go for the ride. Never forget to follow the directions of everyone who is helping you. They want to help you be happy. You don't know it now, but you will figure it out. You'll see! As this thing is happening, you are going to hear things about yourself on the TV or read them in the paper. You are going to want to tell someone that it ain't true. That the news is not being fair. You are going to realize that your Daddy did some really dreadful things to get you where you want to go. Forgive me for them and move the hell on. Forget Ginger, she is way too young for you. Forget Priscilla and Lisa Marie. I will make sure that they are well taken care of.

So, Elvis, are you ready to change your life now? It ain't going to be easy being Joe Everyman, so be sure you want this?"

Elvis looked at Vernon with tears streaming down from his eyes. "Thank you, Daddy. I love you and will always love what you are doing for me. I'll miss you."

"Ah crap, now you're making me cry boy." Vernon gave him a quick hug and then plugged in some electric clippers and ran them through Elvis's thick head of hair. Like when he was in the Army, Elvis was left with a near bald head. Then Vernon ran the clippers through Elvis's eyebrows leaving them bare. He trimmed off all the hair on his face. Then he put a hot wet towel on his head and when he removed it a few minutes later, he sprayed on shaving cream and shaved him totally bald with a razor. When that was done, he cleaned off the residue and placed a woolen stocking cap on his head.

Elvis looked in the mirror in amazement. He did not recognize himself and that was the point. His father fished into his pocket and removed the pills that Elvis's aunt had brought home. He gave him three of them with a glass of water. Elvis drank them down.

Vernon put a light jacket on him and swiftly moved him into the garage without anyone seeing them. By then the sleeping pills were starting to take effect and Elvis was really drowsy. Vernon put him into a delivery van with the name "Memphis Meats" painted on the side. Inside the van was a gym pad and a pillow on the floor. Elvis lay down and went to sleep. As soon as he was out cold. Vernon closed and locked the van. He went back inside the house. A young Yeshiva student was waiting for him in the kitchen. This was the same young man who had hidden Elvis's car when he was staying with the Fried's. Silently, Vernon handed the keys to the young man, who took them and left the house.

Vernon heard the van drive out of Graceland but could not bring himself to look at it as it left the gates.

Chapter Forty-Four

"So, you don't remember leaving Graceland?"

Elie pursed his lips and shook his head. "I'm afraid not. I was out cold. I would stay out for hours. This guy would drive me around Memphis all the rest of the day and into the night. I finally stirred a little. As he said to me later, that's when he knew to turn the truck around and head for the Courts. He pulled up to the delivery dock and helped me out of the truck. It was nearing dusk then and I had no idea that as I had ridden around Memphis in the back of a meat truck, the whole planet had exploded with the news that Elvis Presley was dead.

He helped me up the stairs and knocked on the Fried's door gently. They were waiting for me. Rabbi Fried told the young man to help me to the spare bedroom. He handed Rabbi Fried the envelopes with the remaining sleeping pills. I sat on the edge of the bed as he handed me some pills with a glass of water. Then the two of them got me undressed and put me to bed. I don't remember getting up for two days although the Frieds assured me I had gotten up several times.

When I finally woke up with a sense of being alive, they took me into the kitchen and fed me. I told the Frieds, I wanted to talk to Daddy on the phone. He looked at me and said that I couldn't. He showed me the newspaper and told me that everything in Memphis was upside down. If I called Graceland, certainly, someone could trace it. I sat there dejected, but knew he was right. I was on my journey.

Chapter Forty-Five

For Rabbi Fried, this was simply the hardest decision he would have to make about life and death since the war. The Ukrainians had destroyed his home. The workcamps had nearly killed him and he had spent his life praying for the souls of all that had died and asking forgiveness for having to make choices which resulted in him living and other's dying.

When Vernon had come to their apartment that night, Vernon had no idea how to help his son. He didn't even really understand why Elvis was so messed up. So, it wasn't Vernon who had figured out what was necessary to be done. Rather Rabbi Fried guided him to use his wile and talents to put a plan together to get Elvis out of Graceland.

And the Rabbi felt terrible about it in every respect that could be imagined. He was to repeat a trick that he had used on the Nazis to escape. It had worked then, especially when the Nazis were always looking out for escape attempts. To think that by substituting an already dead body for his own led to his successful escape. Now, well, he didn't want to think about it.

Rabbi Abraham Aaron had escaped Buchenwald and later when he came to the United States, he met a young David Fried as a Yeshiva student in Manhattan. They would walk down to the water together over the hills of Washington Heights and discuss the Torah and life in general. Rabbi Aaron was a Rosh Yeshiva (one of the Head Rabbis) at the great Orthodox Seminary there and David Fried was a penniless student hoping to become a Rabbi someday under Rabbi Aaron's tutelage. It was from Rabbi Aaron that David Fried learned to make peace with his experiences during the war. As the Rabbi was known to say to him on many occasions, "Sometimes we had to make decisions in the war that we should not have had to make. We must trust that G-d guided us to the right decision, even if it didn't seem the right decision in our own mind."

That statement remained crystal clear in Rabbi Fried's mind when he spoke with Vernon Presley. Vernon was an uneducated and somewhat rough-hewn individual. But he was not stupid. In fact, without having to have it spelled out to him in plain words, this seemingly parochial man had been able to deduce what needed to be done. Vernon did not tell the Rabbi how he was going to accomplish this plan, realizing that it would be unfair to the Rabbi to even speculate about the particulars he was dreaming up. Vernon understood that the less people knew of all the details, the better! What he really wanted to know from the Rabbi was, if he could pull it off and really get Elvis out of Graceland, could the Rabbi get him the rest of the way.

Miriam Fried answered that immediately, "We will help you," giving her husband "the look" as he showed reticence. Vernon asked, "How would you do that. Where would you send him?"

She looked first at her husband who was now looking down at the table and then at Vernon. "We will get him where he needs to be. For the same reason, we don't want to know how you are going to get him out of Graceland, we will not tell how we will do this. This would be the best. It would protect you and your family. There is too much at stake and other's will be needed to make it all work. So, we will only tell you that we have been successful." Then he looked at Vernon with deep seriousness, "Or not! But we will tell you nothing else."

"Do you think you can do it?" Vernon asked the couple.

Miriam now answered, "We survived the Nazis and the Ukrainians to get here. Do you think we did that without a little bit of cunning?" Vernon looked at her skeptically. She looked up at him with a hard stare fiddling with a fork on the table in front of her. "We will take care of your boy. We will! I promise you that." Vernon stiffened for a moment and drifted off into his thoughts after hearing the earnestness of this old woman. Then he shook his head and looked down at the floor.

Rabbi Fried looked up from the table. "Mr. Presley, you must understand that if we do this, Elvis must do whatever we say, go wherever we send him and trust the people we tell him to. He cannot do what he wants. He can never deviate. It will endanger everything. I am an old man. My wife and I have been through a lot. Who is to say how long we are to be in this world? You need to understand that we are performing a mitzva for Elvis. He is a Jew, Vernon, a full Jew under our ancient laws. We are in a strange way ransoming him from danger. Not in the way someone is kidnapped and threatened. Not like in the war, where we ransomed people from the Nazis. Rather we are ransoming him from himself, from the damage he has done to himself. Not just the physical body. There is a beautiful soul within him. We call it a Neshama. He has a beautiful Neshama waiting to find its real potential. By helping him we are ransoming that soul from... well... you know. In your own way, you will be doing the same. At least we can hope so."

Vernon looked at them but said nothing. He understood. He shook the Rabbi's hand and went home.

Miriam looked at her husband. She reached up to his face and touched his cheek. He said to her, "Miriam, what have we done just now. Should we really do this? Can we do this?"

She looked at him and didn't say anything. Nothing more needed to be said.

The next few days were spent in phone calls and the writing of letters to Brooklyn.

Chapter Forty-Six

Elvis had awakened to the reality that his former life was now over. He read eagerly in the Memphis Commercial Appeal the details of his "death". In the three days since he had left Graceland, he learned enough to try to figure out the timeline of events over the past few days. Memphis and the world were in shock and certainly his father was using that to his advantage.

From what he could gather from the radio, TV and the papers, Ginger had awakened from a long nap somewhere between 2:00 PM and 2:30 PM. She made a few phone calls and then remembered that he had gone into the bathroom lounge area earlier to read.

Supposedly, Ginger discovered his body on the floor in front of the commode with some reading material strewn on the floor besides him.

Elvis found it fascinating the amount of detail in the reports. "His" body was found in a "kneeling" position. His knees were just about touching his chin. He was sort of resting on his forearms which were bent under him. His head was down, with his face planted in the carpet. Ginger didn't move him at all. She had been frightened just by the sight of him. She called for help and ran out of the bathroom, jumping back into bed, crying. Artie, a friend and employee came upstairs, took one look at the body, but didn't move it. He then ran down and found Vernon. Vernon sent everyone downstairs immediately and called Dr. Nichopolous.

The Memphis Fire Department was also called. Soon, an ambulance from Engine House 29 arrived at Graceland. Even though it was obvious the body had been dead for some time and was in rigor mortis, the paramedic tried to stretch out the body and perform CPR. This was obviously unsuccessful, and they gave up pretty quickly. By 2:48 PM they were transporting the body to Baptist Memorial Hospital which was about seven minutes away. Upon arrival the body was declared DOA. At 3:00 PM Vernon and the rest of the family was told he was dead. A half hour later, a press release announced it to the world.

By 7:30 that evening the Medical Examiner had performed an initial autopsy external viewing of the body. By 8:00 PM, Dr. Nichopolous and Dr. Franco, the Medical Examiner for Shelby County, were interviewed in a press conference.

The next day, the body would lie in state at Graceland, in the foyer by the front door. Elvis thought to himself, "I wonder how Daddy had pulled that off. He must have gotten some makeup artist. That's a lot of people to fool." In fact, it was truly amazing, because some 50,000 to 100,000 paid their respects. Visitors were hustled past the body in very quick order and the doors were closed at 6:30 PM sharp.

A lifelong friend of Elvis described to reporters the mood inside Graceland. "Things are very quiet; they're just sitting around the coffin. Some are crying, most just sitting there subdued, Ginger seemed okay. Priscilla not so well. She was taking it very hard."

On August 19th, a brief funeral service was held in the Music Room in Graceland. The funeral was private. The mourner's left Vernon alone with the coffin after the service was finished. Vernon Presley led the procession with his car at around 3:30 PM. Behind Vernon's car was the white hearse that bore an un-draped coffin. The guests and family members left the grounds behind the hearse. In the car immediately behind the hearse rode Priscilla, holding onto Lisa Marie. They moved along to Forest Hill Midtown Cemetery. The coffin was placed in a mausoleum. Then it was sealed and mortared in place and covered with a marble slab.

Elvis marveled as he read the description of his burial, saying to himself, "So that's how Daddy did it."

Chapter Forty-Seven

Despite the fact that Graceland was in a state of hysterical turmoil, Vernon was as calm and collected as he could be. Once the body was loaded into the ambulance, he jumped into the back with the body. He carried a briefcase with him, and he sat on the end of the gurney while the ambulance flew through the streets of Memphis to the hospital. Once at the hospital, Vernon jumped out of the ambulance and disappeared inside. Soon a doctor appeared in the emergency room. He was not a member of the ER team. He was one of the bigwigs in the hospital. He pushed aside the team of residents and took the body directly into an operating room. He donned a gown, gloves and a mask. He stripped the body of Elvis's robe and laid it straight on the table. Vernon quietly slipped into the room.

"Vernon, give me some of those sheets over there in that rolling bin."

He walked to the other side of the room and reached into a standing bin and took out three folded sheets. They were warm to the touch. They had just been brought up from the Laundry. He handed them to the doctor, who directed Vernon to roll the body on one side. He slipped part of the sheet under the body and had Vernon roll the body over onto its other side. Once the sheet was secure under the body, they stretched it out and wrapped the body carefully. They secured the sheet with some tape around the head, the neck, the elbows, the waist and around the knees. They taped the area around the ankles securely and then placed another sheet on top of the body. They moved the body to another gurney and called the Medical Examiner's office. Vernon handed the briefcase to the doctor before he left the room. Vernon stayed with the body until the men from the ME's office arrived and he walked out to their ambulance with the body. He handed the attendants a manila envelope addressed to the Medical Examiner and marked SPECIMENS - FRAGILE. In that envelope were the three vials of Elvis's blood that had been taken from him in the Dentist's office the night before. Also, inside, was another envelope with two stacks of $100 bills. Vernon waved goodbye to the ambulance as it drove away and went back into the hospital.

Shortly, he would be informed that his son had died from a massive heart attack.

Vernon returned to Graceland to try to get some sleep. He had just laid down in his bed when the phone on the nightstand rang. He rolled over to pick it up. A voice on the other end, whispered briefly in a European accent, "Your beautiful postcard arrived a few minutes ago. Thank you so much for sending it. We will treasure it always." Vernon hung up the phone, smiled and rolled back over and fell deeply asleep.

The next morning, Vernon went into the garage and opened one of the standing bins. He reached inside and with a bit of extra effort, he lifted a mannequin of his son out and laid it on the ground. It was a good likeness, he admitted to himself. Soon, the Medical Examiner's truck would arrive to deliver Elvis's body to Graceland for preparation and viewing. The truck pulled into the garage but was empty. The attendants lifted the covered mannequin into the truck and delivered it to the mortuary. Under the "body", Vernon had placed another envelope. The mortician, finding the envelope, prepared the mannequin and placed him in the coffin that would be used for the viewing and for the burial. The mortuary delivered "Elvis" about an hour later. The coffin was placed by the front door and for the first time ever, Graceland was opened to the public.

People streamed by the coffin and were moved steadily along for hours. Vernon could not believe how many people came through the house. At 6:30 in the evening, he shut it down and closed the coffin. There were still thousands of people waiting to pay their respects. Unfortunately, they would miss out.

Chapter Forty-Eight

Elie had gotten up to go into the house for a few moments. He returned with a stack of plastic bags. Contained inside, untouched for many years, were copies of the Memphis Commercial Appeal, The New York Times, USA Today, Time Magazine and Newsweek. They were taped shut so it was obvious that they were kept as a keepsake, but not otherwise disturbed. Elie showed him these periodicals which all chronicled the day he "died".

"I've had these hidden away in the basement for years. I never knew if I would ever want to read them again." He sighed briefly. "Stan, you take them. They will probably help you more than me. I can only tell you the story. You can read for yourself how they all got the story wrong. But I can't blame them. They had no way of knowing that any of this was going on. I used to look at them occasionally and laugh about how everyone just believed. I used to get afraid when the people who claimed it was a hoax would present something, usually on the internet which they thought "proved" that I was alive."

"Were any of them right?"

"They were all right, I am alive! They just had the details wrong. They're misconceptions were so laughable. It was crazy to read what they thought. They had no idea, I tell you. But once in a while, their craziness got a little too close. Then I would shut off the computer or the radio or wherever, I didn't want to hear or read what they were saying. No one and I mean no one, ever figured out how Daddy pulled it off. Even I have no real idea how he did it. And that was the way he wanted it. Not Priscilla, not Lisa Marie, not the boys, not even Ginger ever knew. Daddy had set the body in such a way that Ginger never saw the face. I will tell you again that nobody ever guessed what happened. If they suspected something, they never mentioned it publicly. I suspect however, that knowing what he had done rested heavily on Daddy. He died less than two years later, on

June 26, 1979. Had a heart attack and that was that! Heck, his mom, my Grandma Minnie Mae outlived him. She died on May 8, 1980 at 89. Daddy was only 63 when he passed. Keeping such a big secret must have just ran the gas out of his tank. That and the smoking and of course, the drinking."

"Elie, I've got to ask this. Vernon pulls off this big hoax and now you are sitting half drugged out, with a shaved head and eyebrows in Rabbi Fried's apartment in the Courts. What happened next to get you to be here in Brooklyn?"

"Fair question."

"Damned straight it is."

Elie and Stan both laughed.

"And I'll tell you that tomorrow. Its late and I'm tired. I'm going go to sleep. You will have to sit on that for a spell. Don't forget the newspapers."

He got up and went inside. Stan collected the papers and went into his house as well.

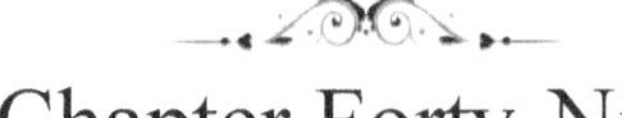

Chapter Forty-Nine

“ “I stayed with the Frieds for two months. Or rather, they watched over me for two months. They fed me and nourished me and probably the most important thing they did was wean me off all of the drugs. That was hard, but it was something I really wanted to do.”

“How did that go? Did you get the shakes or any other kind of physical reactions?”

“I shook a lot at first. Nauseous a lot. Big headaches. They wouldn’t let me take anything for the pain other than an occasional aspirin. Miriam fed me soup for the first week. Soup and tea. That’s all I can remember from the first week. Soup and tea! Then came the Sabbath and they brought me into the dining room for the traditional meal. I ate a lot. More soup, fish, chicken. They didn’t give me wine, only grape juice for the kiddush. She baked yummy challah and I wolfed it all down. Rabbi Fried told me to eat slower, I would get sick otherwise, but I didn’t listen and later that night I paid the price.”

“How so?”

“Threw up and had bad stomach cramps. I should have listened, but my head was still so into indulging my body that I couldn’t resist all the tasty food. By lunch the next day, I ate a whole lot less and felt a whole lot better. No repeat performances, you might say.”

“But what did you do while you were staying with them? What were your days like? Didn’t you want to get out a little?

“Of course! Rabbi Fried knew I couldn’t just stay in their little cramped apartment, especially in the Memphis heat. Every night when it cooled down, he and I would take a long walk around the neighborhood. I wore a black suit with a white shirt. I had tzitzit hanging out, just like a Yeshiva student. In fact, that was where we walked to, many of the nights. To the Yeshiva. We would sit at one of the tables and the Rabbi would take out one of the books and we would learn together. He said to me, that now that I knew for certain that I was a Jew, I should live like one. But he also told me that it would be a "marathon, not a sprint" and I would be challenged throughout my life. He said that he hoped that I would become an observant Jew ultimately. He used the expression "a Shomer Shabbos Jew". Someone who kept the commandments and observed the Sabbath.

I just was following along, keeping my head down and trying not to be noticed. The men in the Yeshiva never took notice of me the entire time. I looked like them and I was learning with the Rabbi. He told me not to shave, just let my beard grow out as much as possible. It itched like crazy for a couple of weeks, but then it stopped, and I was fine." What I found interesting about the process was that my beard was already turning gray. Not like it is today, all white. But enough gray to show my age. My hair started to slowly grow in, but that took a long time. The Rabbi took me for a haircut after about a month. There wasn't much to cut, but at least it looked trimmed and neat. I started to grow side curls, but that would take a long while before becoming like these (pointing to his face). I tried not to mess up the kosher kitchen, but I did mix up some of the silverware initially. Soon I learned where everything went, what to do and what not to do.

I actually got into a rhythm that became familiar and nice. I learned the blessings, how to get up in the morning, pray and become one with G-d and with myself.

After 6 weeks, Rabbi Fried came into my room, and handed me too velvet bags. I opened the larger bad and found a white and black Talis (Prayer Shawl). In the second bag were Tefillin (Phylacteries). You know what those are Stanley?"

Stan nodded," Actually, I still have mine from my Bar Mitzvah."

"When was the last time you put them on?"

"At my Bar Mitzvah." Stan laughed out loud.

"You should put them on. At least once in a while."

"I wouldn't even know how to."

"I can show you. It's really not hard."

"Well maybe, someday."

"Why not right now? Go get them, we'll put them on you"

Stan started to shrink away from doing that. "It's okay, Elie, some other time."

"What are you waiting for Stanley? Go get them! We will do it now!"

Stanley seeing that there was no way out, got up and said, "Well, if you insist"

"I do insist. I think you will be surprised Stanley. It will do you some good."

Stan shrugged and went into the house. He came down after a few minutes with a small Talis bag and his Tefillin. Elie went into the house for a small prayer book.

Stan said the blessing for donning the Talis, then watched as Elie took out the tefillin. First, he placed the hand Tefillin on his arm and told Stanley to repeat the blessing after him. Elie tightened the box in place and wrapped the strap around Stan's arm seven times. Then, he placed the head Tefillin on Stan's head as they said the blessing for the head box. Then finally, he wrapped the strap from the arm onto his fingers. He opened up the prayer book to the Shema and together they read the prayer. As they were doing this, Stanley started to cry. He didn't know why, but he started to tremble, and his insides started to hurt. The tears came freely and copiously. When the prayer was over. He sat back down in his chair and tried to gather himself together.

"Are you alright Stanley?"

Stan dabbed at his eyes with the edge of the Talis and shook his head yes. "Stanley, you have nothing to be afraid of. You are experiencing the power of Tefillin, just like I did when Rabbi Fried taught me to wear mine. It is an overpowering thing. It was for me then and sometimes, even now, I find it overpowering. It's the Pintele Yid in you coming out. Welcome back my friend."

⚬⚬⚬

Chapter Fifty

And just as Isaac said, the phone call came. It was Rabbi Fried, who was mulling over a problem. The problem was called Elvis.

Rabbi Abraham Aaron was now well into his late 80's. While he moved very slowly, his mind remained very quick. Escaping Buchenwald had been no easy task. Like most escapees, he did not dwell on the details, nor the choices that had to be made at the time. Sometimes in moments of quiet contemplation, he would remember and shudder. Those were hard memories to relive. But he always remembered that without G-d's guidance, he would never have gotten to the here and now. He would take a deep breath and return to his Torah.

Isaac had come into his life at various stages in his life. The first time was when he was a boy of six or seven. He did not believe that this man who had appeared to him was real. He told his father about the visitation. His father, Reb Moses was a deeply spiritual man. He asked his Rabbi about what his son had encountered. The Rabbi questioned the boy for some time in his study. When he sent the boy home, he called for the father and told him that his son would someday be a great Rabbi. He also told him that his son had a very unique ability. There would be times when his son would be guided by the great Patriarch Isaac.

Abraham grew up to be that great Rabbi. He survived the war and had taught in the great Yeshiva in Washington Heights for many years. He settled ultimately in Brooklyn and had a large following of people who came to him for advice and comfort.

When Rabbi Fried, his old student called from Memphis, Rabbi Aaron was not surprised. He discussed the problem presented by his friend from Memphis in great detail. Rabbi Aaron understood the world and had always stayed aware of the happenings around him. To Rabbi Fried's surprise, he knew who Elvis Presley was and agreed to help. Abraham knew that this was the person Isaac had spoken of, and he knew why Isaac had come to him to solve this problem. And he would!

He gave instructions to Rabbi Fried and hung up the phone. He mused to himself about whether this Elvis was up to the task. He got up from his table and poured himself a cup of tea. As he sat and contemplated, he knew that if Isaac had visited him about this, then it was out of his hands. The man would be alright, and it would all be good in the end.

Chapter Fifty-One

Vernon had done everything he could to get Elvis out of Graceland. Now that his son was safely ensconced in the Fried's apartment, Vernon looked to keep the Elvis enterprise alive. But he did this wondering when his son would be moved out of Memphis proper. His biggest fear was that Elvis might have a change of heart and just show up one day at Graceland. He had not spoken with the Frieds in six weeks and finally it was too much for him to just not know.

He drove onto a side road and found a phone booth. He pushed some coins into the slot and dialed Rabbi Fried. Miriam answered on the kitchen phone and told him that Elvis was doing fine and that in a couple more weeks, they would send him to his next safe house. Vernon was tempted to ask to talk with his son and Miriam sensed that. She almost offered to let him talk to Elvis, but before she could, Vernon hung up. She realized that putting father and son together on the phone would have been a huge mistake and reproved herself about it.

She did not tell her husband about the conversation with Vernon, figuring it would unnerve him. In the end, Vernon did not call back and stayed at Graceland.

In the meantime, Elvis was getting healthier by the day. He worked very hard at his religious studies and could now read Hebrew pretty well. He still did not really understand what he was reading, but his pronunciation was good, and he knew how to pray the three daily services. On the Sabbath, he knew how to make Kiddush, break bread and say the Grace after Meals. He listened intently when the Rabbi explained something he did not understand. Elvis felt comfortable with the arrangement so far and kept his end of the bargain to not leave by himself.

When Elvis looked in the mirror, he saw a decent growth of beard and his shaved head was now starting to show a very short crop of hair. He saw something different in himself. A peace he had not known, and he was satisfied.

Every evening, after dinner and their walk, the Rabbi would come home and go into his study, close the door and speak on the phone with Rabbi Aaron in Brooklyn. Soon the next phase of Elvis's escape was to come to fruition.

One Wednesday night Rabbi Fried came into Elvis's bedroom,

"Elie, you have been with us for almost two months. You've spent Rosh Hashana and Yom Kippur with us and Sukkot as well. You've done very well. But your journey to a new life must go on now."

Elvis looked up at him slowly, "I've loved being here with you and Miriam. Where am I going from here?"

"I can't tell you, you'll find out when you get there. It is only a waystation to your final destination and your new life."

"How long will I be there?"

"I don't know. I got you this far and now other people will take you further. There will be challenges along the way, but if you remember what I've taught you and practice it, you will be just fine. But Mrs. Fried and I can't keep you here any longer. People will start to question. Surely, they will find you out. "It's best that you go now. Hopefully, I've taught you well enough that you can survive temptation and go back out into the world.

"I won't fail you Rabbi. I promise."

"I appreciate you saying that. I hope so for your sake. The world will be most unkind if you are found out. For me, I am an old man, but for you it could be very tough. Stay strong."

He brought in a big valise that Vernon had sent along with him in the van, when Elvis first left Graceland. Elvis packed his belongings and then came into the kitchen to say goodbye to Miriam and to Rabbi Fried. At around ten, two young men from the Yeshiva knocked on the apartment door. Elvis went down with them into a big Chevy station wagon and got into the back seat. The three of them drove off to the north.

They would drive for 12 hours through the night and into the early morning. They dropped Elvis off by a small house in West Bloomfield, a suburb if Detroit, Michigan. He was brought into the house by a young Orthodox Jewish couple named the Brenner's. They introduced themselves as Chaim and Chana. They called him Elie. They had no idea who he was. They just knew Rabbi Aaron had asked them to house him for a couple of weeks and they agreed to do so.

They had two children. One was a boy around a year and a half. The other was a newborn boy about two months old. They gave Elvis a room upstairs, near the nursery. He unpacked his things and came downstairs. They fed him lunch and then Chaim said to him that it was time for him to go to the Yeshiva. "Would you like to go with me Elie?" Elvis was exhausted from riding the whole night and said to Chaim, "If you don't mind too much, I've been up all night. I think I would like to get some sleep." Chaim nodded and left the house. Elvis went back upstairs and lay down on the bed. Soon, he was fast asleep.

For the next two weeks, he integrated himself with this young family. He got up early and went to synagogue with Chaim. He spent most of the day in the Yeshiva learning and came home and ate with the family and played with the kids. Shabbos came, and he joined fully with them. Rabbi Fried had taught him well and no one was wiser that he grew up completely isolated from the culture.

During his second week with the Brenner's, he started to get cabin fever. One afternoon, he took the bus into Detroit just to get away for the day. As the bus got into Dearborn, he jumped off and walked around. He had been to Detroit before and this looked familiar to him. He was also getting really hungry but had forgotten to take food with him. He was about to fail his first real challenge as a Jew. He walked into a local McDonalds and ordered a couple of Big Macs, some fries, a coke and an apple pie. He sat down and dug right into them.

The food was delicious to him and he sat back finishing off the coke, very satisfied. When he left the restaurant, he walked a while and then started to feel badly. His belly started to hurt and then he threw up in the street. He didn't know whether he felt badly because he had deliberately eaten non-kosher food or because he felt guilty for breaking his promise to Rabbi Fried. Either way, it didn't matter. He got on a bus back to West Bloomfield and never ate non-kosher food again.

Right after his second Sabbath, he was visited by the two young men who had brought him to Michigan. They told him that it was time to travel again. He packed his bags, said goodbye to the Brenner's and got back into the station wagon that had brought him this far for the next leg of his journey.

Chapter Fifty-Two

The three men drove east through the night. They passed Cleveland, Ohio. Then on to Pittsburgh. From there, they traveled across Pennsylvania, passing through Philadelphia, before finally reaching the Town of Lakewood, New Jersey in mid-morning. There in Lakewood was the Great Yeshiva. There he was dropped off in front of the building, with his possessions on the sidewalk. He was a little confused. Some young men saw his predicament and helped him by grabbing his bags and escorting him to the office.

When he introduced himself in the office, to his surprise, he was expected. He was handed the key to a dorm room, which he would share with no one else. Looking around the room, he saw that it was a neat little room with two beds and desks with two closets for clothing. There was a sink for washing and some sheets and pillowcases on the foot of the bed. He quickly unpacked, and being tired from the long trip, he promptly fell asleep in his clothes.

Elie awoke in time for dinner. He walked down to the dining room and saw a cavernous room full of young men and older boys. He gingerly made his way to the serving line. The fellow running the line said to him, "Your new here?" Elie nodded. "No problem," he said, "take a plate and serve yourself." He walked down the line taking a piece of chicken, some potato kugel, some bread and some juice. He went to wash and sat down to eat. After he ate, he looked for the study hall. To his amazement, there must have been at least a thousand men in there. The din was deafening to him. All these men sitting in little groups learning the Torah. They seemed oblivious to the noise. He wondered if he would ever get to the point where he would not hear all the goings on around him. He wandered through the whole room and looked around dazed. Finally, Elie sat down at an empty seat waiting for the Evening Service to be called. Soon he heard a bang on the Lectern and all the men became quiet and the

Evening Service commenced. When it was over, a lot of the men left, but a respectable number stayed and continued to learn. He looked around and finally buried his head in his prayer book, not knowing what else to do.

Chapter Fifty-Three

"So, I end up in the Great Yeshiva in Lakewood. There are those who liked to brag that it was the largest Yeshiva in the world.

Some of the men had also studied in the Mir Yeshiva in Jerusalem. Those men would argue that Mir was bigger. I don't know if that's true or not, I've never seen the Mir. All I know was that this was one huge school. I was so lost that first night. Of course, I knew nobody, and I wasn't really sure what to do. But the next day that would change.

I came down in the morning to pray. The room was full of men dressed in their Talises and Tefillin. They were swaying and bowing in this repetitive way, that I had seen before, but never really understood. I tried to pray but was distracted by everything around me. After we were done, everyone moved into the dining hall for breakfast. I grabbed some bread and some eggs and sat down to eat. People sat down next to me and greeted me quickly and proceeded to eat in the fastest possible manner. Really, it was like watching machines eat. They would finish and quickly pray the Grace after Meals. Then they were out of there. All around me I looked, it was the same! Maybe a few people lingered over their food. I remember shaking my head, kind of in disbelief. I turned back to my food and ate at my own pace. I got up and made a coffee and sat back down. Soon, I was aware of a tall man standing next to me. He wore one of those long coats that Rabbis are known to wear. He had a large black hat on which he took off as he sat down next to me at the table.

"Elijah?" he said to me as he reached out to shake my hand. I looked at him and he smiled. I answered, "Yes that's me! Most people call me Elie."

He smiled again and said "Elie it is! Welcome, I am Rabbi Menachem Zweig. I am one of the Rosh Yeshivas here in Lakewood. Rabbi Aaron in Brooklyn and I have had several conversations about you."

I asked him," What do you know about me, sir?"

"I know what I know. It's only important that you want to live this new life. I run the program here for Baalei Teshuva (people becoming religious). I am here to help you achieve as much as you can while you stay here."

"Do you know how long that will be?"

He shook his head, "I am not sure exactly how long. It's almost Chanukah time. You will stay at least until before Passover. It could be longer. That is partially up to you."

"Do you know where I will ultimately end up?"

"That will be up to Rabbi Aaron. I'm sure it will be in due time."

"Who is this Rabbi Aaron, I've heard his named used in hushed tones. Will I meet him someday?"

Rabbi Zweig laughed gently, "Almost certainly. He is very old, but very vigorous. He will certainly want to meet you and he will help you in many ways. For now, Elie, let's get you set up. The first order of the day is to go shopping for clothes. Are you finished eating?"

I nodded and told him I had to pray the Grace after Meals. He nodded and pointed to the lobby. "When you're done, meet me there."

I was taken to a men's store and outfitted with four black suits, six white shirts, two black ties, two black skullcaps and a black Fedora hat. I also got two pair of black shoes and a bunch of black socks. I didn't need underwear, but I was also given three pair of tzitzit.

"Because of your age, you will learn with the married men in the Kollel. There is a small stipend to help you with incidentals. Now, you will be able to fit right in. Keep growing your beard. It is a good sign and will help you." I didn't understand that then. I do now!"

Stan looked at him quizzically, "How so?"

"Oh, my friend, a long beard is a sign for prosperity, and I don't mean just financial. Many wonderful things have happened in my life. I say to myself that is in part, because I grew this long beard."

"Elie, you realize that's just ridiculous."

"To you, it would seem so. To me everything that has happened to me is the work of G-d. In every way, I sit here today because G-d willed it. I just followed the plan."

"But Elie, what about the cancer?"

"That's also G-d's plan. I can't fight that. I live as long as he allows me to. No doctor can change that because no doctor is G-d. The only thing a doctor can do is carry out the will of G-d. If more doctors understood that, we would have much better doctors. Don't you think?"

Stan was quiet for a moment, "Well, I guess."

Elie laughed, "Well I don't. That's the difference between us my friend. But it's alright. Someday, you too will understand."

Stan just shook his head in wonderment.

"Anyway", Elie continued, "For the next six months, I stayed in the Yeshiva in Lakewood. I sat every morning and afternoon in the study hall. My Hebrew got much better and I learned all these amazing texts, like the Talmud and the Code of Jewish Law. I fit in just fine, lived quietly and made some friends amongst the older Kollel students. I was invited to their homes for the Sabbath and the holidays. When Purim came, I got a little bit drunk, but not so much that I lost my inhibitions. Rabbi Zweig saw me every day and made sure that if I needed anything, I was able to get it. I would go out in town some nights to walk around. It was a very cold winter that year. You remember the Blizzards of 1977-1978? I was walking around outside. The temperature dropped 31 degrees over the course of four hours. Man was it cold and we were all snowed in. But life inside the Yeshiva changed little during the cleanup, which took days. It was even worse in Buffalo. They were trapped inside for weeks."

"I remember" Stanley said, "I was trapped inside. Thought I was going to go stark raving mad trapped in the apartment."

"Soon, however, it started to warm up and life returned to some sense of normal. One Sabbath, we had a Scholar in Residence, the great Rabbi Abraham Aaron from Brooklyn. This was about two weeks before Passover. He came into the Study hall and lectured for some two hours after the morning service, Riveting stuff. I didn't want to leave. He spoke about the meaning of the Exodus from Egypt and how it impacted us even to this day. After he was finished speaking, I went up to the front and introduced myself. He was a small man, you know, kind of wiry. Black 3-piece suit, the big hat you see some of the Rabbis wear, with the upturned brim. He shook my hand swiftly and briefly looked up at my face. Then he left the room without saying another word to me.

I must tell you I was kind of shocked. I mean, this was the person to whom I had entrusted my entire existence and he barely acknowledged me. An ugly thought entered my head. Doesn't he know who I am? I am Elvis Presley! The Great Elvis Presley!

I was so pissed off that I stomped out of the study hall and went up to my room. Rabbi Zweig had quietly watched my reaction from the side of the room. He intercepted me as I was about to go up the stairs.

"Elie don't get mad"

"Why not?"

Rabbi Zweig sighed. He knew so little about this man whom he had mentored for months. He had often wondered about his protégé and what the big deal was. Rabbi Aaron had only instructed him to mentor Elie, see to his needs and ensure that he continued to grow in his learning and practice.

He said to Elie, looking up at him from the bottom of the stairway. "Listen, I don't know your whole story Elie. I don't know who you were before you came to Lakewood, but whomever you are or were, I think it would be safe to say that Rabbi Aaron was not going to acknowledge you in front of everyone. Believe me, he knows you are here, and he will talk to you soon. Just don't get excited."

Elie looked down at the Rabbi, nodded his head gently and turned back to climb up the stairs.

Chapter Fifty-Four

Abraham looked up at the man who had reached out to shake his hand. With a fleeting look, he tried to size him up. The man was taller than he thought he would be. As he walked out of the study hall, he said to himself, "So, this is Elvis Presley?" On some level, Rabbi Aaron felt a sense of surprise that Elie was even still there. But he understood that was the skeptic in him. But he did not fail to recognize the hand of G-d, in the fact that Elvis stood in front of him.

He was met by Rabbi Zweig as they exited the building. He was walking nearby to have lunch with some friends. Rabbi Zweig walked alongside him.

"Is he ready?" Abraham asked quietly.

"I think so."

"Any problems with him?"

"None! Actually, he has kind of melted into the Yeshiva without anyone taking particular notice. Elie has a learning partner, maybe a few friends or rather acquaintances. Otherwise, he is just another Kollel guy."

"I want to meet with him after Shabbos."

"He wants to meet you. I think he was disappointed that you barely acknowledged him."

"He will get over it"

"I will arrange for you two to meet. Do you want to meet at the Yeshiva or someplace else?"

"Not the Yeshiva! Everyone would know about it soon enough. Too many questions. No, not there." He pondered quietly as they walked. "Bring him home with you after Maariv (the evening service). I will come soon after. We will talk there."

"Ok," Rabbi Zweig answered. Then stopping in his tracks, he turned to Rabbi Aaron and asked, "Rabbi, who is this man? I have taken care of him for nearly five months. He is a wonderful person. I have had him in my home for Sabbath meals and he is so polite and so nice. You asked me to take this man on and really, he's been a pleasure. But I have to wonder who he is and why you sent him to me. Really, what is his purpose being here?"

Abraham turned to him and put his hand on his colleague's shoulder. He smiled briefly and said, "Menachem" and then shook his head no. Then he looked down at the pavement for a moment. He seemed to want to say something. But he didn't. He simply turned Rabbi Zweig around and continued walking without saying another word.

They walked on in silence for a short while. Then Abraham arrived at his host's home. He said goodbye to Rabbi Zweig and went inside.

Rabbi Zweig continued on, thinking about how Elie had been with him for months and he still didn't know who he was or why he was so important to Rabbi Abraham Aaron.

Chapter Fifty-Five

"After the Sabbath was over, Rabbi Zweig took me to his home for what I thought was going to be a light dinner. When we arrived, Mrs. Zweig offered me a seat in the dining room and the Rabbi went into his study for a few moments. He came out and the family gathered to make Havdalah, (a set of prayers formally closing out the Sabbath). After that, we all sat down to eat. The Rabbi periodically looked down at his watch and then would rejoin the conversation at the table.

Around an hour after we had come home, the doorbell rang. Rabbi Zweig left the table to answer the door and in came Rabbi Aaron. He removed his coat and hat and joined us all at the table. He looked at me briefly, gave a quick wave to Mrs. Zweig and took some food onto his plate. He got up to wash and broke bread and started talking with Rabbi Zweig about a curious case he was learning in the Talmud.

Soon, the meal was finished. We recited the Grace after Meals and I was invited to join the two Rabbis in the Zweig study. Rabbi Aaron settled into a chair and invited me to do the same. Rabbi Zweig however, left the study and closed the door behind him.

He stared at me for what seemed like forever. However, it was just a few seconds. Piercing blue eyes and a long white beard, for such a small man, he had a huge presence. Dressed immaculately in a black three-piece suit with a pocket watch chain across the bottom of his vest, he adjusted his skullcap towards the back of his head and leaned forward in his chair. I was drawn to his shoes and the way he had his right foot turned in at the ankle, in what looked like an impossible and very painful angle. At least to me, it would seem so. But he was indifferent to it as if it had always been his way to sit.

"Elvis Presley?"

"Yes sir, that is me." I answered.

He nodded, "I know. I am sorry that you may have felt slighted by my greeting in the Study Hall. I did not want to bring any unnecessary attention to you in front of all those men."

"I understand, sir. It's alright. Thank you."

"Are you well Elvis?" I nodded yes. "I know it has to have been very disorienting for you up until now." He stopped and pinched at the inside corners of his eyes. "You've done a very good job so far staying… let us just say, "under the radar". He smiled for a moment and leaned back into the chair. Then he put his hand to his mouth and thought quietly for a moment.

"Elvis is this what you really wanted?"

"I don't understand, sir."

"What I mean is that you gave up everything in your life. Everything! Your family, your father, even your little girl. You gave up your friends, your money, your fame. You have let us take you far from what you know, what you grew up with."

I started to jump in to protest but he told me to let him finish. I sat back quietly.

"Elvis let's talk about this. I have helped you to get to this place and did it willingly because of circumstances which I can never explain to you. You are obviously a good man who has gone through a lot of troubles. But the reality of all this is that you sit here having faked your own death!"

"When he said that to me, I just wanted to crawl into a hole. Really, I could have died right there and that would have been that!

Rabbi Aaron continued, "Not necessarily you, Elvis. But people who loved you. They took extraordinary risks to get you here now. So, I have to ask you, was your life so bad before, that you felt compelled to make such a drastic change?"

I answered him with one word, "Yes".

He paused for a moment and closed his eyes in thought.

"Why?" he asked me. He looked at me directly when he asked that.

I stopped and thought deeply about the question. At first, escaping my life was about relieving the stress. At that point Stanley, I had become pretty calm. My life had a routine, limited as it might be, but I felt comfortable that every day was essentially the same. When I thought about it though, I sometimes missed the road trips and making movies with the beautiful women and all of that attention.

"Rabbi, I will not pretend to you that sometimes, I do miss it all."

"Not surprising, you had an incredible life. Just no self-control!"

I grinned and nodded yes. "That's definitely the truth, sir."

"You have been off the drugs for many months. Do you ever feel the need for them?"

"The truth is that I haven't felt the need since I left Memphis. No that's not true. I sort of forgot about all that once I came here to Lakewood."

"Do you like it here?"

"Most of the time. Sometimes I'm lonely. I thought about going into New York a few times, but I was afraid someone would recognize me."

"Why would anyone recognize you? And even if they thought they did, I guarantee you Elvis, most everybody thinks you're dead."

"But I'm not."

Rabbi Aaron then laughed heartily.

"No, you most certainly are not dead. More important though, if you had the choice, which life would you want?"

I sat there without answering him for what seemed like a long time. He sat there in the chair opposite me, not saying a word, just looking at me.

Stan asked, "What was that like? Was he staring at you?"

"No. He just looked at me. He seemed to be deep in thought though. I was trying to answer him, but I was shaken by the question.

"How so, Elie?"

"Since the beginning, I was told, I had to just follow the directions of people that I did not necessarily know, and trust that they would lead me to a proverbial "Promised Land". I never really thought about whether I had free choice. Now this Rabbi, who was obviously in charge of getting me to a place where I could start a new life, was point blank asking me if this is what I truly wanted. For the first time, I really had to make a choice."

"Why do you think Rabbi Aaron said nothing?"

"To be honest, I have no idea, even now. But this was my moment of truth! I had thought that my moment of truth was when Daddy got me out of Graceland. But I was sick then and couldn't really think clearly. I was all emotions. Just wanted to run away and not be recognized. I wanted to stop being a goldfish in a giant fish tank. Does that make sense Stanley?"

"Certainly. You were exhausted, and your system was full of drugs."

"And I was afraid!"

"You were that as well." Stan stopped to think a moment. "I guess I have the same question for you that Rabbi Aaron was asking you way back then. Only I think I am asking it in a different way. What exactly were you afraid of?"

"You know, I am not so sure now. I have had decades to think about it. I guess that if I had returned to my music career, at some point, I would feel choked by the whole entourage thing. People telling me where to go, what to do."

"And the life you ultimately chose, has this been free of being told where to go and what to do?"

Elie thought about it for a little while, "It's different. Of course, life cannot be lived with total freedom to do anything you want. But this has been different. For one, Shoshana has loved me in a way no other woman besides Mama has ever done. She loves me because I am a big doofus." Elie laughed. "Everyone else in my life loved me because I was Elvis Presley. Even Priscilla as a young teenager was dealing with a big famous person, even if I was so immature. Everything was in the context of all that money, all that fame. Even in the Army, it never really let up. I was always under someone's thumb. That's why my whole relationship with Priscilla was so ridiculous. I was a grown man, but psychologically, I was younger than her, even when she was a young teen. It was free and easy because I was such a baby. The only one who ever really called me on that was Linda Thompson. She really cared for me, but I was a human train wreck. A grown man tornado, filled with impulsive behavior, drinking, drugs and selfishness. With Shoshana, I never did that. To answer your question Stanley, I'm not really sure what I was so afraid of, but it was a powerful fear that drove me."

"Why do you think that you never acted out with Shoshana?" Stan asked.

"She would never put up with that."

"Really?"

"Yeah, when we got married, all she knew was that I was a Baal Teshuva. In a sense, she taught me everything I know about being a responsible man. Look at my family Stanley. All these kids and grandchildren. With Shoshie, all the anger just evaporated from my life. It has been a wonderful marriage for me. I am so blessed that I met her."

"How did you meet?"

"She is Rabbi Aaron's daughter."

Stanley almost fell out of his chair. "Really? She is Rabbi Aaron's daughter? You've got to be kidding me! Wow! That must be some story."

"Actually, it's a rather simple story. And it goes back to what I was saying about my talking with the Rabbi the first time."

"Yeah, let's get back to that. So, when you didn't answer him right away, what happened?

"Well, some time passed with the two of us just sitting there, saying nothing."

"How long do you think you stayed that way Elie?"

"Can't guess, it just seemed like forever. But during that time, I really thought about what going back to that life would look like. I felt something I had not felt in months. My chest started to hurt, and I couldn't seem to catch my breath. My thoughts ran wild. I thought about going on stage in one of those big concert locales. I felt frozen. Thoughts about dealing with Colonel Parker made me nauseous. I started sweating profusely. I reached into my pocket for a handkerchief to wipe my face. All that time Rabbi Aaron just sat there looking at me, not saying a word.

"Did he know you were having a panic attack?"

"I think he could see that, but it was like I was being tested or something."

"Were you?"

"At the time, I didn't know. Later on, Rabbi Aaron would admit to me that in a sense, he was testing me."

"Testing you for what reason?"

"He wanted to see if this was really what I wanted."

"Why?"

"He had invested a lot of effort to get me to that point. He told me, he wanted to make sure that this was the life for me. He didn't want me to suddenly change my mind after he executed the final part of the plan. So, he watched me quietly, trying to watch my reactions to his question."

"Very interesting Elie. I could see that."

"So could I. Look, he was already an elderly man. He lost his entire family in the war. He came to the United States, married again, had new children, started a new life."

"Was he married in Europe?"

"Yes, he lost his wife and six children in the camps. Two sons and four daughters"

"Wow, six kids. Must have destroyed him."

"At the time, yes, but because of it, he found a way to escape and came to this country."

"Escape? Where in Europe was he?"

"He escaped from Buchenwald."

"Really, that must be a heck of a story?"

"I'm sure it was. He never spoke about it. I know none of the details."

"Still it must have been hell"

"I imagine it was."

"Getting back to the story. Finally, I just looked at him and shrugged."

"Really? What did he do?"

"He got up and left the room."

"No!" Stan exclaimed.

"Actually yes. He got up and went into the kitchen."

"What did you do then?"

"I didn't know what to do. I was kind of paralyzed. I didn't know what to think other than that I had just screwed it all up and was done for."

"Well obviously not. You ended up marrying his daughter."

"Uh, huh! I finally got the courage to get out of the chair and leave the room myself. I kind of drifted into the kitchen, where Rabbis Zweig and Aaron were sitting drinking some tea and noshing on some chocolate cookies on a plate. Rabbi Aaron said to me, "Elie sit down and have some tea." I was kinda dumbfounded but sat down. Mrs. Zweig poured me a tea and then went into the living room. The two men looked at me. I took a sip of the tea. Rabbi Aaron pushed the plate of cookies towards me and motioned that I should take one.

Rabbi Zweig excused himself and put his teacup in the sink. He joined his wife in the living room. Rabbi Aaron finally spoke, "I asked you a tough question Elvis. But I didn't expect you to answer it so quickly. You have choices even if you don't think you do. If you went back to be a musician, like you were before, you can control your life! That is something you had to learn for yourself. I see you don't believe that."

"No sir, I am not so sure. That would be very hard."

"Or it could be very easy. It depends upon you Elvis. If you have learned to trust in total strangers during these past few months, then you can learn to trust yourself as well. If there is anything that you have learned from all this, is that you have that power. If you didn't have that power, then nothing we have done for you would have made any difference. You would have relapsed and then you would have absolutely nothing."

I looked at him and asked, "Rabbi, why did you so this for me? After all…."

Rabbi Aaron got up from his chair and stood right next to me with his face to mine. He placed one arm on my shoulder. "I did it because I was commanded to."

I didn't get it.

"Elvis, you are here now because this is where you should be. That is why! Think of it as a Heavenly Decree! That is why I am asking you, is this what you really want?"

"What other choice do I have?"

"Oh, come now, you could walk out of here tomorrow and announce to the world, you are alive. You would become instantly famous again. You could give interviews of how you managed to pull it off and after all the uproar dies down, everyone will think it's a terrific story. You would be back singing in short order. Don't you realize that?"

"I sat there dazed. It had never occurred to me, that despite everything, I could probably return to my old life. A few envelopes of money would probably silence all the law guys and the outrage would probably fade rather quickly. I thought to myself, "How did this old Rabbi have this all figured out?"

I sat in a state of amazement at this old man who obviously was much more in the world than I ever expected him to be. He walked out of the kitchen and returned a few minutes later with a brown manila envelope. He handed it to me and said, "These are from your father."

I tore into the envelope with such fury. I don't know what I expected from Daddy in that envelope. A letter, pictures, anything like that. Instead I pulled out a Birth Certificate from Tupelo, a new Passport, a new driver's license from Mississippi and a new Social Security Card. All of these papers came with the name Elijah Pressler. I just looked at them in awe. Then I heard a voice breakthrough my fog. It was Rabbi Aaron.

"Go back to the Yeshiva and pack all of your belongings. You are coming to Brooklyn to live with me for a while. There we can help you set up your new life. It will be good Elie. It will be a blessing for you." Then he laughed, "You see, I didn't call you Elvis. And I won't ever again call you that. You are Elijah and your past is the past. Welcome to your new life."

Chapter Fifty-Six

66Brooklyn was different than anything I had expected it to be. Without actually vocalizing it, Rabbi Aaron had instinctively understood that I really did not want to return to Graceland and that old life. I never said it outright, but it didn't matter. For in the end, I had actually made a choice. And it was a choice I made, on my own. Sure, you could say that Rabbi Aaron had stacked the deck and I was somehow "brainwashed". But no. I really wanted this. I felt connected to G-d and to my heritage and you know what, Stanley, I just really wanted this!"

"Elie, you sound as if you were so certain at that moment in your life. I wonder though, how could you be sure? You had been living for months either in someone's small apartment or buried away in a large Yeshiva far from home in Memphis. For an extended period of time, that's all you knew! That's all you had! They fed you, they clothed you. They kept you close to the vest."

Elie was shaking his head no, but Stan continued, "Elie have you ever heard about something called the Stockholm Syndrome?"

"I know! It might seem like that, but it wasn't that. Believe me, I am no Patty Hearst."

"Well, of course not. But you were closely watched and steered."

Elie shook his head. "Probably so in some ways, but the intent was different. They had to watch me and steer me. I was one of the biggest personalities in the world. And Stanley, I really wanted out of the entertainment business. That was a far bigger "Stockholm Syndrome" for me. Graceland with all the people and the Colonel controlling my entire life, that was far more confining and difficult for me than any of the things I was going through, at the moment Rabbi Aaron packed me into his car and we drove to Brooklyn."

"Where did he live?"

"Right around the corner, so to speak. East 10th Street between Avenues N and O"

"And so, you ended up relatively close to his home when you bought this house."

"Honestly, it was not by design. We were looking at a house in Boro Park on 57th Street between 12th and 13th Avenues. We had put a binder on the house. Then a young couple put in a much higher offer. I think their parents financed the purchase. So suddenly Shoshie and I had to find another house, as our apartment in Boro Park was getting too small for us, with the kids coming and all. Someone in Rabbi Aaron's Synagogue was selling their deceased parent's house to close out the estate. It happened to be this house. Shoshie and I looked at it. She liked it. The house is smaller than the Boro Park house would have been, but not by much. It was close to her parents. The neighborhood was changing into a more Orthodox one. So, in the end, we bought this house. For the most part, it has been good, very good. We raised an entire family here and the grandkids come and stay for visits. Wish it were a little bigger, but then again, things could be worse." He laughed gently for a moment pointing back at the house with an expansive swing of his arms, "My Graceland 2!" He chuckled again.

"Where did you stay when you first got to Brooklyn?"

"With the Aarons. They had converted the basement into a little apartment. It had its own entrance and was separated from the rest of the house by a locked door on the side of the house. I would go straight into my own apartment after my day. If I needed something from the Aarons or were invited for a meal, I could knock on the inside door on the top of the basement stairs and not have to go outside to come into their home. Mrs. Aaron would simply open the door for me to come in. This way, I had my privacy, and yet they were there for me if I needed them for anything."

"How did you meet Shoshana. I assume she was living in the house."

"Actually not. Believe it not, she went to law school and was a practicing attorney for a firm in Midtown Manhattan. She had her own place on the Upper East Side, a studio apartment near the Park East Synagogue. She would come home for most Sabbaths and for the holidays, but during the week, she stayed in the city. She worked crazy hours anyway, so it was more convenient for her to live in the city."

"Did she continue practicing law after you were married?"

"For a short while. Elie laughed briefly. How we got together was a completely different story."

"Now you've opened the Pandora's Box. What went on between the two of you?"

"It's a long story."

"Ah, come on now, spill it."

"Tomorrow's another day. See you then." Elie grinned as he got up and went into the house. Stan shook his head wondering about how those two got together right under the Aaron's noses. Or maybe not!

Chapter Fifty-Seven

The drive from Lakewood to Brooklyn takes a little under two hours if there is no traffic. They left about 11 o'clock Saturday night and arrived by Rabbi Aaron's home around 1 o'clock in the morning. Elie slid himself out of the car, helped the Rabbi with the bags and followed him into the house. It was dark and quiet inside. Mrs. Aaron had long gone to sleep, and so had the other inhabitants of the house. They left the bags in the vestibule and Elie followed Rabbi Aaron into the kitchen. The old man flipped on a light switch and the kitchen was bathed in the white light of a circular fluorescent bulb on the ceiling. After so many hours in the darkness, the bright light startled Elie. The Rabbi filled a teapot with some water and put it on the stove to boil. He stuck his head into the refrigerator and shuffled some things around until he found what he was looking for. He placed a round chocolate cake on the kitchen table and pulled out two plates, a knife and two forks. When the water boiled, he turned to Elie, "Coffee or Tea?" Elie yawned loudly, "Coffee". The Rabbi stirred in a spoonful of instant coffee into both cups. "Sugar?", Elie nodded yes. "Milk?", Elie nodded again.

Once the coffees were prepared, they sat down at the table. Elie cut two slices of cake and the two of them sat silently, drinking their coffee's and eating the cake. Once they finished, they cleared the table and put everything away.

Rabbi Aaron opened the door adjacent to the kitchen on the side of the house. He turned on the light. He motioned to Elie to get his belongings and follow him downstairs. He turned on the basement light and Elie saw for the first time, his new home. It was a small basement apartment. Some chairs, a small couch and a bed off to one side. There was a small kitchenette unit and a bathroom with a shower in the back. Elie was shown where there were towels and bed makings. The Rabbi, satisfied that Elie had what he needed, bid him good night and went upstairs. Elie heard the door lock and sat alone in his new surroundings. He looked around the room. It was clean and neat, but he was too tired to make the bed. He removed his shoes and lay his head down on a pillow. He pulled a blanket around himself and soon was fast asleep.

Chapter Fifty-Eight

“You seem perplexed Abraham!”

Rabbi Aaron looked up from his seat in the kitchen, where he had returned after setting Elie up in the basement. He saw Isaac sitting across from him. Abraham scratched at the back of his scalp and pushed his skullcap back into position.

“Well?”

“I am perplexed, actually.”

“About what? You accomplished what I asked you to do.”

“It seems deceitful.”

“How so?”

“We faked a death!”

“Did we?”

“Of course, we did. I thought that was past me. I guess not. Shame on me. It has brought up so many memories, so much pain. I’m an old man, I had put it all to bed a very long time ago.”

“You think so? Abraham, you never put that to bed. Maybe you are looking at it wrong?”

“Looking at it wrong? I conspired to fake a death, not just once, but twice. The first time to save my own life. I can live with that. As hard as it has been for me, I can live with that. The Nazis would have ultimately killed me and besides, they murdered my family. All I had was myself and nothing to lose. Now, I did it for a second time. There was no danger of Nazis killing him or working him to death. There was no imminent danger. I faked the death of a perfectly healthy man. Tell me Isaac, how can that possibly be good?” Pointing his old bony finger right at Isaac, he asked angrily, “Why did you ask me to do that?” Then pointing the same finger at his own chest, “And why did I agree?” He made a fist and pounded at his chest in anger.

Isaac got up from the table and walked around to the sink. He leaned his back against it as he stroked his beard and pondered.

"Maybe you're right."

"Maybe, I'm right?" Abraham's eyes opened widely.

"Yes. Maybe you are right. Maybe, G-d asked too much of you this time! Maybe, more than you could tolerate. Possibly, more than you should have been asked to do. Could be! Yes, could be!"

Abraham sat there in tears looking at Isaac. "How can you say that? I have always given my life to perform whatever G-d asked me to do." He said shaking his head no.

"Then why is this so troubling to you?"

"I don't know. It would seem that for once, I am without answers."

Isaac stroked at his beard and was silent for some time. Abraham got up and turned the fire on under the teapot. He stood facing the pot silently for some time until the kettle started to whistle. He reached into the cupboard and removed a new cup and a teabag. He poured the water and dropped in the teabag. He looked down as the water started to turn orange, saying nothing. He walked back to the table and poured some sugar into the cup and mixed it with his finger.

"Isn't that hot?", Isaac said to him.

Abraham just shrugged. "I barely noticed it was hot."

"Why is that"

"I lost most feeling in this hand in the freezing cold at Birkenau."

"Never came back?"

"Nah. My feet, they are always cold, but in my hands, for some reason they lost most of their sensitivity to heat or cold."

Isaac said to him, "Your feet, you need. Your whole weight rests on them. The feet need to be able to feel so you can negotiate your surroundings. Everything you are rests on those feet. Your hands....eh.... they are how you express yourself. Normally, they are the most sensitive of your limbs. If they've lost sensitivity, it is because, something in you has lost sensitivity. It may be a deliberate thing, that your mind has done. On the other side, however, it may just reflect that you do not want to "handle" your pain about something and it shows up in your ability to stick your finger in boiling hot water and well...."

Abraham gave Isaac a look of annoyance. "I've done everything you asked me to do."

"I didn't tell you how to do it."

"Yes, you did! You told me to use the skills I learned at Birkenau."

"And you did! And you have rescued a man, just the same as you rescued yourself."

"How can you compare the two. I was facing certain death. It's not the same."

"Why? What makes you think that Elvis was not facing certain death. You don't know what the Heavenly Court had in mind."

Abraham grew silent. Isaac continued, "Even the most righteous amongst us, in this plane of existence, do not know what our Maker intends. Maybe Elvis' self-struggle was his way of understanding that his life had another purpose. You do not know what his interaction with you is about but let me tell you that it is not coincidental, and it is certainly not random.

Abraham, you may be an old man and you have lived two distinct lives. That which was before the war and that which came afterwards. Through all of that, one thing has held true to you. It is that G-d had a purpose for all the suffering as well as for all the subsequent success and joys. You have seen a whole new family grow around you and have lived the life of many persons. And yet, still, you wonder why old pains still feel the same. But it is not the same world and the pain is not the same. You, my friend, are judging yourself far too harshly! Elvis came into your life for a reason. Look around you and determine why?"

Abraham looked up to say something to Isaac, but he was gone. All he had at the moment in front of him was a cup of tea, a man he hardly knew sleeping in his basement, and his family sleeping above him in their beds. His mind wandered back to his home in Europe. He started to cry to his long dead wife, "Oh Chava, what do I do?" In his mind's eye, he could see her most clearly giving him her knowing look and her sweet smile. He wiped his eyes with his shirt sleeve. Then he put the cup in the sink and rinsed it out with some water and climbed the stairs seemingly renewing his new life. He quietly undressed, slipping into his bed next to his wife Devora.

Chapter Fifty-Nine

Elie knocked on the door that lead into the main part of the Aaron's house. It was late Friday afternoon and he was going to synagogue with the Rabbi. He knocked again, lightly, and soon the door was opened by a young woman in a long black dress. She had a pale complexion and was very slim, almost skinny. What stood out to Elie the most was her bright red hair and big blue eyes, although the large square glasses she wore kind of hid her eyes. She wore an apron around her waist as she was helping with the cooking in the kitchen.

"You must be Elie. The one staying in the basement." She said it in a matter of fact way and returned to what she was doing. Elie stood there at the entrance to the kitchen not knowing what to say or do with himself.

"I think I will go into the living room until the Rabbi comes down", he said to her as he passed by her on his way out of the kitchen.

"You do that! He will be down soon." She said to him without glancing back at him. Elie stood there for a moment not quite knowing what to say, then he shrugged and went into the living room and sat down on the sofa.

Rabbi Aaron and his wife Devora soon came down the stairs and greeted him. He went to the front closet and put on his coat and hat and motioned to Elie to follow him. As they walked out of the house and down the stoop, Rabbi Aaron asked Elie if he had met his daughter Shoshana.

Elie had been living in the Aaron's basement for about three weeks and had gotten used to the rhythm and routine of the house. This was his third Sabbath with them. However, their daughter Shoshana had been away those first two Sabbaths. This was the first time he had met her.

"Yes, she let me into the house."

"Good, she is usually home every Sabbath, but was away on

vacation for the last two weeks. She lives in Manhattan during the week because it's close to her work"

"What does she do?" Elie asked.

Rabbi Aaron shrugged as if in amazement. Then he half chuckled. "She's a lawyer. With a very prestigious firm in Manhattan. Works very hard."

"You don't seem pleased."

"Actually, I am quite proud of her. She is very good at what she does. I just never saw her growing up to be a lawyer as a little girl. She was always such a quiet girl. Always with a book, reading for hours at a time. Devora and I have hoped she would be married by now, but she has her own ideas and has fought any idea of a matchmaker."

They walked together towards the synagogue. It was a cool spring evening. Passover was in a few more weeks and the winter weather was no longer blowing cold.

"Rabbi, you would prefer her being married to her being a successful lawyer?"

"I'd like her to be both. Elie, it is not good for a person to be alone. It is not about the loneliness, although that can be very powerful. After the war, with my Chava gone......?" He stopped walking for a moment and reached into his jacket for a handkerchief. He opened it slowly and touched it to his eyes and then carefully folded it back, holding it in his right hand as he started to walk again. Elie followed alongside. "I mean that being alone brings out the selfishness in a person, even if they do not intend it to be. Reliance on oneself is good, but not at the cost of having shared experiences. Being together, children, grandchildren. You know what I mean!"

Elie shook his head yes as they reached the synagogue. Rabbi Aaron continued as he walked in, "She's a tough girl! Life has made her that way. That's why she is good at what she does. She tells me that she loves her work. But work is not a life. Work is work! I hope that someday, she finds someone to share her life with." He hung up his coat and walked to the front of the synagogue, greeting his congregants as he worked his way forward. Elie hung back and took a seat in the back pew. The Sabbath service began.

Chapter Sixty

Shoshana had seen many young men stay in the basement over the years. She always felt that her parents were trying to set her up for a marriage. This was, of course, the truth. They were trying to set her up.

She however, had other ideas. She enrolled in Brooklyn College after High School, rather than going to Seminary or to Israel for a year or two. Her parents were opposed to that at first but seeing that she had her mind set on the matter, they ultimately relented. Their only insistence was that she had to live at home. To that she agreed, and every morning, no matter the weather, she boarded the train at Kings Highway and East 16th Street and went off to school. Even in the heat of the summer and the blowing snows of winter, she rode the subway to school.

She graduated three years later, and her parents were relieved and proud. But she then informed them that she had applied to law school and was accepted to Columbia Law School in Manhattan. So, for the next three years, she again rode the subway into Manhattan early in the morning and then late into the night to get home.

She came to like Manhattan. She liked to walk and soon learned to travel downtown to the theater and to the concerts in Lincoln Center. On days when her schedule allowed, she would sit out in Central Park and take in the sun and watch all the people wandering around. Shoshana especially loved to walk through FAO Schwartz, the greatest toy store in New York. She looked at all the children with their parents and felt the first tugs of the desire to be a mother someday. But that did not deter her from her mission to become a lawyer. She studied hard and acquired a voice and persuasiveness she didn't know she had within her.

She graduated near the top of her class and was offered a clerkship with a Federal Judge. She was also offered a job at a very prestigious law firm in Manhattan. The pay was very generous and would allow her to help her parents who had mortgaged their house in Brooklyn to send her to Law School. So she turned down the clerkship and took the job with the law firm. By doing this, it also allowed her to live in Manhattan. She really wanted to stay in Manhattan and soon found a small one-bedroom apartment in a Pre-War building on East 66th Street, a short walk to the Park East Synagogue in a neighborhood with Orthodox Jews and kosher restaurants nearby. It was a relatively short subway ride to her office near Wall Street. She decorated the apartment comfortably and began her life as a young lawyer in New York. She made it her business to try to come back to her parents' home in Brooklyn every Sabbath. This did not always work out due to her workload, but she was successful in returning home most weekends to spend with her family.

When Elie knocked on the inner door in the Aaron's house, he had no idea what to expect when she opened the door to let him into the kitchen. She kind of looked him up and down when first greeting him and then turned back to her work in the kitchen.

Elie, not being sure what to do, went into the living room to wait for Rabbi Aaron. Soon, the two left to go to the synagogue. Devora Aaron came into the kitchen soon after and began her final preparations for the Sabbath. Soon Shoshana and her mother lit the Sabbath candles and finished the table.

As was the Aaron's custom, there were several guests who dined with them on Shabbos. Rabbi Aaron was always inviting people from Synagogue back to join him for the Sabbath meals. Most were young men from the Yeshiva or older men who were widowed and alone. Between the family and guests there were often a dozen or more people eating with them.

Elie, now accustomed to the happenings of a Sabbath meal, readily joined in the eating, singing and conversation. Periodically he looked down the length of the table where Shoshana was sitting, but she was too involved in the conversation with the women sitting near here to pay attention to Elie's looking at her. His innate shyness made it almost impossible to try to engage her in conversation. He found that surprising to himself as he had been with so many beautiful women in his life and in his previous life, Shoshana would never have even gotten a passing glance from him.

Soon the meal was over, and the guests got up and left. Elie helped to clear the table and then said his good nights and went back down to his apartment in the basement.

He was not yet sleepy, so he sat down in an old armchair that the Aaron's had placed in the basement. He stretched out his legs and leaned the back of his neck against the top cushion of the chair. He opened a book to read and soon drifted off to sleep in the chair.

He slept for a few hours in the chair and woke up about 2:00 AM. He was no longer tired, so he got up and went to his little kitchen and poured a glass of water from the sink. He sat down at the small round kitchen table, intending to continue reading his book.

But something was strangely off to him. He read through a few pages, but that odd feeling did not escape him. He looked up from his book and was startled to see an old man sitting in the chair opposite to him.

"Sorry to have made you jump."

"Who the heck are you?"

"What's a heck?"

"Huh?"

"What's a heck? You asked me who the heck I am. I want to know what's a heck?"

"It's just an expression. You caught me by surprise. But really, who are you and how did you get in here?

The old man was dressed in a long black robe and sandals. His white beard was long and flowing. His hair also was white, long and flowing. He had piercing eyes that seem to penetrate Elie's soul.

"My name was originally Jacob, but it was changed later to Israel."

"Why?"

"Because G-d willed it so!"

Elie shook his head as he was so confused.

"Elvis, my father's name is Isaac. His father's name is Abraham. Does that make it easier?"

Elie jaw dropped. Then he stood up and just stared at the man.

"You have nothing to say? You seem shocked."

"I am! Are you real or am I having some sort of dream?"

"You're not dreaming. I am very real. Come touch my arm. You will see that I am very real."

Elie reached out and placed his finger on the man's arm. It felt real.

"How can this be? You are dead!"

"Elvis, the world thinks you are dead. How is this any different?"

"But you've been dead for thousands of years. You are buried in a cave in Israel."

"Elvis, time is a human concept. In your learning have you ever heard the expression that Yaakov Avino Lo Mais (Jacob the Patriarch did not die)?"

Elie nodded yes. Jacob continued, "Well, it's true! Physically, I passed away, but spiritually?" Jacob shrugged.

Elie grabbed his head and sat back down in his chair. He closed his eyes tightly and breathed deeply for a few moments thinking he was just dreaming. Then he opened his eyes slowly and the man was still sitting there opposite him.

"Convinced yet?"

"No, I must be dreaming!"

"Aren't we all dreaming?

"What?"

"You heard me! Aren't we all dreaming? Is it possible that this life is really a dream?

Elie was quite shaken by that thought, But Jacob quickly calmed him down.

"Your life is very real Elvis, but you are separated from what is the true existence of G-d. Anything is possible, if you believe."

"Why are you here?"

"Why are you?"

"I don't understand!"

"What are you doing here Elvis Presley? Everything in your life was so big. And yet, you walked away from all of that. Now you are living in the basement of an old Rabbi's house in Brooklyn. It is far from where you grew up, far from whatever you previously knew. Yet here you are! Quite miraculous, you might say. What brought you here Elvis?

Elie looked up at him. "Well you see my life was a mess and Rabbi Fried took me in and with Rabbi Aaron…."

"No! No. no, no Elvis, I know how you physically got here! That's not what I am asking. You asked me why I am here now? I asked you, in exchange, why you are here? So, Elvis, why are you here?"

"Don't call me Elvis. My name is Elie… "At which point Elie stopped for a moment to really ponder Jacob's question. "Jacob why am I here?" he asked quietly with his head down to the table.

Neither spoke for a few minutes. Jacob looked at the man across the table. Elie was rubbing the back of his neck and quietly crying.

"I don't know all the reasons you are here Elie. You see I called you Elie now, because you are no longer Elvis. How could you be anymore? I don't know all the reasons your journey brought you to this place at this time. Really, I don't know that. I do know, however, one of the reasons,"

Elie looked up at him. "So, what's the reason then?

"One of the reasons you are here is ..." Jacob sighed for a second, then his eyes looked up towards the ceiling. "She is sleeping upstairs right now."

"Shoshana?"

Jacob nodded.

"I don't understand. She barely acknowledged my existence."

"Things are like that sometimes. Trust me when I tell you that it is decreed from above."

Elie closed his eyes trying to formulate his thoughts. He had a bunch of questions, he now wanted to ask Jacob, but when he reopened his eyes, Jacob was gone. Elie shook his head and looked around, but the house was quiet, and his rooms empty. He was not sure if he had just dreamed it all up or what. He quickly got undressed and went to his bed. And for the first time in years, sleep came to him easily and restfully.

Chapter Sixty-One

Shoshana woke up in a state of fright. She thought someone had touched her, but as her eyes scanned the dark bedroom, she saw that the room was empty except for her. She calmed down and fell back to sleep.

She slept fitfully for a couple of hours. She looked at the clock radio by her bed and saw that it was almost 4:00 in the morning. She rolled over to her other side and tried to sleep, but soon realized that she was unable to. She got up, put on her robe and slippers and went down to the kitchen. She poured herself some hot water from the urn set up for the Sabbath and made herself a cup of tea. She sat down at the table and flipped through some magazines while she sipped on her tea.

It had been a very hard week at work. She had worked well into the night almost every day that week, preparing her cases for trial or settlement. She was glad that she had become a person the firm could rely on for large billing hours. She hoped that this would put her on the Partner track someday.

Now she was just tired and unable to sleep. She closed her eyes for a moment and yawned. When her eyes reopened, she stared out at a truly beautiful woman sitting opposite her. She closed her eyes again, thinking it was just a dream, but as her eyes reopened, she saw that the woman was still sitting there in front of her, smiling. She closed her eyes a third time, but the result was the same as she reopened them.

"You don't trust your eyes Shoshana?" the woman said to her.

Shoshana looked at her directly and shook her head, "I'm not sure. Who are you?

"My name is Rachel."

Shoshana furrowed her brow, "Rachel who?"

"Rachel"

"I know that. What is your last name?

"Last name? What is that?"

Shoshana spoke in an irritated tone, "Your last name. You know, your family name."

Rachel looked confused. "I am not sure what you mean. I am Rachel daughter of Laban, sister of Leah, wife of Jacob."

Shoshana sat up straight in her chair. Part of her thought this was a hoax or a seriously ill young woman who had in some way wandered into her house.

"Rachel are you feeling alright?" she said to the woman while getting up and walking over to the other side of the table to see if maybe the woman needed her help.

"I'm fine. Thank you. Are you alright Shoshana? You seem so tired."

"Where are you from Rachel? And how do you know my name?"

Rachel just smiled. Shoshana became very concerned that the young woman was mentally ill. She thought to herself to go upstairs and wake her mother, but before she could Rachel said to her, "Don't wake your mother. I am not crazed or otherwise mentally ill. I will not harm you."

"Then what are you doing here?"

"Shoshana, you are not getting any younger. You work so hard, but your life is ... incomplete?"

Shoshana asked sharply, "How do you know anything about me?"

"I've known about you for some time. My father in law speaks periodically with your father."

"What?", Shoshana replied incredulously. "Your father in law? Who is he?

"Isaac, who did you think I was talking about?"

"Either this is the craziest thing, or I am still asleep."

"Do you feel like you are asleep?"

"No, actually I don't. I feel quite awake and very confused. What do you want?"

"It's not what I want that brings me here. It's what you want, even if you are not aware of it."

"And what exactly do I want?", Shoshana asked angrily, implying that this Rachel could not possibly know what she wanted.

Rachel watched as Shoshana returned to her chair and sat down.

"So, what is it exactly that I want?" Shoshana demanded again of the young woman.

Rachel looked up at Shoshana and smiled broadly. Her teeth were bright white and straight. She wore a long dress with her hair wrapped up in a kerchief. Her eyes were clear, but the corners of her eyes showed the little lines of someone who cried often. Shoshana looked at her, still not believing that this was taking place.

"There is a man sleeping in the basement right now."

"Yes, I know, we often have guests. They stay down there."

"This is no ordinary guest."

"What? I don't understand."

"He is your intended and I was sent to tell you that."

Shoshana laughed out loud. "Are you kidding me? Him?"

"Trust me when I tell you he is a person of importance."

"What are you talking about. I met him for the first-time last night. We barely spoke. He is not a man of importance. He is just an older bachelor that my father has taken an interest in. Believe me, this has happened before! I've seen this happen many times over the years."

Shoshana was getting tired of the whole conversation and just wanted the woman to leave. "Who are you? Really! Are you some matchmaker? My parents promised they wouldn't try setting me up."

Rachel looked up towards the ceiling. Shoshana followed Rachel's head as she looked upward. "Shoshana, would an ordinary matchmaker be sitting in this kitchen at 4:30 in the morning talking with you about some man sleeping in your basement?

Shoshana was quiet. The answer was self-evident. She had to admit to herself the truth in that statement. Looking across the table at Rachel.

"He is much older than me."

"Maybe so, nonetheless ..."

"Nonetheless what?"

Rachel raised her hands and shrugged. "He's a complicated man, but a good man. This one has a great heart and a huge capacity to love. He will take loving care of you, but he will need a lot of care himself. You may resent that at first, but soon you will see the innate greatness in him. I can assure you that he will try very hard for you."

Shoshana shook her head no. "Thank you, but I don't think so! I have a life of my own. My work is exciting, and I adore living in Manhattan. Someday, if G-d wills it, I will find a sophisticated, urbane Jewish gentleman and we will live in the city and raise a family. I just know it."

Rachel pondered that for a moment, "You have it all planned out?"

"As a matter of fact, I planned it out a long time ago."

"Why hasn't it worked out?"

"Who says it hasn't"

"Well has it?"

Shoshana sat there quietly, reflecting for a moment. When she was deep in thought, she had a habit of biting her lower lip. She was doing it now.

Rachel looked at her. "We all made plans. Jacob and I, we waited seven long years. And in the end, My sister Leah! Then Leah had children and I didn't for a very long time. Nothing goes as we plan it, because despite our best efforts, we don't control the world.

"So, you are telling me ... what?"

"I'm telling you nothing I haven't already said."

Shoshana got up and put her teacup in the sink. She ran some water into it to rinse it out. She turned back to continue talking with Rachel, but she was gone.

She looked in the dining room and the living room, but they were quiet. She walked back into the kitchen. She opened the door to the basement stairs and listened quietly. She heard nothing. She stepped quietly down a few steps and looked at the bed. She saw Elie sleeping soundly and turned back up the stairs to the kitchen. Finally, she closed and locked the door and climbed the front stairs to her own room. She took off her robe and slipped into bed. As her head lay on the pillow, she realized that she was crying softly. Rolling over, she finally returned to sleep.

Chapter Sixty-Two

They were married six months later. Rabbi Aaron cried when he read the blessings which united the couple. Elie looked so happy and Shoshana looked radiant in her white gown and red hair. As she approached the Chuppah she could see that Elie was smiling so broadly.

She walked around him seven times with her mother lifting the train to her gown. Then they stood next to each other and he placed the ring on her finger saying in Hebrew, "With this ring, you are consecrated to me according to the law of Moses and Israel." Various Rabbis and family members from the Aaron's side said the seven blessings and the couple drank the wine. Then a glass cup was wrapped in a napkin. Elie stepped on it and the crowd yelled Mazel Tov and they were married.

They moved into an apartment in Boro Park in Brooklyn. After a short time, Elie was recognized for his singing. A local Cantor soon began teaching him the services. Soon he was asked to be a cantor for the High Holiday and with much trepidation and encouragement from Shoshana, he soon mastered the service and was hired by a synagogue in Florida to come lead their services. Shoshana and Elie traveled down South and stayed through the holidays while he led the services. Later on, he would become a full time Cantor in a synagogue in Flatbush, where they ultimately would move to.

Shortly thereafter, Shoshana became pregnant and there was such joy when a little girl was born. They named her Bathsheba and Elie loved them both with all his being. He had never known such love since his mother had died.

Soon, a son was born, Moses Jacob and it became obvious to Elie, that they needed a bigger place to live in. They looked at many houses in Boro Park in Brooklyn and finally put a binder on one they really liked. But it fell through and as luck would have it a house became available from someone in Rabbi Aaron's Synagogue. The house was located at 1652 East 7th Street between Avenues O & P in Flatbush. They liked the house and bought it. Shoshana was glad they moved to this house because she wanted to be in close proximity to her parents. Her father was now in his nineties, although still vigorous, so it worked out well for them.

Over the next few years, they would have three more children, another little girl named Rachel. They also had twins, both boys. The older twin was named Abraham in memory of Shoshana's father who passed away, the year before. The other twin was named Sholom for he symbolized the peace that Shoshana and Elie felt as a family. With Rabbi Aaron's passing a great sadness descended upon the family. He was responsible for everything Elie now had in his life. For Shoshana, it was a terrible loss. There was also great mourning in the community as the simple man was greatly beloved by all who knew him. It would take a while for the family to recover.

Chapter Sixty-Three

Stanley sat in a chair next to Elie's bed in Coney Island Hospital.

"So, in the end you never told her you were sick?" Stanley shook his head disapprovingly at Elie. Elie looked back at him in his hospital gown. Tubes and I.V.'s hung from his bed and his arms.

Elie shrugged and shook his head no.

"Must have been a hell of a shock to her?"

Elie smiled weakly and shrugged his shoulders.

Stanley looked at him sadly. Changing the subject, he said, "Do you think her father ever told her about who you were?"

"No, I kind of doubt that he would have ever told her. He wanted her to have a quiet Jewish life. If she knew who I had been, she never would have married me. Rabbi Aaron once told me that I should never tell anyone and with the exception of you, I have never told a soul."

There was quiet between the two men for a few moments. Then Elie said to Stanley, The Doctor wants me try Chemotherapy. I don't want to."

"Why not? What have you got to lose by trying it?"

"Stanley, it will make me very sick."

"Like you're not very sick anyway? Look at you! You're in the hospital. If Chemo gave you a few more months, wouldn't it be worth it? For your wife, your kids?"

"I know, but it will make me really, really sick. The doctors told me what to expect. The big pain in my belly is enough for me. What good would it do for my family?"

"Idiot, they would have you!"

"But at what cost. They will remember their father as a sick old man. I would make them miserable."

"You don't know that."

Elie scrunched up his face. "It would be no good."

Stanley threw up his hands in exasperation and got up from his chair.

"Now, you are being a martyr. And a selfish one at that."

Elie looked over at the nurse in the door. She came in and took his vital signs, shooing Stan into the hallway. As he stood outside the room door, leaning against the wall, Shoshana came into view at the other end of the hallway. Moving towards him, she recognized Stanley and looked at him quizzically.

"What are you doing here Stanley?"

"Came by to see my friend." Stanley looked down at his shoes.

"Did you know that he was sick?"

Stan continued to look down and said nothing.

"Why didn't he tell me?"

"He didn't want you to worry."

"But he told you?

Stan looked up at her and shrugged.

She gave him a look of disgust, shaking her head from side to side.

"Is there anything else he hasn't told me? You seem to be so close that he felt he could tell you he was sick, but not his wife. No, he couldn't seem to do that! Couldn't tell his wife he was dying, but the neighbor ..." With that, she broke down into tears. Stanley reached for her, but she pulled back.

"Shoshana, I told him he should tell you. I think that for him, telling you would mean he had to acknowledge to himself that he was so sick."

She looked at him and wiped at her tears with a tissue. She lightly bit at her lower lip but composed herself.

"I am not angry with you Stanley. You kept him going these past few months. Whatever you talked about brought him back to life. He seemed to have lost that for several months before you moved in next door."

She touched his arm. "You are a good man Stanley. I'm sure you tried to convince him to tell me." She then shrugged and walked into Elie's room. She closed the door behind her with a resounding bang.

Chapter Sixty-Four

Stanley walked away from the hospital and down to the subway. Rather than return to his house, he went back to the office. The sunset was before him as he looked out the window of the subway car. Soon the train descended into the tunnel between Brooklyn and Manhattan.

He came into the newsroom and sat at his desk. It was mostly quiet. There were only a few people working on stories in the overnight. He tried working on a feature story for the weekend edition, but soon gave up. His head was in turmoil. He got up and went down to a bar around the corner. Ordering a beer and a hamburger, Stan sat by himself at the bar.

He pondered how Elie could have lived with Shoshana for so many years and never even give her a hint of what his life was before he met her. How Elie must have wanted to share that with her in their most intimate moments? But he had felt duty bound not to. That was remarkable restraint from a man known in his younger days for his unquestionable lack thereof.

Soon, it would all be over. They would be burying a man who once had the entire world in his hand. And he would be buried as a simple old Jew, in a grave belying the fact that he had known greatness and wealth beyond anyone's imagination.

Stanley thought it remarkable that Elie had given it all up. He knew that he would not have done the same in the same circumstances. Hell, he would have ridden that wave to the bitter end. Anyone else would probably have as well. All Stanley could think of was all those women!

He shook his head and thought how Elie, who could have had almost any woman he wanted, chose to live out almost half his life with a pale, plain, skinny woman who always was besieged with the tumult in her house.

He wondered why? What did Elie see in her? What did he know inherently? What did the two of them have to talk about? Stan could not see any commonality between them at all. But what did he know? He had messed up his own relationships.

Stan took a bite of his burger and then took a long draw on his beer. Trying to figure out Elvis Presley was as perplexing as anything he had encountered. But fate had brought him together with the biggest story of his life. Now he was not sure that he even wanted to spill the beans. Maybe it would be better if Elie were just allowed to rest in peace with the life he had chosen so long ago.

But he had made a promise. He promised Elie that he would tell the story and share the money with Shoshana and the children. It was a quandary for Stanley. He had been shaken by the question she had posed to him in the hospital, "Is there anything else he hasn't told me?" If his illness was a shock to her, the knowledge of his previous life would be a catastrophe.

Furthermore, he did not want to be the one who told her of the Elvis part of his life. That was for Elie to do. But he did not know how to get Elie to do it. Finishing his meal, he paid his bill and headed for the subway to Brooklyn. Sighing as he went down the stairs to the train, he was very troubled. When the train pulled into the station, Stan stepped on and found a seat. He closed his eyes, stretched his neck back and tried to escape all of his thoughts.

"Is there anything else he hasn't told me?" That question kept playing in his head all the way back to Brooklyn and in the end, Stan got no escape from his thoughts.

Chapter Sixty-Five

Stan went to the hospital directly after work. Elie could not decide whether to start chemotherapy. Shoshana had been with him all day and when Stan walked in, she looked so relieved.

"Stanley, I'm glad you are here. I've been here all day. I must get a cup of coffee and take a short walk outside to get some air. Can you look after him while I go out for a while?"

"Of course. Take your time. I'll sit with him for a bit."

"Maybe you can talk some sense into that fat head of his."

Shoshana collected her bag and coat and turning to Elie, she said, "Be back in a little while." Elie nodded his head and sighed deeply. Shoshana waved at Stan and left the room.

"Well buddy, how you doing?" Stanley said, as he sat down in the chair by the bed. As he descended into the chair, he gave a light slap to Elie's knees which were under the blanket. Elie laughed briefly. He looked terrible. His eyes had dark circles under them. He sat propped up with a pillow spilling out from behind his head. His skullcap was askew. Stanley moved it more squarely onto his head.

"Having fun?"

"Tons. I am a human pin cushion."

Stanley looked at him. He was hooked up to a bunch of equipment monitoring everything. There seemed to be a million tubes and wires attached to his friend. It was a sorry state.

"What did your wife mean by telling me to talk some sense into you?"

She wants me to start the chemo."

"So, do I, my friend. Your giving up too easily."

"What if this is my time? Maybe G-d is calling me home?"

"Listen to yourself. You sound like an idiot. You may be really sick now, and the Chemo may make you even sicker. But if it works, you could have …?"

"More time?"

"Yes"

"How much? Maybe a few months. Is it worth it? This will bankrupt my family and it is already destroying the kids. They come here and cry." He started to tear up. "What do I tell them?"

Stan shook his head. "You tell them to be strong for you, so you can be strong for them."

Elie shrugged, wiping his eyes with a tissue. He looked up at the T.V. in the room. It was playing the news. Elie looked away. "What rubbish on the television. I used to be addicted to watching it at Graceland. I haven't watched it in years. I see that it has gotten much worse. Such garbage. I'm glad my children don't watch."

"At least you can't shoot at it in here." They both laughed.

Elie laughed again "If I had a gun now, I definitely would shoot it out." Stanley looked away. Elie just chuckled. A young girl brought in a hospital tray and put on the rolling table in front of him.

"Well my friend, at least they feed you here." Stan said jokingly. He reached to open the cover for Elie. "Looks pretty good." On the tray was a small piece of fish, some mash potatoes and green beans. There was a small jello and some hot tea. Stanley carefully opened the package with plastic utensils and placed the teabag into the hot water. He stuffed a napkin under Elie's chin. Mixing some sugar into the tea, he looked at his friend and saw that he had no interest in eating anything.

"Elie, eat something!"

Elie made a face and looked around at the tea. "Well maybe the jello and some tea to wash it down."

"Elie, you've got to eat more than that."

Elie made a face of disgust. The smell of the fish was making him nauseous." No, really, I am alright with the jello and tea."

"The hell you are! Listen my friend, eat your damn food. You ain't allowed to die right now. And I have selfish reasons."

"Really? And what could those be?"

Grabbing Elie under his chin and tilting his head up to his own face "You know damned well what those reasons are. You still have a lot to tell me and I won't let you die until you're finished with me. So there!"

"So there", Elie said and stuck out his tongue. They both started to laugh. Elie protested, "Don't make me laugh Stan, it hurts."

"Then eat your food."

"Okay, if you insist." Digging into the plate with a plastic fork. He took a mouthful of fish and shrugged. "Eh, not so bad. Shoshana does it much better."

"You're a spoiled brat," Stanley said with a smile.

Elie nodded, "I guess I am."

"No s--t Sherlock."

"Well of course I am! After all, I am, ta da, Elvis Presley.

"Ain't you ever!"

They both laughed.

"You're never going to tell her."

Elie shook his head slowly, "No. I don't think so."

Stanley walked to the window and looked out. "Is she the one you really loved?"

"I love Shoshana very much."

"But she isn't the one you loved the most?"

Elie sat quietly for a moment. "Stanley, why does that matter so much to you?

"I don't know. Well actually" Then stopping for a moment Stan settled into thought. "Forget that… Actually, it matters, my friend because it gives a tremendous value to your life."

"I don't understand."

"You gave up your greatest love to find happiness in a new life. You must think of her often and compare for yourself what might have been if you had been mature enough to handle it."

"Stanley, who are you talking about?"

Stan looked at him quizzically, "Priscilla, of course."

"What makes you think that Priscilla was my greatest love?"

Stan looked at Elie closely. Elie sat up a little taller in the bed.

"Stanley, why do you assume that the great love of my life was Priscilla?"

Now Stan was very confused. He stammered, "Well… Well I just kind of assumed, you know."

"Because we were together so long? Yes, we were together from the time she was a young teenage girl. Yes, she was a tremendous part of my life and a great love. But believe it or not, she couldn't hold a candle to Shoshana."

"Huh. Who was it then? Linda Thompson?"

Elie shook his head no.

"Ginger Alden?"

Elie made a face.

"Then who?" Stan started to pace around the room. "I got it. Of course, it was Ann-Margaret."

Elie smiled broadly. Stan laughed triumphantly, "I knew it. I knew it. I'm right, Elie aren't I. I should have guessed that first."

"If you guessed that first, you would still be wrong."

"What? Well, if it wasn't Ann-Margaret ...?"

Elie just sat there with a smile like the Cheshire cat. Stan walked close to him. They looked at each other. Elie smiled but Stan looked away.

"If it wasn't one of these women, then whom?"

"Come on Stanley, you know the answer to that."

Stanley sat back down. He scratched at his head and looked down at the floor. He shook his head in total confusion. Elie interrupted his thoughts.

"Stanley, there is one person, I would do anything for..." He said quietly.

Stan looked up at him, still confused. Elie continued, "One person, I would do anything for..."

Stan, seized with a thought, jumped up from his chair., "Not your mother?"

Elie smiled.

"Your mother? Gladys? When I said that you had given up your greatest love, I meant a woman who... you know had a relationship with."

"I did have a relationship with her. Just not the kind you are thinking of."

"But your mother was dead, long before you ran away to this life."

"Yes. That is true, but without her constantly reminding me of my real roots, I would never have had the courage to abandon my unhappy state and live the life I have lived here in Brooklyn. Gladys was my one true love. All other women are a distant second."

"Even Shoshana?"

"Yes, even her."

"But." Stan closed his eyes. "I don't understand. You and Shoshana have been together for years."

"Yes, she has been the woman in my life longer than everyone else. And she is as different from Gladys as I am from you. But it worked. It worked well. And I have loved her more than any other woman in my life. But never more than my mother.”

“Doesn’t that strike you as strange, Elie?”

“Sometimes! Yes, sometimes, it seems odd. But no one ever loved me like my mother. No one ever sacrificed her everything like Mama.”

“Elie, don’t you realize that if you had given your wife the same kind of unfettered love that you retained in your head for your mother, she would have loved you the way you were loved by Gladys.”

Elie lay there silent. Then he closed his eyes and a tear dropped down onto his cheek.

“Do you think it’s too late for me and Shoshana?

Stan shrugged. “Who knows? But you will never know unless you start your chemo!”

Chapter Sixty-Six

Shoshana sat in the hospital cafeteria sipping on a coffee. She was exhausted. She had been with Elie almost the entire day. Her friend Breindy Frankel was watching the kids. It was a good thing that Stanley had come by to visit. It freed her up to recharge a little before going home. She reached into her pocketbook and pulled out a candy bar. Opening it, she shoved a piece into her mouth. She swallowed hard and followed up with a sip of her coffee. She felt the candy going down hard and she reached for her belly and rubbed it until the pain subsided.

Finishing the candy and swallowing down the rest of her coffee quickly, she got up and walked towards the elevator bank. She thought to herself that she would say a quick good night to Elie, go home, collect her kids and collapse. The elevator opened up and she wove her way around nurses and patients on the way to returning to Elie's room. Stan was sitting in the chair next to Elie. They were talking quietly when she came in. Elie saw her come in and interrupted his conversation with Stan.

"Shoshie, I want you to know that I've decided to start the chemo."

"Oh, thank G-d," she said as her eyes began to tear up. "Thank G-d. Stanley, what did you say to him to make him change his mind?"

Stan flashed a quick look at Elie and then turned to Shoshana and said, "You got me! We talked. He changed his mind. Did I get that right Elie?"

Elie shook his head yes. Shoshana looked quizzically at Stan. "Well, however you did it. Thanks. I couldn't get him to agree. I'm glad you were able to do it Stanley."

"No problem, glad I could help."

"Elie are you sure about this."

"Yes."

"I mean you were pretty sure you didn't want to do this."

Stan interrupted the conversation. "Shoshana, leave it alone! He agreed to it. Let's try not to overanalyze this. He agreed. Period. Don't try to dissect it. Okay?"

She looked at him, then at Elie. Speaking very slowly, "Okay! I'll leave it alone."

"Good."

She nodded and then walked over to her husband's bed. She bent down to give him a kiss. "I will see you tomorrow. Try to sleep well."

Elie kissed her back. "If they will let me sleep and not keep sticking me in the middle of the night."

"I'll talk to the nurse."

"Thank you honey."

Stanley suddenly stirred in his chair agitatedly. Elie and Shoshana looked at him with curiosity. He finally blurted out to Elie, "When are you finally going to tell her? Does she have to find out after your dead?"

Pointing to Elie, then to himself, "I don't want that responsibility Elie. I don't! After all we have talked about tonight, don't you think it's time she knew?

"Know what?" Shoshana asked alarmed. She looked at her husband. "What's going on Elie?"

Elie shifted uneasily in his bed. Stan stood up and yelled at Elie. Damn it! Elie tell her who you were before you came to New York. Tell her now! Tell her now or I will, right this moment."

"Tell me what's going on Elie. What are you guys talking about?" She asked angrily.

Elie fell silent. He was terrified and couldn't speak. Shoshana walked up to Stan and pointed her finger into his chest. "What's going on here? What is it that I need to know? Why are you yelling at my husband?"

He looked right past her towards Elie's bed, "Tell her Elie or I will… right now!"

Elie closed his eyes and opened them again slowly. His mouth started to move, but no words came out. Stan yelled at him again, "Tell her, damn it!"

Elie couldn't get himself together. He was breathing heavily and sweating profusely. Stan looked at him in disgust. "Don't you think she has a right to know that you …."

"That he ... What?"

Stanley took a deep breath, looking at Elie and then turning to Shoshana. He spoke softly to her, not wanting to shock her too badly.

"Elie, in light of all the possibilities that could happen over the next few weeks, she needs to know that before you came to New York, you were a very famous person."

Shoshana tensed up visibly. "Shoshana, your husband is ..."

She interrupted him and finished his sentence, "actually Elvis Presley!"

There was total silence in the room.

"Yes, I know! I've always known!

Elie looked stricken. "How long have you known?

"Since before we were married. Father told me."

Elie looked past her as if he was talking to himself. " He told me to never tell a soul. You knew and you were still willing to marry me?"

She looked at him as if he was asking a stupid question."

"Of course, I married you, didn't I?"

Stanley rubbed his forehead and sat down. He didn't know whether to stay or leave.

"But why? Elie stammered tenderly.

Shoshana walked over to the other chair in the room and dragged it over to Elie's bedside. "Because I loved you! Why do you think? You were trying so hard to turn your life around and I saw that. I still love you Elie."

She started to choke up and then suddenly laughed at herself.

Elie looked at her. "Why didn't you tell me you knew?

"Why didn't you tell me yourself? You've had 35 years to do so. One might have thought that a secret like that was a very big deal. No?"

Elie shook his head silently. Shoshana looked at him.

Stan, seeing that this might be the right moment to leave them alone, slowly rose from his chair and started to move to the door. Shoshana stopped him.

"Where are you going?"

"I just thought this might be an appropriate time to leave you two alone. I would say you have a lot of things to discuss."

"Stanley, sit down. Do you think, I don't know what you have been talking about these past few months?"

Elie and Stan looked at each other.

"Well, I don't know ..."

"I am a lawyer. It may seem that I am just an ordinary overwhelmed housewife, but I am still a lawyer. I even renew my license in case I ever need it." She looked Stanley right in the eyes.

"Oh!? He responded sheepishly as he slipped back into his chair.

"You two would sit on the porch and talk. Well my little private space, my office as you could call it, is right behind that window. And I hate to break the news to you guys. I could hear every word."

Stan turned red in the face. "I'm sorry Shoshana."

"For what?"

Stan started to say something, then just stopped and looked away.

"You're sorry for what Stanley?"

Stan threw up his arms and shrugged. "You know, like everything. It was wrong!"

"What was wrong?" Elie started to interject into the conversation. Shoshana said to him, "Stay out of this Elie."

"But he was trying to help me."

She looked at her husband, "Maybe!" She looked towards Stan. "You are a big name in the newspapers here. I sometimes read your stories myself."

Stanley started to smile. Shoshana continued, "If it was up to me, I don't know if I would have chosen you to tell this story. I mean really, a sportswriter to chronicle my husband's life, but ..." She started to smile slightly. "I always worried that someone would figure it out. I was sure that when it happened," She turned to Elie, "our lives would have gone to holy hell in a moment."

Turning back to Stan, "You could have broken this story a long time ago. Stanley, you could have, and I wouldn't have blamed you if you had. I know that it must have taken something very special for you not to. What that was, I don't know and frankly, I don't care. I am only thankful you didn't. It must have killed you to sit on the biggest story of your life."

Stan sat there mesmerized.

She continued, "So, tell it well Stanley. There is a lot you still don't know, and time is not our friend here. You need to speak to me as well. There is a lot I can fill in."

Stan sat back in his chair trying to control his breathing. "Thank you, Shoshana."

She shook her head softly. Then turning to her husband, "And as for you, Chemo! Starting tomorrow. Yes?"

Elie looked at her and felt such love and admiration for her. "Yes."

"Good. And whatever deal you guys cooked up about this, you will run it by me. You hear me guys. Run it by me, because it involves the children and I. Elie, we will talk more about this tomorrow. Get some sleep." She got up and kissed him.

"Come on Stanley, let him get some rest," she said as she motioned him out the door and followed him out of the hospital.

Chapter Sixty-Seven

Shoshana sat at her parent's kitchen table. She was wearing a robe and slippers and was sipping from a cup of coffee. A plate of cookies was on the table covered with plastic wrap. Tempting treats to look at. Pondering whether to take one, her finger lit lightly onto the plastic. Lifting up the edge of the plate she brought it to her nose and sniffed at the cookies. Finally, looking down at her waist, she put them back and pushed them away beyond her easy reach. She moved the chair next to her and pulled it alongside, so she could rest her feet on it. Thumbing through a bridal magazine for what seemed like the hundredth time, she looked up at the clock above the refrigerator and saw that it was after 1 in the morning. Sighing deeply, she took another sip.

She got up to put the cup in the sink, but it slipped from her grasp and fell, shattering onto the floor. Quietly muttering to herself, she grabbed the broom and shovel and was in the middle of cleaning up when her father appeared in the door.

"Is everything alright?"

Grunting as he bent down to hold the shovel for her, she looked up saying to her father, "It's okay, I just dropped my coffee cup. I am cleaning it up."

"You didn't cut yourself; heaven forbid?"

"No, No, All good!"

Rabbi Aaron smiled. He looked at his daughter. In less than a week, she would be getting married. At long last, the child he worried so much about would take the big step of marrying. He stood there with a smile at the kitchen entrance in his robe and slippers with his skullcap curiously perched on his head. His glasses were skewed down on the right. She didn't know how he could see from them.

"Papa." She reached for his glasses and removed them. She straightened the metal rims. Clearly, he had been reading when he fell asleep with the glasses still on. They must have bent when his head touched the pillow. She laughed and put them back on his nose.

"Thank you my dear. What are you doing up so late?"

She shrugged.

"Are you worried about the wedding?

She sat down again and looked up at him.

"I wouldn't say worried." Her father looked at her curiously.

"Not worried. Then what?"

"Concerned."

"About what? Has Elie done anything to make you have doubts?"

She made a face and looked down for a moment. Getting up from the table, she said, "Papa, would you like some tea?"

He looked at her. He knew she was troubled about something. He wouldn't drink tea at this hour, he was there to listen. "Yes, A tea would be nice. Some chamomile please, so I can sleep."

She rustled her hands in the cupboard and pulled out a box of tea. She set the water to boil and wiped down the sink with a towel. When the pot started to whistle, she poured a cup and placed it in front of her father who was sitting at the table opposite her.

"None for you?"

"I just had coffee, Papa. I think I've had enough for tonight."

"So be it. Shoshana, could I have a plate. I would like to take a cookie. Your mother outdid herself it would seem."

"I made them Papa."

"Well then, you outdid yourself. So, what troubles you Shoshanela?"

"I am not really sure, but to answer your question, Elie has done nothing wrong. He is a good man."

"Are you concerned that he is much older than you?"

"No. In many ways, he really is not."

"Not what?"

"Older!"

"I am afraid, I do not understand."

"Elie may be older than me chronologically, but he is so naïve about things. Often I feel that I am so much more worldly than he is."

The Rabbi smiled to himself as he drank some of his tea. He put the cup down and looked at his daughter. Such a smart girl. No, a woman. He remembered her as a baby. The first baby of his new life.

The baby that defied the odds just by being born. His head stretched into thoughts of Europe. She was the symbol for him of how he beat the Nazis.

And now she was getting married to a man she loved, but she really knew nothing about him. Yet he knew that Elie loved her with all his heart. On paper, none of this should work. But on paper, he should be dead along with the family he lost. And just like he had defied the odds and beat the Nazis, Elie had defied the odds and defeated his demons.

He had been determined that Shoshana should never know about those demons. As it became increasingly clear that Shoshana and Elie were getting close, he held his breath. He did not want Shoshana hurt; nor did he want Elie to be hurt either.

He had spoken to Elie about the challenges ahead of him. He also had elicited a pledge from Elie not to tell her about his past as Elvis Presley. He wanted his daughter to have a normal life, free from doubts and distractions that knowing Elie's past would certainly bring upon the couple.

But he knew better. He sighed deeply. Shoshana looked at him quizzically.

"Papa, why the sigh?"

Looking at his daughter, he smiled softly. Such a joy! What a wonderful daughter! Self-reliant, strong, determined. She had such a sweet spot for Elie. Her kindness bubbled over when she looked at him. Elie was so much younger than her in that emotional way of men. As her father, he thought to himself how Shoshana will be so good for Elie. She was so much more grounded than any of the other women he had been involved with in his life.

"I sigh because I want so much for you and Elie."

"So why sigh? It's a good thing to want for us to have a life together with all that entails."

"I know. It is a good thing." He pushed his teacup to the side and leaned into the table speaking in a very hushed tone.

"Shoshana, there is something you must know about Elie, but you must promise to never tell him you know. In fact, you can tell no one else, ever…., even your Mother and siblings."

"Papa, what are you talking about. You're scaring me."

"There is nothing to be frightened about and if you truly love Elie, you will understand why you must always keep this secret."

"What is this secret? And I am to keep this secret even from Elie?"

"Yes. He must never know that you know! And what's more I made him promise to never tell you."

"So, both of us will know this secret, but we can never tell each other that we know of it?"

"I'm afraid so."

She started to say something but stopped herself. She looked at her father carefully. She had not seen him so serious in a long time. He would not ask her this unless there was a special reason. She took a deep breath. "Okay Papa."

"Well you see, my dear Shoshana, it goes like this..."

Chapter Sixty-Eight

"You like being alone, don't you?" Shoshana stood by his side of the bed. Elie stirred slightly and rolled over to see her in the darkness of their bedroom.

"Huh?"

"You heard me! You like being alone!"

Elie reached for his glasses on the nightstand and put them on to see her better.

"I don't think so!"

"Sure, you do!"

"No. Really, I don't think so.

Elie had been home for six weeks. The chemotherapy he was going through knocked him out and made him feel awful. He didn't want Shoshana and the kids to see him suffering, so mainly he stayed in the basement stretched out on the old couch down there. He would come up for meals if he felt up to it, but otherwise, he would stay put in the basement.

When he came down to the kitchen, she was waiting for him. She handed him the guitar that had been gathering dust in the basement for years.

"Play this for me. You are Elvis Presley and I, your wife, have never heard you play. In fact, I have never heard you sing anything other than Jewish music. I want to know what the big deal was. So, let me hear!"

Elie looked up at her as he cradled the guitar in his arms and smiled. He reached up to tune the guitar and when it was ready, he strummed it lightly. The sound was like a breath of fresh air to him. It had been years since he last picked it up. Elie smiled again and then put the guitar down on the table.

Shoshana looked confused. "You don't want to play it?"

Elie put his palm on the face of the guitar, "Oh yes. Yes, I do! It's been a long time. How can I explain it?

She sat down next to him. Reaching for the guitar, she took it from his grasp and placed it on her lap. She strummed the strings and smiled. She strummed then again, then she picked at the strings with her fingers. "When I was a young girl, I always wanted a man who could play the guitar. Who knew, I always had a guy like that. I knew you were Elvis Presley, but I never knew what it meant until now. I have started listening to your music. I went out and bought a bunch of your albums."

He looked at her quizzically. She answered the unspoken question, "Yes, even your gospel and Christmas albums. I've also seen all your movies.

"When, we don't have a television or a VCR?"

"I borrowed a TV from one of our friends. It had a VCR built into it. It was not large, maybe 13 inches, but it was large enough for me to see you act. I saw them while you were in the hospital. Some of them were rather silly. I can understand why you hated making them. But most of them were funny and cute. I liked them. I wish we could have shared them years ago."

He looked at her eyes, "Me too! It would have been fun!"

"Yes, it would have been." She handed him back the guitar. "Play for me now."

He nodded as he strummed the strings and then started to sing for her. Tears ran down her eyes. Speaking to the guitar as if it was human, she said, "Say hello again to your old friend Elie. You see, it's been crying out for you. Sing for me, Elie, as you sang for your Mama. I love you that much too."

Chapter Sixty-Nine

Stanley kicked at the dirt alongside the gravestone. His toe loosened up a round stone, which he bent over and picked up, placing it on top of the marker. Leaning against the gravestone was one of the folding lawn chairs that had sat on Elie's front porch. He had asked Shoshana if he could borrow it for the day while he visited Elie's grave in Queens. He looked at the gravestone. In front of the stone were evergreen bushes. The marker had musical notes carved on them and then in Hebrew letters, Elie's Hebrew name and date of death. Hidden behind the outgrowth of the evergreens, if you looked very carefully, one could see in English, in small carved letters, the words: Elvis Aaron Presley, surrounded by a carved heart. It was the only indication to the uninitiated that this was Elvis Presley's final resting place.

Stanley opened the chair in front of the grave and sat down. He reached into the pocket of his windbreaker and pulled out a small flask. Opening it up and taking a small sip, he said "L'Chaim," and pointed the flask at the grave as if to offer Elie a drink. He took another sip said "L'Chaim" again and screwed the cover back on. He put the flask on the grass in front of him and started to speak.

"Well buddy, how the heck are you?" In the absence of a response, he continued to talk. "Buddy that was a great way to end a show." Then, inexplicably, Stanley started to cry.

It was only a few months since they had all gathered together to bury Elie. It now seemed surreal to Stanley. Elie had become a great friend to him in the short time they had known each other. Now the loss felt particularly profound. He had been to the grave again, when Shoshana had erected the marker, but since that time, he resisted, half out of being so busy, half out of an uncomfortable feeling that he would not be able to tolerate seeing the grave.

It had been over a year since Elie had passed on and finally Stanley summoned the nerve to visit. It was a sunny, unusually warm spring day in April, and he ventured out to St. Albans in

Queens to the Old Cemetery where Elie was buried. The grave was on small hill like rise next to a tiny pathway. He parked in the parking lot near the cemetery office and walked the short distance to the grave, carrying the lawn chair. From the pathway, you could clearly see the gravestone as no other graves were blocking the view.

As he sat, Stanley thought back to the last few months he had spent with Elie. While undergoing the chemotherapy, Elie had initially holed up in his basement and refused to come out except for a few visits with Stan. Each visit had been short and frankly, Elie looked worse every time Stan saw him. Maybe Elie had been right after all, about how difficult the chemo would be.

Then suddenly, one Sunday morning on a warm autumn day, Stanley heard the strumming of a guitar and soft singing on the porch. He stepped out of his front vestibule and saw Elie playing and singing. Shoshana sat next to him in the other lawn chair and smiled broadly as he sang. After each song, she would reach out to touch his shoulder or take his hand in hers. Recharged, he would sing some more to her. They were like two teenagers and he was showing off to her. Stanley just looked at them for a moment.

"Stanley, how you doing?" Elie called out to him.

Stan looked down for a moment and then said to them. "Now you two behave yourselves." They all laughed for a moment.

Shoshana looked at Stanley, "He looks pretty good today, doesn't he?"

Stan shook his head yes and then chuckling to himself, walked back into his house. He could hear them continuing for quite a while.

Over the next few months, this scene would repeat itself several times. Sometimes, Shoshana would sit with him, other times one or more of the kids or grandkids. But each time Stanley witnessed it, he could see that Elie was getting stronger.

Sometimes, Elie would sit alone on the porch and play by himself as if he was trying to work out some sort of musical puzzle in his head. The tears would flow copiously from his eyes and he would have to stop and take a break until he was able to gather himself together.

The Chemo went on for several months. It would sap Elie's energy for a week or so, but soon he was back out on the porch, even on a cold day, playing his guitar and singing softly. When it got too cold, he would play inside. Sometimes, Stanley could hear Elie playing the piano from the other side of the demising wall between their houses.

During all of this time, in little spurts of energy, Elie filled in the gaps in Stan's notebook. He also sat with Shoshana and got her side of the story.

They had lived a surprisingly good life. Money was often tight, but they managed to raise a family and Elie felt safe with her. By Elvis Presley standards, their life could be seen as very dull. But by Elie Pressler standards, their life was full and rewarding and happy,

As the Spring warmed the air, Elie returned to playing on the porch. One day, Stanley and Elie were sitting out when Stan asked: "Elie, now that I see you playing the guitar so often and singing your old songs… do you ever, I mean just for a second, wonder what it would be like to go out on stage…? Then Stan stopped, not quite knowing how to finish the sentence. Elie finished it for him, "and play for an audience one more time?" He peered over at Stan, "Is that what you're asking, my friend?"

Stan looked up at his friend, "Well, sort of, something like that". He chuckled for a moment.

Elie laughed as well, "All the time, all the time, my friend!"

The two of them looked at each in silence for a moment. Stan said to him, "Really! I thought you had this all figured out?"

"I did, but it was always a passing thought. I never took it seriously and of course, now…. The closest I have ever gotten to that is when I sang as a Cantor in Synagogue. I would say to myself, "if they only knew who was singing for them right now, they would go wild". I would smile to myself and it would give me the lift to go on. But I never was going to betray myself or my family or any of my mentors."

Stan sat transfixed. Elie had never let the dream die inside of himself. He had transformed it and controlled it. And because he was able to do just that, he had built himself a life to be proud of.

"Elie, if the chance ever came up, would you do it?"

"What's the chance of that ever happening? You're kidding around."

"But Elie, really, what if say that opportunity really did happen…?"

"Miraculously!"

Stan leaned over on his chair. He punched himself lightly on the noggin. "Yeah, miraculously, would you do it?

"Hypothetically, sure!"

"What if it wasn't hypothetical? What if it was real? No hypothetical nonsense, the real deal."

Squinting at Stan, Elie was a bit confused. "How can I contemplate something like that. First of all, listen to this conversation. We are two old men talking about a fantasy. Secondly, I chose not to do that a very long time ago."

"But Elie that was when you were younger and healthy. And you would have had to take up where you had left off. Now, you are old, and you know…"

"Sick!"

"Yes! However now, it could be a one-shot deal."

"Are you talking about me doing an open mike or a real full concert?

"The full Monty, a regular concert. Then you could disappear again into obscurity."

Elie frowned, "Stan, are you talking about me revealing myself?"

"That I am, my man."

"That's crazy, they would think I was some old Elvis impersonator."

"Could be! But not if the venue was so big, that there would be no denying that it was you."

"Right…! Never happen!"

"But if it could?" Stanley smiled at Elie. Elie leaned back and closed his eyes, stoking his beard.

"Ah, isn't craziness fun?"

Stan got up and opened the screen door to Elie's house. "I'm going to have a little conversation with Shoshana."

Chapter Seventy

Everyone likes to keep a big secret. The trick is finding the right people who know how to and are willing to wait for the big reveal without giving it away!

Stanley had rubbed shoulders with bigwigs for decades, he knew how to do this! Sort of like Vernon who knew how to make Elvis disappear!

Chapter Seventy-One

Madison Square Garden had always been a great venue for a music concert. The acoustics sucked, but the energy was hyper-drive alive. That night, the Grammys proved it. Great performances dominated the evening from all the genres of music.

To end the show an assembly of great bands and musicians crowded onto the stage to produce one of the greatest group efforts of music ever seen on a stage. It didn't matter that they were rockers or country, or rappers or jazz guys, these artists blew the house away. Just as they ended and took their bows, suddenly, the lights went dark and the announcer called out to the crowd.

"Ladies and Gentlemen, we are not done yet. We have a special guest coming to the stage."

A dim spotlight pointed to stage left. A tall, very thin man with a walker, wearing a white shirt with suspenders and simple black trousers glided slowly across the stage guided by a young woman with her hand on his right arm, followed by the spotlight. Otherwise, the stadium was black. This man wore a black velvet skullcap and white fringes hanging from his waist. He had a long white beard and wore silver rimmed glasses. A stool had been placed centerstage. As they approached the stool, she let him go. He stopped, folded up the walker, and handed it to a stagehand. Then he walked the few steps to the stool, climbed up onboard and was handed a guitar.

There was some confusion in the crowd as this was all happening. A lot of murmuring. Nobody knew who this "Special Guest" was! People whispered to each other trying to figure out who was onstage.

Smiling at the crowd, the man plucked at some strings to see if they were in tune. Satisfied, he smiled at the crowd again and then started to sing, ever so softly…

"Love me tender,
Love me sweet,
Never let me go.
You have made my life complete,
And I love you so."

He didn't look at the audience. Rather, he peered intently at the frets on the guitar neck, as he played out the notes. The audience didn't know what to think or whom they were seeing. But some of them thought they recognized the voice. Some whispers, some jostling. The man continued.

"Love me tender,
Love me true,
All my dreams fulfilled.
For my darlin' I love you,
And I always will."

Curiosity was now turning to excitement. People in the audience were not sure what they were experiencing, but they knew it was quite special. For some of the older people in the audience, the voice they heard told them that they were witnessing something amazing. For they recognized the voice and they recognized that it was the real thing.

"Love me tender,
Love me long,
Take me to your heart.
For it's there that I belong,
And we'll never part.

Someone in the audience yelled out, "Hey man, who are you? The man just smiled and continued,

"Love me tender,
Love me dear,
Tell me you are mine.
I'll be yours through all the years,
Till the end of time."

"Someone else yelled out, "Are you a Jewish Elvis impersonator. The singer laughed and pointed to the audience. Now some of the musicians still on the stage started to move forward to listen more intently as they started to realize that this "guest" was somebody very special.

"When at last my dreams come true
Darling this I know
Happiness will follow you
Everywhere you go."

Then suddenly, with great energy, he jumped off the stool, started swinging his hips and strumming the guitar really hard,

"Well, it's one for the money,
Two for the show,
Three to get ready,
Now go, cat, go.

But don't you step on my blue suede shoes.
You can do anything but lay off of my blue suede shoes."

With the broadest smile, he started dancing around the stage. For a man who walked onto the stage with a walker, he strutted the stage with an energy that surprised everyone onstage and in the audience. The crowd went wild, even though they still didn't know who he was. Elie looked offstage to see Shoshana and Stanley standing there. Shoshana was clapping and dancing with tears running down her eyes. Stanley just looked out at him and gave him a thumbs up.

"Well, you can knock me down,
Step in my face,
Slander my name
All over the place.

Do anything that you want to do, but uh-uh,
Honey, lay off of my shoes
Don't you step on my blue suede shoes.
You can do anything but lay off of my blue suede shoes.

You can burn my house,
Steal my car,
Drink my liquor
From an old fruit jar.
Do anything that you want to do, but uh-uh,
Honey, lay off of my shoes
Don't you step on my blue suede shoes.
You can do anything but lay off of my blue suede shoes."

"Well, it's one for the money,
Two for the show,
Three to get ready,
Now go, cat, go.

But don't you step on my blue suede shoes.
You can do anything but lay off of my blue suede shoes.

He bowed deeply and spoke for the first time to the crowd. "Thank you, thank you very much", he said in that southern drawl that was unmistakably Elvis. He launched right into his next song, still on his feet, now stalking both ends of the stage. He waved to the back of the stage to all the musicians still up there, calling them all forward to join him on the front of the stage. They were not sure exactly who he was, but he was singing up a storm and they wanted to be a part of it.

"You ain't nothin' but a hound dog
Cryin' all the time
You ain't nothin' but a hound dog
Cryin' all the time
Well, you ain't never caught a rabbit
And you ain't no friend of mine

Well they said you was high-classed
Well, that was just a lie
Yeah they said you was high-classed
Well, that was just a lie
Well, you ain't never caught a rabbit

And you ain't no friend of mine"

A voice yelled out from the audience, "Hey, you're Elvis Presley!" That was acknowledged with a shake of his head up and down as he moved swiftly around the stage. One of the musicians came up and started playing with him and the whole Madison Square Garden was going wild.

"You ain't nothin' but a hound dog
Cryin' all the time
You ain't nothin' but a hound dog
Cryin' all the time
Well, you ain't never caught a rabbit
And you ain't no friend of mine

Well they said you was high-classed
Well, that was just a lie
Yeah they said you was high-classed
Well, that was just a lie
Well, you ain't never caught a rabbit
And you ain't no friend of mine

His energy seemed relentless. His voice was strong and true.

Well they said you was high-classed
Well, that was just a lie
Ya know they said you was high-classed
Well, that was just a lie
Well, you ain't never caught a rabbit
And you ain't no friend of mine

You ain't nothin' but a hound dog
Cryin' all the time
You ain't nothin' but a hound dog
Cryin' all the time
Well, you ain't never caught a rabbit
You ain't no friend of mine"

He took a deep bow, high fived the musicians on the stage and

230

returned to the stool. The crowd quickly quieted as he re-tuned the guitar. Adjusting the microphone he spoke to the audience with the ease of a performer who had been doing this all his life.

"Thank you all. Thank you so much. My name is Elie Pressler, but you probably remember me by my old name… Elvis Presley." The audience went silent, then it went wild. Reporters started running to the front of the stage. The lights dimmed again, and a spotlight pointed at the stool. Elie looked longingly at the neck of the guitar, closed his eyes and sang…

"And now the end is near
So I face the final curtain
My friend, I'll say it clear
I'll state my case of which I'm certain

I've lived a life that's full
I've traveled each and every highway
And more, much more than this
I did it my way

Regrets, I've had a few
But then again, too few to mention
I did what I had to do
And saw it through without exception

I planned each charted course
Each careful step along the byway
Oh, and more, much more than this
I did it my way
Yes, there were times, I'm sure you knew
When I bit off more than I could chew
But through it all when there was doubt
I ate it up and spit it out
I faced it all and I stood tall
And did it my way

I've loved, I've laughed and cried
I've had my fill, my share of losing
And now as tears subside

I find it all so amusing
To think I did all that
And may I say, not in a shy way
Oh, no, no not me
I did it my way

For what is a man, what has he got
If not himself, then he has not
To say the words he truly feels
And not the words of one who kneels

The record shows I took the blows
And did it my way
The record shows I took the blows
And did it my way!"

Elie took off his glasses. He was crying and reached into his pocket for a tissue to wipe his eyes. He leaned into the microphone, "Thank you very much. G-d Bless you all. Then he stood up as the crowd jumped to their feet and gave him an extended standing ovation. The musicians on stage all came up and shook his hand and hugged him. He bowed to the audience one last time and then the arena went dark.

When the lights came on Elie was gone from the stage and an announcement was made, "Ladies and Gentlemen, Elvis has left the building."

Chapter Seventy-Two

They jumped into the back of a white construction van like kids who were happily partying and were free with abandon. They laughed and high-fived each other as the van sped out from under Madison Square Garden. Sitting on the floor of the van they held onto the shelving in the van and steadied themselves as the truck raced up 8th Avenue, hoping to avoid the press. By 72nd Street, it appeared that no one was chasing them, so they turned right and sped across Manhattan to the FDR Drive and headed south eventually ending up in the Battery Tunnel and working their way eventually to Ocean Parkway and then to their home. They piled out of the van in front of the house. Stanley hugged Elie tightly, patting him heartily on the back. Stanley looked at Shoshana and winked at her. Shoshana then reached out to him and gave him a big hug. This surprised her as much as it surprised Stanley. They said their good nights and went into their respective homes.

Back at Madison Square Garden, it was pandemonium. The press, caught flat footed, did not know what to do. They did not know where Elie was heading, and they didn't know the vehicle. There were crowds milling around, with the press interviewing major artists about the story that had turned the night on its head. It was very late, so the major networks coverage was limited, but the internet was lit up. There were so few details that the story just seemed to simmer in rumors and half-truths. By the time the press figured out who Elie was and where he lived, it was the early morning. News vans could not find where to park in front of Elie's house and the police had to force them onto Avenue P to keep the travel lane open.

None of this was really going to help them, because as soon as Elie and Shoshana had walked in the door, they grabbed suitcases and the children and drove upstate to a little hotel in Orange County, where they had a reservation for two rooms. They checked in around 2 AM and soon the children were asleep in one bedroom and Elie and Shoshana climbed into bed in the other room.

In the morning, Shoshana awoke as the sunlight streamed into their room. She got out of bed and put on a robe. Coming over to Elie's side of the bed, she sat down and gently touched him on his shoulder to wake him. Usually, he would slowly start to move his shoulder and then would roll over to speak with her. This time she got no response. She shook him a little harder and still there was no movement. She reached over and rolled him over to her. Lifting his eyelids, she saw only then, that that he had passed on in his sleep. She kissed his head and pulled the covers around his neck and adjusted his Yarmulke. Then she picked up her phone and called Stanley.

_______ ᴏ̇ᴄ̇ᴏ̇ _______

Chapter Seventy-Three

Stanley woke up the next morning to the hullabaloo in front of his door. He smiled when the reporters recognized him but could not honestly tell them where Elie had gone. When asked what he knew about his neighbor, he smiled and shook his head closing the door. His cell phone was ringing off the hook. He put it in silence mode and took a shower. He dressed for work and walked out towards the subway with a line of reporters following him. But he knew that if anyone got this entire story, it was going to be under his by-line. When he got to the office, everyone crowded around him, but he just walked into the Editor-in-Chief's office. This story was his and only his.

When he was done with the editor, he stepped briefly over to his desk. He had left his cellphone on a pile of papers. It was ringing and as he looked at it, there were many calls from Shoshana. He called her back and she broke the news to him.

They buried him that afternoon. The majority of the mourners standing graveside did not yet know they were burying Elvis Presley. The news of Elie's performance had exploded all over the news, just as the news of his first death had shaken the world.

Now Elie was really gone, and a handful of men and women laid him to rest. Stanley stood off to the side looking at the scene. Tears rolled down his eyes. as the family and friends threw shovelfuls of dirt into the grave. Shoshana looked to him and waved him over to pick up a shove. He shook his head no, but she walked over to him and whispered into his ear. He slowly walked to the pile of dirt and placed the shovel into the pile and then threw the dirt into the grave. He heard the thud of the dirt hit the casket and shook his head. Placing the shovel back in the dirt for another person to use, he turned and returned to where he had been standing. Shoshana was still there.

"Stanley, you didn't kill him! He wanted it and we all agreed to it.

235

We thought that the whole idea would never happen. We dreamed of the impossible and you helped make the impossible happen."

Stan looked down, then up at her. "I know! It was an incredible long-shot."

"That's right. It was! You know how you smile about a dream you never think will happen? Like winning the lottery. We got lucky. We won the lottery! You're a lucky man Stanley, you helped him make his final dream come true. He was able to come full circle and still maintain himself as the man he really wanted to be and was. I hope someday, you get to understand that." She turned and walked back to the grave.

Soon the grave was filled, and the mourners recited the Kaddish. Stanley just let the tears flow to the ground. After the mourners had moved back toward the cars, Stan stood in front of the grave and stared at the mound of earth and the little marker provided by the funeral society. It read "Elijah Pressler". He reached down to touch the marker gently, then stepped back and went to his car.

Chapter Seventy-Four

"A Conversation with the King" was a tremendous literary success. It sold millions of volumes, was made into audiobooks and eventually was sold as a movie.

Stanley embarked on a book tour which lasted several months throughout the United States, then to Europe and the Far East. After hundreds of signings and radio and television interviews, he finally came home in the middle of the night and stood on his stoop. He looked to the left at the Pressler stoop as if half expecting Elie to be sitting there with his guitar.

He wanted to knock on their door but thought better of it. Surely, Shoshana and the kids had long gone to sleep.

He reached into his pocket for his keys and let himself in. He placed his bags in the vestibule and walked back to the kitchen. He filled the coffeemaker with water and coffee, letting it brew. Stan sat down reviewing the piles of mail that Shoshana had neatly placed on his table while he was away.

After a few moments, he sighed deeply. The interviews were not over yet. He still had several scheduled in New York, but the tour was over, and he could at least hope for a relatively normal existence. The Elvis story was so compelling. A faked death, a long life under the radar and an amazing reveal followed by a quick death. What a story! Stanley had written many biographies before. This biography got under his skin...

The question interviewers had asked the most was where Elie had been buried. Stan never revealed the location, nor would he ever think to do so. He knew that if it ever was known, it would soon be overrun by Elvis fans who would have turned it into a makeshift memorial or worse, it might have been vandalized by those who wanted some sort of memorabilia from the grave.

Elie could rest in peace that the proceeds from the book and tours left Shoshana and the kids financially secure for life. Stanley had also secured his future with the proceeds, so if he wanted to, he could have retired to someplace warm and never worked again. But he wasn't ready for that!

Over the next few months, Stanley returned to the paper and to reporting sports. But a restlessness stayed with him all of the time. One morning, he walked into Elie's old synagogue and asked to speak to the Rabbi. The next morning, he returned and brought his old phylacteries with him. He put on his Prayer Shawl and his Phylacteries and sat down and prayed.

And that's how it was everyday afterward.

END

About the Author

D.M. Freedman caught the writing bug when he was a young teenager and has been writing ever since. Starting out with his first article for the Staten Island Historian while in High School, he has contributed off and on to a number of publications, both in the military and locally on Long Island, most notably in the South Shore Standard where his bi-weekly opinion pieces delved into the political and local scenes. He has authored two books, the last one named *A Butterfly on the Gowanus Expressway*, published in 1985.

Born in Brooklyn, he lives in Long Island with his wife and two children. He is also a Rabbi, NY State Chaplain, an architect, engineer and a teacher.